PRAISE FOR
THE ART OF BENDING TIME

"Quinn Jamison, author of *The Art of Time*, is full of surprises. From her book's innovative opening, where the protagonist falls through a painting into a past world, to the ups and downs of her love affair, to the plot twist at the end, you learn to expect the unexpected. But when you finish the book and flip back to Jamison's bio, you discover her biggest surprise: she wrote *The Art of Time* during three months of the covid outbreak—when she was sixteen years old. An author to watch, for sure."
—Chris Coward, author of *Perpendicular Women: Adventures in the Multiverse*

"Quinn Jamison's *The Art of Bending Time: A Forbidden Return* is a fast-paced time-traveling, historical fiction YA romance novel with a gutsy heroine and a spellbinding love-story that spans time and space. A real page-turning perilous race against all odds to save her soulmate husband from his doomed fate!"
—AnneMarie Mazotti Gouveia, author of *Drifters Realm, Book 1*, *Mirror Tree, Book 2*, and *Brave Falls, Book 3*, of the Drifters Realm book series

"Breathtaking prose. Compelling voice. Quinn Jamison has simultaneously created a high-stakes adventure and an endearing romance that transcends time, all set to an amazing playlist! A triumph!"
—Kara Jacobson, author of *The Intra-Earth Chronicles, Book II: The Aswan Device*

THE ART OF BENDING TIME

A FORBIDDEN RETURN - BOOK II

Quinn Jamison

atmosphere press

© 2024 Quinn Jamison

Published by Atmosphere Press

Cover design by Kevin Stone

Interior character illustration by Esther Burns (Instagram: @eburnsillustrations)
Interior hourglass illustration by Elada Vasilyeva on Pixabay

No part of this book may be reproduced without permission from the author except in brief quotations and in reviews. This is a work of fiction, and any resemblance to real places, persons, or events is entirely coincidental.

Atmospherepress.com

This story contains elements of battle, war, hand-to-hand combat, alcohol use, blood, gore, mature themes, brief thoughts of suicide, graphic violence, and death/murder.

Readers who may be sensitive to these, please continue with caution.

For my readers who inspire me to keep writing and to those who wish for a happy ending.

"I was stunned when a familiar strong hand caught mine, and I saw those dreamy sea-green eyes."

PLAYLIST

Prologue ~ 'The First Time Ever I Saw Your Face' Cover by Geroge Michael & 'When I Saw You' by Mariah Carey

Chapter 1 ~ 'Time After Time' by Cyndi Lauper

Chapter 2 ~ 'Like I'm Gonna Lose You' by Jasmine Thompson & 'Wait' by M83

Chapter 3 ~ 'What Was I Made For?' by Billie Eilish

Chapter 4 ~ 'One Moment in Time' by Whitney Houston

Chapter 5 ~ 'The Story' by Brandi Carlile

Chapter 6 ~ 'Ghost' by Justin Bieber

Chapter 7 ~ 'Love Again' by Celine Dion

Chapter 8 ~ 'Where Forgiveness Is' by Sidewalk Prophets & 'Like a Lion' by Bryan Lanning

Chapter 9 ~ 'Destiny' by Jim Brickman ft. Jordan Hill

Chapter 10 ~ 'When We Stand Together' by Nickelback

Chapter 11 ~ 'I'll Come Back For You' by MAX

Chapter 12 ~ 'All I Want' by Kodaline

Chapter 13 ~ 'Go For Gold' by Autum Kings x The Song House

Chapter 14 ~ 'Warrior Spirit' by Samuel Day

Chapter 15 ~ 'Iris' by Goo Goo Dolls

Chapter 16 ~ 'Can't Turn Back Time' by Danielle Juliette

Chapter 17 ~ 'Rescue' by Lauren Daigle, 'In the Air Tonight' Cover by Natalie Taylor, & 'Angel in the Fire' by Natalie Taylor

Chapter 18 ~ 'Titanium' by David Guetta ft. Sia

Chapter 19 ~ 'Somewhere Only We Know' by Keane

Chapter 20 ~ 'The Scientist' by Coldplay

Chapter 21 ~ 'To Build a Home' by The Cinematic Orchestra & 'My Tears Are Becoming a Sea' by M83

Playlist Link ~ https://shorturl.at/9nyRV

TABLE OF CONTENTS

Prologue: First Meet 1

Chapter 1: Lost Memories 11

Chapter 2: Wind the Clock 30

Chapter 3: Breakthrough 44

Chapter 4: The Plan.. 51

Chapter 5: Telling My Story... 68

Chapter 6: Timing Can be Everything at Times 74

Chapter 7: Blurred Figures 89

Chapter 8: Forgive But Don't Forget 95

Chapter 9: The Gift and the Curse 109

Chapter 10: We Stand Together Calmly 123

Chapter 11: Mysteries 131

Chapter 12: Paint Colors of Wisdom 146

Chapter 13: The Clock is Ticking... 166

Chapter 14: The Way of the Fight.. 179

Chapter 15: Strange Voices 188

Chapter 16: No Turning Back Time.......................................198

Chapter 17: Stopping it All 205

Chapter 18: Hope... 220

Chapter 19: The Smell of Home 228

Chapter 20: Dancing into a Corner..252

Chapter 21: Ascend Through Darkness................................ 262

PROLOGUE
FIRST MEET

ARMOND

There has only been one woman on earth who made me a fool with a single look.

From the time I was a boy, I thought the world was our biggest enemy until I learned my father made it seem that way. The truth lies in the fact that our worst enemy lives in the mirror. I gained courage through my own reflection.

I was young when I found out a man shouldn't hurt a woman. My father tried to instill the opposite in me. But instead, he created an internal scar deep inside me, and ever since, I have never been the same. A piece of myself had broken and found its way back to me again the moment I met Lavinia Melrose. Once I knew a man was not superior to a woman, I strived to be a true gentleman. They may be of different heights, but they are equal. They protect each other.

I was eight years of age the first time I went out of my way to do favors for women. The older I became, the more I realized being a man was different than being a gentleman. A man would never take that extra step that a gentleman would. Eventually, I questioned if my father ever became a man at all.

He acted like a child that had never grown up.

The day I officially wanted to be a gentleman for one woman, the boyishness in me vanished and bloomed into a true wise man ...

My father's *cavalieres* and I had just come back from a long trip on horseback when we were informed food had been stolen from town. I was on edge as we veered through the forest, looking for the poor, hungry soul. I felt as if something more profound than punishing a thief was about to happen.

"Can't we tell him to return the food and give him some of our own?" I attempted to suggest to my father.

"What an excellent idea, boy." My father's voice was full of sarcasm. I should have known he would not be persuaded. He deadpanned, "We'll give him a reason to come steal food from us in the future."

"That's not going to—"

"Don't speak anymore. We must hurry and try not to alert the fellow."

"As you wish, Father," I whispered bitterly and obediently, which I despised hearing in my tone.

Minutes went by before bushes rustled in the distance, a twig snapping like a crack of a whip. I stayed calm as I slowly scanned the area.

"Over here! I see the red-faced runt!" one of the *cavalieres* shouted, pointing.

I gave Midnight a command before we took off faster. My father and I made our way to the front to lead them as I spotted the short, hungry man in tethered clothing making a beeline for the trees. I shifted my reins in his direction, and we all followed the fast man in a gallop as he ran quickly around a tree and ...

He slammed right into somebody and knocked them flat onto the ground.

"Oh my ... Father! Did you see that?" I asked loudly. I encouraged Midnight to pick up pace, then squinted my eyes to see ahead. They widened when I realized a woman was under the homeless so-called thief. I gave my horse more low shouts of encouragement. "*Vai*, Midnight. *Vai!* Faster!"

"See him make a fool of himself, you mean? I do have eyes, Armond; what's your point?"

I ignored him because he was oblivious to anything I tried to say. The girl looked so frightened as the man yelled something in her face and then took off. I watched her head turn fast at the sound of us approaching.

"*Fermo! Subito! Malvivente!*" My father suddenly took on a much more obnoxiously loud tone as he shouted that. I realized he really did not care to take notice of a lady who was alone, vulnerable, and afraid.

Everyone began drawing their pistols and swords except for me. I didn't want to scare the girl more. They made their shots and their weapons ready, but the man started to lose us. As I watched her struggle to reach her feet and fall back into a tree, I knew I had to step in and help.

"*Aspetta, fermati! Non sparate! C'e una signora!*" I commanded.

"*Sì, sono una signora!*" her soft and frantic yell penetrated the air, and she waved her hands to catch the other's attention as well, I gathered.

"*Non mi interessa! Abbiamo quasi preso il malvivente!*" my father snapped at me.

But I was fueled by his disagreement and the fact that this woman didn't deserve to be out alone with nobody to watch over her. I told him we should stop and that if he did not, he was less honorable than I thought. He replied heatedly, saying he would stop to help just this once. He ordered some men to follow the criminal and others to halt in place. The young woman's brown eyes frantically landed on each battle-ready man as we removed our helmets. Before I could take off mine, instinct took over, and I dismounted without thinking twice, striding toward her.

Dirt clung to her odd clothing and skin, and her blonde waves were knotted against her head. When her gaze met mine, lightning bolted through me. The sun lit her eyes, revealing a stunning cognac color. Her long eyelashes brushed her cheeks as she blinked in my direction. She concealed her fear well as she straightened her spine and pushed her shoulders back. I held back my amusement. Luckily, she could not see my soft grin behind my helmet.

I spoke first in polite haste. "*Una ragazza dolce come te non dovrebbe vagare da sola; non è sicuro. Dov'è la tua scorta? Non sta facendo un buon lavoro per proteggerti.*"

A furrow appeared between her brows. "*Non ho una scorta.*"

No man to keep her company? If she could have seen my face, surprise would be there, but it was not lost in my tone. "*Non sei sposata.*"

Her head shook with a softly spoken monosyllable in reply. "No."

My eyes dropped to her hand as my head tilted to the side slightly. No ring. My eyes trailed over her body, then back to her face. "*Cosa indossi?*" I asked, full of perplexion.

Her chin bowed to her chest to look down at herself as if she had forgotten what she was wearing before pinning a glare on me. She did not answer, clearly offended.

I had to ask, "*Qualcuno ti ha ferito? Ti sei fatto del male?*"

"*No, non sono ferita. So badare a me stessa,*" she responded, quick as a whip, assuring me she was uninjured and could look after herself. She still paid no attention to my confusion about her attire.

"*Sono sicuro che tu ne sia capace. Non fraintendermi. I boschi lo sono—*" I began, but she interrupted by saying it was a free country, that she could wander wherever she pleased. My mirth displayed a chuckle as the others chortled scornfully.

"*Guarda qui! È impazzita!*" my father bellowed cruelly. The men's laughter hurt my ears. The woman did not look happy to hear him voice his opinion that she had gone mad. However, her mostly collected features made me believe I was more offended than her. In truth, the comments that followed caused my blood to boil.

I tried to distract her by apologizing for their rudeness.

"*Va tutto bene*," she said unconvincingly. But their behavior was not acceptable; it was inexcusable.

I explained to her how they were confused by what I meant by "free," and her eyebrows formed that frown again.

"What are you talking about?" she blurted in English with staggering sharpness. It was so unexpected that a cough flew up my throat. The American accent immediately intrigued me. Her voice was so much softer when she spoke the language despite her irate tone.

I snorted lightheartedly. "*Ohimè*, you are not from here."

Her body suffered a chill as I finished speaking, which only confused me more. "No, I'm not. I live in—" Her words stopped short. Something seemed to occur to her by the slight widening of her eyes while they traveled from knight to knight. Their laughter roared once again, and my fists clenched. I couldn't stand hearing it any longer. A clearing of her throat distracted me and brought my attention back to her. "Uh, I live in the colonies."

"America, eh? I thought I detected the accent," I admitted. "Then again, I don't hear it a lot."

She became very nervous, an edgy chuckle escaping her. "Yes. America. That's what I was going to say. It's just that I'm old fashioned and still like ... to ..." Humiliation surfaced, painting her expression clearly.

She was strange, but I didn't prefer anything less than that. "Can I ask you again why you are here alone in the middle of the woods?" I tried again.

"That's really none of your business." She stuck her chin in the air defiantly. "Maybe I just like the forest."

I suspected she had something to hide. I only didn't know

what could have happened to make her think she couldn't tell me. But a gentleman would not ask. My throat cleared. "Of course. Forgive me." I reached up to lift my helmet away from my head. "I am Armond Alessandro. May I ask who you are?"

Her eyes could not have been wider. I heard her sharp intake of breath as her jaw dropped. Her expression sent a crawl of chills down my back. For several long moments, she only stood there stiffer than a board before she stuttered out her answer. "Uh—uh I am—erm … Lavinia. Lavinia Melrose. Yes, that's my name."

"Lavinia Melrose …" I whispered, the name rolling off my tongue nicely. Such a pretty name for a *bella* woman. I could not fight a grin.

Her smile, in return, lit something deep down inside me that had been dark for a long time. My eyes roved over the rest of her features, taking her beauty in. A small mark above her lip I had not seen before moved as she spoke again.

"You … are a knight?" she questioned in revelation.

I wasn't even aware I had been staring long enough for there to be a silence for her to break. I must have appeared rude. I almost stuttered my reply. "A squire in all important respects. I will become a knight at the age of one and twenty," I specified, sounding as if those words were rehearsed and burrowed inside my head. "We prefer the term *cavaliere*."

Before she could give me her answer, my father interrupted rudely. "Well, let's not tell the lady your whole life story! We shall be going!"

I held in the urge to throw him a look and instead put forward a proposal. "Of course, Father. If we bring Lavinia with us."

My father immediately ripped his helmet away to reveal his revulsion and affront. His lip curled further as he looked toward the poor girl. Begrudgingly, he replied, "Very well. If we must." His expression became more disgusted. "We'll have Iseppa fix her up; she requires a serious bath and … dressing."

Lavinia did not appreciate his comment. In all honesty, I hadn't either. Her features contorted in annoyance when she snapped, "Excuse me! You don't know the half of what I've—"

I knew my father would not like her standing up to him long before his irate response: "I suggest you shut that pretty mouth of yours, or I'll leave you out here for the animals to eat!"

His tone caused her to shake slightly, but she stood her ground. She was smart enough not to argue with him more. "I apologize, sir; I have had a rough and … confusing night, and even that is no excuse. I should not have raised my voice."

I could not handle seeing her look so defeated. My heart swelled. I had to speak up. "Don't dwell on it. Whatever has happened, I'll make sure you're safe from now on," I told her softly and reassuringly. I offered her a pleasant smile so she would feel more comforted.

She seemed to calm slightly. "Thank you, sir. I appreciate your kindness," she said demurely.

Her faint simper only made me angrier at my father.

"It is my greatest pleasure." She couldn't have known how great. I lent her my hand. "Come with me."

Her cognac eyes fell on my open palm. Moments went by as if she was considering her options until she grasped her tiny hand in mine, the softest skin brushing against me. I brought her to my horse and assisted her on to Midnight, following suit behind her. So very close. The second my eyes began to wander, I stopped myself.

"I have never seen a lady of good breeding wear such odd-looking men's clothes before," I murmured to distract my wayward line of thinking. Luckily, she could not read my mind.

Her scoff caught me off guard. "I'm no 'lady of good breeding,' trust me," she told me quietly in a grumble.

I didn't think it was meant to be heard, but I questioned her words anyway. "You mean you are a man?"

"No!" she cut in loudly.

I struggled to keep in my chuckle. "Oh, forgive me."

Her head shook. "There's nothing to forgive. I just mean that no one refers to me as 'lady' whatever. I'm not highly praised or royalty, just an ordinary girl."

She was most definitely not ordinary, and I would assure her ... until she believed it if I was given the chance. "You are still a lady in my eyes, and not an ordinary one at that."

Her head turned to face me, and the look she gave me could have knocked me off my horse. I couldn't help but stare back as her eyes searched mine, our noses almost touching.

She merely told me, "Thank you." Her voice was softer than a feather, so pleasing to hear. However, I didn't miss the sudden shakiness to her tone.

"It is simply the truth." I spoke unwaveringly, and she did not deem a reply necessary, only focused back ahead of her.

Father ordered us to go, and the horses ran onward, causing Lavinia to fall into me. I chuckled, and once I knew she was all right, I continued our journey to my home. Minutes later, she asked me where we were headed, and I told her so.

I noticed the longer it took to meet our destination, the more tired she became. She began to slouch, and I heard her sigh drowsily every once in a while.

When the roof of my home came into view, she seemed to perk up. Her shoulders squared as she stared fixedly ahead of us.

"Wait—Is this ..."

"This is my family's villa," I confirmed for her.

"Get out! You live there?" Her excitement was as confusing as her words.

What on Earth ...

My brows furrowed into a frown. "Get out? Is there a problem?"

"Sorry ..." she apologized, embarrassed. "I don't mean literally."

"Oh." That was good to hear. "Well, to answer your question, yes, I do."

"Well, to answer yours, it's not a problem at all. I love it here!" she exclaimed, eyes lighting up.

I only became more perplexed. "You have been here? I must say I do not recall ever seeing your face." If I had, I would have remembered and surely approached her.

"Um, err—I just mean it's so beautiful!"

My mood darkened. On the outside, it was a sight for sore eyes; on the inside, there lived a man I called my father. He lured people in, good or bad, by building it exactly as it appeared. "That's one word for it."

"You don't agree?" she asked, bewildered.

"It's more ostentatious than anything." I certainly wanted to spare her the awful details. It was difficult enough to speak about him and all he had done.

She did not respond, and I was grateful. I wouldn't have been able to look her in the eye.

We entered the gardens, and I watched her look around in awe, jaw dropped, soft gasps falling from her lips, until we stopped by the stables. I dismounted, and she turned to slip down, but I grasped her waist and brought her to the ground instead.

"Armond!" my sister's voice cried out. Chiara quickly rushed to me and wrapped her arms so tightly around me that it was hard to breathe correctly. "*Finalmente, sei a casa!*"

"*Sì, ho qualcosa per te*," I told her, reaching into my satchel to give her a Russian souvenir nesting doll I found. She had always wanted one of them.

"*Grazie, Armond, le adoro*," she thanked me and soon met eyes with Lavinia. An immediate grin upturned her lips. "*Chi è questo, Armond?*"

"This is Lavinia Melrose. She is from America," I informed her, unable to help a smile.

"*Ohimè!* I will be sure to speak English, then. Nice meeting you, Lavinia. I'm Chiara, this one's sister." Her hand patted my shoulder twice, gently.

"Nice to meet you too, Chiara," Lavinia told her politely.

Chiara threw me an odd look I had never seen before. "You are quite pretty. Don't you think, Armond?" She wiggled her eyebrows at me, shoving her pointy elbow into my rib cage.

I would have teased her had I not been distracted by looking into Lavinia's eyes, scrutinizing every detail of her face. "*Sì*, she is *bellissima*," I whispered, not afraid to tell her so.

Her eyelashes fluttered in surprise as I didn't dare take my gaze off her until my sister spoke again.

"Well, you could use a change of clothes," she voiced with confusion, looking at Lavinia's attire. "What is it that you're wearing? What is A-did-ass?"

I wondered the same.

"Ad-dee-das," Lavinia pronounced for her with a shrug of her shoulders. She clutched the helm of her ... shirt. "The three-stripe company. It's ... new in America."

Chiara's brow arched questioningly before glancing my way, as if I could help her understand. Only, I had no clue, either. "Here," she began, "I'll bring you to Iseppa so you don't look like you've just been swept ashore and have purposely rolled around in the dirt. She will take good care of you."

Lavinia's laugh drifted away with her. I grasped Midnight by a rein and tugged it forward to bring him to the stables. I did not believe she had noticed, but I was watching even as the door closed behind her.

And I didn't care to ever stop.

CHAPTER 1

LOST MEMORIES

LAVINIA

Time gave me love, and in the end, it failed me. That did not mean I would fail myself or *him*, no matter what else I'd soon face. Even as tender memories flooded back in a torrential downpour. The warm summer breeze brushed past my dress. Green blades caught between my toes as I ran barefoot in the tall grass. I giggled and kept running regardless. I had no care in this world, a world where no pain existed. In this world, there was only serenity.

I glanced behind me for that mop of curls and locked on a pair of green eyes belonging to the man chasing me. His mouth tugged in a smile as more giggles slipped from my lips until they ceased in response to the stunning view ahead of me. My hasty steps slowed to admire every single detail of the large and shapely cork oak tree. Round leaves ended in a narrow point, swaying in the gentle wind. I watched as they sporadically fell from the curly branches to the ground. Its long and broad trunk curved slightly to the right, standing strong with our carved initials encased in a pointy heart just above a spiral in the bark. Thick overlapping roots at the bottom disappeared in the high weeds and then deep into the earth.

Out of the blue, his body knocked me to the soft ground. Taking the brunt of the roll, I grunted, but the bright grin I was met with swept away any discomfort. The sun shone down on us and peeked through the strands of his hair, revealing the light tresses that hid in dark and dimly lit rooms. He looked like an angel. He was one, dead or alive.

"Hey!" I exclaimed. "That wasn't fair!"

"I hardly care, *cuore*." He leaned in to capture my lips and leave a chaste kiss on them. "I was able to do that."

I smiled and rolled us over, now looking down at him, and his beautiful face glowed in the sunlight. "I love you," I whispered.

His green eyes sparkled. "And I you."

Once our lips touched, it was not much longer until his mouth became stone cold beneath mine. My eyes flew open, and a cry lodged in my throat.

"Armond ..." I gasped.

The clouds moved in and obscured all rays of sunshine, casting a dark shadow over his paling face. Rain danced its evil dance upon us. Thunder rolled across the meadow and a whirlwind of leaves circled around us as blustering gales slashed at me harshly. I sat in pools of his blood, attempting to shake him awake as I begged ... just begged for him to open his eyes, at least once more.

But he didn't ... and he wouldn't.

I sprung awake and found my mom's remorseful expression, her brows pulled inward, forming the deep lines there. I had woken her with my screaming again, just like almost every other night. She was always quick to jerk me away from the terror so I wouldn't be left to endure more and she wouldn't have to withstand hearing my loud pleas. I swear I saw tears begin to rim her eyes. I swiftly averted my gaze.

Each morning, I was roused by painful images of Armond and a lacerated heart. No matter how much I hoped and begged for him to reappear, his face only became visible in my soundless sleep. There had been a time when I was rarely unhappy, but those days seemed over. I had started to believe time had failed me. Time may have given me love, but in the end, I had lost it.

"I have to take a shower," I muttered stoically.

My shoulder brushed against hers as I rushed to the bathroom, but not without glimpsing my clock's big hand nearing the four. I hadn't admitted every detail of my nightmares to her. I didn't have to say much for her to know who starred in the dream and how it ended. I could decipher the understanding in her eyes alone. That was enough. I was nowhere near ready to speak the words.

My emotions shut off shortly after he died. I couldn't stand not being able to breathe when I thought of him. There had been times I crouched in a ball and merely wailed on the floor or in bed for hours. The emotional pain was so intense it became physical. I felt as if his soul had been forcefully ripped from mine, and that tore me to shreds, a part of my own soul leaving with him. I felt my world had betrayed me and gone dark the moment his face paled and arms went slack. I could still hear him take his final breath, as if my brain kept the sound playing just to torture my soul more.

So, I grew tired of feeling that way. I welcomed numbness, blocked out every feeling that threatened to push me over the edge.

That was easier.

Naturally, it was not for long, but I did it anyway, knowing it wasn't best for my health. I was willing to suffer the consequences later for the sake of my unborn baby. The baby would feel every sad emotion I did. I had to focus on what made me happy, or at least content.

Again, easier said than done.

Within the first week of my return, I had only a few bites to eat, too busy spending my days staring out of a window. I talked to no one and paid nothing much attention other than what was in my view outside or in my bedroom. For nearly three months, I was void of complete emotion, barely feeling alive. I would have continued that behavior had I not been in school. I didn't want to blow all my hard work, but I struggled to keep up. I practically forced myself to readapt to the world I had left behind, thrown into the life my other self had created while I was gone.

As summer approached, my mom suggested I had fresh air for a few minutes daily. Once I began sitting on the porch, I didn't stop. I sat there every day to eat my breakfast, watching with the hope that he'd emerge from somewhere. I sat and listened intently until my body and mind could no longer take it.

And sometimes at night, if I was angry enough, I'd sneak into the basement and punch the heavy bag until my knuckles almost bled.

I wished so many times to forget the memory of him gone, like the million mundane moments lost in the depths of my mind. But the image of his lifeless face always weaseled its way into my thoughts. I wished now that the hot water flowing over me could melt the ice in my mangled heart and wash away the hurt to make it whole and alive again.

But I was human, not a robot, and life didn't abide by that.

The shower curtain abruptly slid to the side as I sat crunched in a ball on the tub floor. I couldn't find the strength to move my head in my mom's direction. I barely even heard her calling my name. Echoed white noise I normally wouldn't care to listen to overpowered my senses.

"Lavinia," she spoke louder, firmer, and not too loud to startle me.

I remained fixated on the shower wall. "Yes?"

"Oh, honey. Are you okay? You've been here for a long time."

"No, Ma. I haven't been for a while now."

"I–I know. I just ..."

"I know," I whispered, my voice cracking.

She didn't need to explain, and neither did I. We often could just about read one another's minds, usually silently acknowledging the other's potential thoughts. Today was especially difficult for me. I'd had a nightmare, which meant I was extra sleep-deprived, and it was a Sunday, so I would go back to my classes the next day. And well, it was also the specific day I preferred for going to therapy, even though I dreaded it.

She sighed and planted herself on the edge of the tub, asking hopefully, "What would you like for breakfast? I can make your favorite for today."

I finally lifted my eyes up to her empathetic ones. "Thank you. That sounds perfect."

"Of course, baby." She kissed my forehead and walked through the doorway, shutting the door softly.

I breathed in the hot steam and exhaled deeply, burying my face between my knees. It had been six months. Half a year without him. My pain had not lessened since what had occurred on that cruel battlefield and terrible day. Mom had said it took a while before her anguish began to pass after my dad died, and I yearned for the day mine would lessen even a little bit. Life wasn't yet any better or any easier.

I peeled myself off the tub floor, forced my hands to wash my hair, and prepared myself for the day. For another phony therapist to pick inside my brain.

The first time I had tried therapy had been a couple of months ago, the fifth month Armond was gone. The lady had been confident she could make me talk, so I had deliberately chosen not to speak a word. I hadn't wanted to anyway. Every time I had met with her, I had only sat there and stared at her for the entire session. I had visited a total of five times in the period of two weeks. Finally, she had said it wasn't working and we weren't a good fit. Really, she just hadn't appreciated my attitude. My mom had advised me not to piss off any others if I wanted actual help. I had almost laughed.

Almost.

The next one had told me I needed to see a psychologist after I spent one hour with him. He had recommended someone who ended up creeping me out, and I had never gone back. I had decided to get a second opinion and chose a well-known and revered therapist, Dr. Birkenstein.

She was middle-aged and spoke very clipped in her raspy voice. Always dressed the same. Her clothes were mostly beige, and she always wore white socks with the same white sneakers. The first day I had gone, I had convinced myself I would try, no matter what I thought or felt once I took my seat in her office. It had gone well enough, so I had kept going back. Eventually, I had decided I would spit out the truth.

But once I had confided in her that my husband had died over a hundred years ago, she hadn't believed me. I hadn't completely trusted her from the beginning and should have known not to tell her anything of the sort. She hadn't been willing to listen to me after hearing that I "claimed" to have time-traveled through a painting. Automatically saying so created assumptions that I was delusional. So much for a second opinion; she had wanted to send me straight to a psychologist as well. I had shut down her suggestion and left her so fast her stupid white socks had blown off.

I had almost had a mental breakdown, which hadn't helped the situation, but I had been so angry for putting myself in that position just to be told I needed to be evaluated immediately. Again. She had actually believed I wasn't sane enough to make the right decision going forward. Of course, my mom being my mom, the headstrong surgeon, had reamed her into the ground with her words.

Things had gone uphill but, at the same time, downhill from there. Uphill because my mom had rendered her speechless, downhill because that hadn't kept Dr. Birkenstein quiet.

I met my mom in the kitchen and watched her slide a couple of fairly big pancakes onto a dish. The delicious aroma filled my nostrils, and a weak smile graced my lips. I had entered just in time.

"Here you are!" my mom chirped proudly. "Two blueberry pancakes with whipped cream, strawberries, and lots and lots of syrup." She presented the plate in front of me on the outside porch table with a wide smile. "Just like how your father used to make it."

"Thank you," I whispered gratefully.

"Don't mention it. Are you feeling ready?"

I picked at a stray blueberry that hadn't stayed inside the pancake with my fork. "I don't know if I should go. I'm not up for it."

If I was going to give therapy another try, I had to really figure out whether or not I could divulge very much. I planned on withholding most information. But I didn't know how much someone could help me if I couldn't tell them everything.

"Vinnie, you don't have to go. Therapy is for when you want it. But you should try again. I'm telling you, you will find the right person. Sometimes, it really does take a bit before you do."

I sighed heavily. My mom had gone to therapy when my dad died, and she swore by it. Her smile dipped as I looked down solemnly at my pancakes.

"Hey," she murmured, lifting my chin with her hand to meet my eyes. "I'm going to be very honest with you, Vinnie." She tucked a blonde wave behind my ear. "This will help, and you're going to meet many people who will also help. Although, the pain never leaves. It only gradually fades and doesn't carry on all-consumingly."

I swallowed the lump that never seemed to leave either. "Yeah, well, it doesn't seem like anyone will ever believe me. That doesn't help. At all."

She shook her head dejectedly and let out a tight breath. "As I said, you'll find the right person. There is always someone out there who will listen." She didn't say, "Like Armond."

She patted my arm. "I'm going to grab you a glass of orange juice. Eat, please."

I nodded and cut off a piece of pancake to put in my mouth. A bird tweeted, and I glanced up to find a familiar cardinal on the railing post.

"Oh, it's you again." I cracked a smile. "Hi, mister. You didn't visit yesterday. I missed you."

"*Tweet, tweet!*"

"Looking bright today. I hope you weren't too busy cleaning your feathers for me."

The bird tweeted at me more curiously.

"I thought so." I ate another piece of pancake off my fork, then chewed and swallowed before speaking again. "Should I go to therapy today, Baby Red?"

"*Tweet, tweet, tweet,*" he chirped enthusiastically.

"Yeah, maybe you're right."

He tilted his head back and forth quickly, as if to say he knew he was right.

I laughed and shook my head. "Oh, look at me! I'm talking to a bird and think it talks back. Maybe I am crazy."

Baby Red flapped his wings and flew onto the table, hopping a few times.

"Hmm," I hummed. "You're just as crazy as I am."

He hopped onto my plate and poked his beak into a stray blueberry.

I pulled my dish back. "Hey, you can't have this!"

The bird actually glared at me, then fluttered his wings and chirped once loudly. I rolled my eyes. He really wanted the dang blueberry.

"Oh, fine! Here!" I tossed it forward.

If a bird could smirk, he did, then practically dove for the piece of fruit.

The porch door opened, scaring the cardinal. He flew away in a hurry with his blueberry trapped in his beak. The harsh ache from my sorrow returned to my chest. Cardinals are said to be a sign of a loved one who passed on being with us in spirit. I liked to believe this cardinal was him. Of course, it wasn't the same as being around Armond, but it was better than nothing.

My mom set down my drink on the round table. As I sipped the glass, the delicious orange flavor refreshed my taste buds.

"I think I'm gonna go," I whispered finally.

My mom's head whipped in my direction, her bright grin reaching her eyes. "Oh, Vinnie! Good. I'm proud of you either way."

I smiled faintly. "Thanks, Mom."

After I finished my breakfast, I took my time getting ready. The appointment was in several hours, and the place wasn't too far. My mom offered to drive me and pick me up afterward. I was thankful because I didn't know where my mind would be once the session was over. The ride was smooth. We found where to go with ease, arriving ten minutes early.

My mom dropped me off by the front entrance. The building was modern and stark. I entered and checked in, then was told to take a seat, approaching the long hallway lined with doors. I found a door marked Dr. Terri Fields and further read the sign hanging there, which said she was still in session.

Minutes went by. I waited anxiously, bouncing my leg up and down in anticipation as I looked around. The hall was decorated plainly with glossy, blond parquet flooring, the walls bone white. Too white. I sat on a worn-out, dull-green chair that had already begun to hurt my bottom. A middle-aged woman came to take a seat down by one of the other rooms to wait and never glanced my way. Her expression was so melancholy. I wondered if she was in the same position as me or worse.

Dr. Fields' door finally opened. A young man came out and offered me a small smile before walking down the hall. I surmised that the woman standing by the door must be my therapist, who greeted me with a pleasant smile and welcomed me inside. I hesitantly planted myself on her bright blue couch and put my hands flat on my thighs, taking in the room nervously.

The immaculate office gave off a much more pleasant and exuberant vibe. The array of colors in the room made me feel more at home. I glanced at the stiff couch beneath me and the tissues on the table beside me that I refused to use, then finally focused on the doctor.

She smiled softly at me as a distracting ticking sound filled my ears. The noise of a ticking clock never annoyed me more than when I had to listen to it for a full, painstakingly long sixty minutes. I planned on not opening my mouth to say a single word for any of those seconds.

"Hi, Lavinia. Nice to finally meet you. I'm Dr. Terri Fields. How are you today?" she asked in a sweet voice, pushing up her cute and stylish glasses. Her shoulder-length, dark hair was in loose curls, and caramel-colored skin complimented her toffee eyes. She was pretty and sophisticated.

Tick tock tick tock tick tock.

I shook my head and stared at her with my face blank, continuing to keep my trap shut. I used the time to analyze her just as much as she would me. It was a therapist's job, after all, but I didn't particularly like my every action and word being analyzed, especially once Dr. Birkenstein had learned my secrets and considered me a nutcase. I believed my therapists secretly always did. That woman might have tried to throw me in an institution, but my mom was a bull. Never in a million years would she allow that unless I actually needed it. My mental state was clear; there was no reason. I had made a vow to never tell a therapist the whole truth again. Still, a small part of me hoped that Dr. Fields would be different.

Tick tock tick tock tick tock.

"So not good?"

I shrugged and shook my head again.

She cleared her throat and gave me a pretty, pearly white,

warm smile. "That's okay. You don't have to talk, just coming and being here is a good step forward."

I tilted my head and raised an eyebrow. That was what they always said; maybe she wasn't different.

"But I am going to ask you a few yes or no questions. Have you been to therapy before?"

I nodded slowly.

"So, you have an idea of what this is like. Was it a good experience for you?"

I shook my head, curling my lips into a deep frown.

Her face fell. "Oh, I'm sorry. It's good you are still trying. Does it feel good to try again?"

I tilted my head back and forth.

Not really, lady.

"Understandable. Were you mistreated?"

I nodded.

"I'm sorry. That has nothing to do with you. It's their job to be better than that."

I nodded with a shrug.

She sighed, looking down at her papers and shuffling them around for a moment. "Have you had trouble coping with the problems that brought you here?"

I swallowed thickly, nodding.

"Do you have trouble getting up in the morning?"

I nodded once.

"Do you feel groggy or unmotivated?"

I reluctantly nodded.

"Any trouble sleeping?"

My lips quivered, and I pressed them together, nodding gently.

She nodded as well. "Would you like to write about your past experiences? Perhaps you can do it in your free time and bring it back to me."

That sounded ... reasonable. *If* I came back to see her and kept out the fact that I time-traveled. I nodded anyway.

Tick tock tick tock tick tock.

Dr. Fields sighed. "I'm sure you have your reasons. It is important that you only talk to me when you feel ready."

Understanding and respectful. Those were good qualities but really the bare minimum.

"I can give you a list of my questions as well so you can write down your answers. Some patients find that easier."

She was right; I'd give her credit for that one. That did sound easier. I nodded with a small smile.

"Perfect. I can get that ready for you when we're done to take home." She began jotting a few things down, then put her pen behind her ear. She stared at me for a moment before she spoke again. "Are you expecting?" She pointed to my stomach.

I gasped, and instinctively, my hand went to my growing belly. I looked down and smiled slightly, and then my expression dropped a little. I was eight months pregnant, and *he* wasn't even here to celebrate. My breathing became shallower. I shook my head.

"No," I muttered, grabbing my forehead and fighting back the urge to vomit at the painful images in my mind. Things I had imagined so easily before were too much. Images of a future taken from me. What would it have been like to see him rubbing my growing belly and talking to the baby in a funny voice again? What would he look like holding our son for the first time? How would he make him smile? How would we laugh together? Play together?

We wouldn't.

Dr. Fields smiled for a second, maybe at the fact I actually uttered a word, then frowned. "No?" she said. "Oh, I'm sorry, I thought—"

"No, I am ... but—" I stopped myself. I was talking. She had actually got me to talk.

"But?"

I shook my head.

"Well, congratulations; that is wonderful."

I nodded and looked down at my sneaker-clad feet.

Tick tock tick tock tick tock.

"You don't seem ecstatic."

That rubbed me the wrong way. "Of course I'm ecstatic. My baby is a miracle."

She smiled. "That's beautiful. I'm sure you'll be a great mom," she told me. "But something is making you unhappy about this."

I hated that she was right and decided to ignore her. She probably assumed the pregnancy wasn't planned and the guy I was with couldn't handle a baby. But if there was anything Armond had taught me, it was to not be so quick to judge. Hopefully, she wasn't either.

Tick tock tick tock tick tock.

Dr. Fields didn't bring it up again.

"Can you tell me why you are seeking therapy at this time?" she questioned.

I blinked and shrugged like it was obvious.

I'm not doing well, and I need help.

"It's not completely clear to me why you are here unless you tell me," she said. "You seem very bright and mentally stable. I think maybe you have recently gone through a rough patch and need help overcoming it. Maybe you have trouble expressing your emotions and can only confide in someone when you trust them."

She had read me like an open book, but at least she approached it in a non-judgmental, positive regard. Except, I would say it was worse than just a rough patch.

Tick tock tick tock tick tock.

Dr. Fields checked her watch, trying to be discreet about it. Of course, that was how they kept track of time, but it unsettled me. It was like they didn't care to listen to people's problems and couldn't wait for the session to be done with.

"Please don't answer if you feel uncomfortable," she whispered quickly, genuinely.

My mind went back to Armond again. He had always made sure I was comfortable. I squeezed my eyes shut and sighed shakily, warding off those memories.

"You're right," I said, shocking myself. "I have been going through a ... rough patch—actually, an ugly, terrifying bump in the road that I can't really seem to get over."

"Mmh," she hummed. "I understand. We've all been there. You aren't alone in that." She paused. "How is your relationship with your family?"

I bit my lip and closed my eyes.

What is your family like? His pleasant and velvety voice echoed in my mind. It was the only thing I really cared to hear once more.

Instead ... *tick tock tick tock tick tock.*

"Lavinia?" Dr. Fields' voice pulled me from my thoughts. "Are you okay?"

"What?"

"You spaced out for a minute there."

Tick tock tick tock tick tock.

Beads of sweat began to form on my forehead, and my breathing quickened. "Uh—sorry, I ... I can't."

"You can," she assured me. "You just don't have to say, not now. Take baby steps."

I rubbed the back of my neck and sighed deeply in an attempt to push back my nausea. It didn't work very well.

"No, I really can't. I need a second."

I jumped off the stiff couch, stumbled to the door, and quickly threw it open to find the women's room. When I asked the lady at the front desk to direct me, she must have seen how green I looked. She pointed frantically and gave me directions. I almost lost my footing on the way there. As I barged inside, I let the heavy door fall closed on the girl behind me. I ignored her irritation, rushing to one of the stalls, and emptied the contents of my stomach. For several minutes, I heaved over the toilet. I tried breathing in and out deeply to calm my nervous system, but it hardly worked. I covered my mouth to hold in any more vomit and my loud sobs before standing up and opening the stall to wash my hands.

The mirror revealed my sunken eyes and pale face. I could see in my reflection that my eyes' cognac color had gone dark, the life in them consumed by blackness, dulled to a deep brown. I looked so unbelievably exhausted. And I was. I really was. I couldn't remember the last time I slept well. My harbored nightmares about *his* death ruined any amount of sleep I had. That wasn't very healthy for a pregnant person. The last good night's sleep I had was probably in the arms of my dead husband.

A tear creeped out of my eye and slipped down my cheek. I wiped it away angrily, repeating in my head what I said to myself every day:

I miss you. I love you. And more than anything, I want you back. But you are gone. I need to accept that.

Dr. Fields waited in the room with her legs crossed patiently and hands folded professionally. She didn't speak as I reentered, not mentioning anything about my sudden leave. A large breath of relief fell from my lips as I regained my seat on the couch.

"It's good, the best really," I told her. "My relationship with my family."

Dr. Fields gave me a small smile. "That's good," she murmured. "Are those the supportive people in your life?"

I nodded. "Yes, and ... a—a few others were too."

"Friends?"

"I had a lot of those ..."

"You are using the past tense."

I narrowed my eyes. "I'm aware of that."

"So, you *had* a lot of friends?" She wrote something down. "What happened to them?"

I shook my head. "It's not very easy to explain."

"I'm willing to listen," Dr. Fields pressed gently.

I shook my head. "It's hard to make more in college when everyone looks at you weird for being pregnant and whispers about you."

She frowned deeply, a flash of vexation in her eyes. "I understand," she muttered, downcast. "How are you doing with that?"

"It's fine. Bullying is nothing new to me. I just let it go. I'll find the people who matter eventually."

She hummed and nodded, then cleared her throat. "You're absolutely right, you will. Do you really let it completely go, though?" she asked, tilting her head. I swallowed, lips parting to answer, stuck on what to say, but she changed the subject before I replied. "Where do you attend?"

I sighed in relief. "California University."

"Oh, wow. Impressive. That's great," she gushed. "What are you studying?"

"Fine arts. I'm considering a degree in arts administration." I shrugged. "I don't know."

Her eyes lit up. "That's a wonderful idea. What kind of fine art are you interested in?"

"Painting. And drawing, more recently."

"Amazing." She kept asking me more questions about my interests and subtly checked her watch every few minutes. I didn't really want to talk about school, but I answered the best I could. Painting had brought me little joy recently. All I thought about was Armond when I touched a paint brush. I anticipated the moment I could walk out of there and be free, so when she checked her watch again and then glanced at the wall clock, I sighed in annoyance.

That's it! I'm tired of not getting to the bottom of this!

I scoffed. "Are you bored?" I blurted curtly.

"Bored? Not in the slightest, why?"

"You therapists constantly check the time. Are you sure you can stand to listen to me blab about college? I don't really feel like talking about that anyway."

"Fair enough. We can talk about whatever you'd like." She uncrossed her legs and put her papers down, leaning forward with her elbows on her knees. "But you should know, Miss Melrose, I *am* listening either way. I multitask well. My time is devoted to you. I always give my patients my full attention."

"Well, you should. Unfortunately, that's more than I can say about the therapists I've had. But it's still distracting. It makes me feel … well, uncomfortable. You said you don't want to make me to be uncomfortable."

"Nobody *makes* you feel anything."

My lips thinned at that comment. I held back a groan, and then silence ensued except for …

Tick tock tick tock tick tock.

"Aren't you going to ask why I left the room earlier?" I questioned, my irritation clear in my tone.

"No," she said matter of fact. "You don't want me to."

I leaned back onto the couch and clapped my hands slowly. "Right you are."

She cracked a smile and chuckled lightly. "You're funny."

I laughed humorlessly. "I used to be."

"And what makes you think you can't be anymore?"

I opened my mouth to answer but snapped it shut. I chose not to say a word, listening to those aggravating ticks of the clock instead.

Tick tock tick tock tick tock.

A minute of quiet, and still, I was speechless.

"Whatever it is that is bothering you, only you have the power to choose how you can be. You influence you, just like you influence others."

I took in her words, pondered them for a while. Dr. Fields was definitely wise, wiser than I had given her credit for when I first sat down. I froze, uncertain of what to say, if I should say anything.

"What happened, Lavinia? Why are you here?"

A lump formed in my throat again, blocking all the words

from escaping. "I'm ... miserable."

"As we all are sometimes. Go on."

I shook my head, burying my face in my hands. "I can't."

"You can," she assured me as I continued to hide my expression. "It's on the tip of your tongue. You don't want to tell me most things yet. You're not quite there, which is normal. We'll work on getting to know each other and reaching the point where you *are* ready."

I lifted my eyes, narrowing them at her. "I never said I'd be coming back."

Dr. Fields tilted her head and smiled. "Well, that's all up to you," she whispered softly, understanding in her gaze. "So"—she straightened herself out—"what do you want to accomplish out of this?"

"As you said, I want to overcome a rough patch. Therapy is supposed to help."

"All right. And you don't want to specify, correct?"

"Uh—no, I ... I can't." I sighed and shut my eyes, shaking my head. "I've been dealing with ..." I paused, then said, "An extremely difficult loss."

Dr. Fields' comforting face turned sympathetic. "That is devastating and definitely very difficult. I am deeply sorry you have lost someone." She gave me a sad smile, the upturned ends of her lips lifting slightly. "How long ago?"

"Um ..." I pushed away the flashbacks and focused on answering. "About six months." I stumbled over my words and involuntarily touched my stomach.

Her eyes darted to my hand, then back to my face, a thoughtful look on her own. "Do you feel better or worse after telling me this?"

"I feel ..." I sucked in a sharp breath. "I feel shaky, but almost like a little weight has been taken off my chest. I have never told a therapist that easily before."

"I am glad to hear that. My goal is for you to feel as at ease as possible so you *can* tell me these things. It brings me joy to have done that for you."

"Well, I'm not ready to spill my guts out to you, but I am able to—I guess, answer your questions."

Dr. Fields nodded with a pleasant, close-lipped grin. "Of course," she said. "Maybe next time. That concludes our session, Miss Melrose." I blinked and glanced at the clock.

2:00 PM.

"Uh—how ..."

She laughed and shook her head. "I look forward to seeing you again. I do hope you choose to come back. You're a great girl, a brilliant one. I respect your decision, whatever it may be."

My lips parted in such shock that I could only nod and offer a tiny smile. "Maybe. Thanks, Dr. Fields."

"Oh, please, call me Terri." She beamed, holding out her hand for me to shake. Our hands joined and bobbed once. "And you're very welcome. I believe we have made some good progress."

I managed to give her another smile, a mere lift from the corners of my lips. "I think so, Terri."

We had made progress, indeed, but naturally, seeing her once wouldn't change much. I still felt bonded to a chair, forced to sit and watch the memories that were no longer him. No matter how much I knew that I couldn't let them have power over me, I sat and watched, hoping that Armond would somehow come back to life.

CHAPTER 2

WIND THE CLOCK

**ROME
1848**

If I was not dreaming, I would have to be dead, though my sixth sense and the feeling of consciousness contradicted all logic. Blinding sunlight penetrated my eyelids, and my senses were deluged with timeless smells I knew I couldn't conjure up in a dream. Citrus blossoms and a mix of flora pervaded the air, as well as the smell of pine and green earth flowing into my nose. Those were unique scents I remember from being in the forest of Italy.

I tried to move, but a flash of falling from a great height caused me to cringe into the soft ground beneath me. I recalled the blackness before the complete sunshine, the blunt landing that should have killed me. I struggled to peel my eyes open, peeking through branches and squinting at the sun shining its rays that rendered me sightless. With a wince, my hand instinctively lifted to block the sun, except my hand did not look like my hand. At least not like it had in several years. A smooth and soft surface had replaced my slightly aged skin.

I blinked, and in that second that my eyes shut, I saw

myself falling down that deep pit of darkness, like dropping from the night sky with no parachute. My heart stopped for a whole beat, then began pounding against my chest as fast as a horse's hooves racing in the dirt. Every doubt I once had began melting away.

No dream. I was not dead either.

In the past—my past—I had thought time and time again about the possibility of seeing *him*, imagined it for years, but had hardly believed it might actually happen. I had assumed those trying years were wasted once I had been let down after the short time that I did believe it was possible. I couldn't have known how close I came to figuring it all out; it was near impossible. I hadn't yet seen what light lay at the end of a dark tunnel. Finally, I just made it through the bend, the light a clear beacon of hope.

A newfound energy coursed through me.

Springing to my feet, I began to run so quickly my legs could hardly keep up. I dodged the trees in my path and jumped over every ditch because I knew my way to him by heart this time. I hoped when I found him, he'd be the living, breathing kind of angel, not the kind who looked over me anymore. I didn't care that I wasn't utterly confident I could make a strong enough impact to change his fate. All I cared about at the moment was reaching him.

I found it hard to believe I had traveled back in time again, falling down that endless hole that had startled me. I had been let down many times for so long. Eventually, the possibility had become too ideal. My faith had been shredded. I had thought my chance was lost forever. I'd had to pick up the pieces and move forward with my life.

I had planned to visit the museum as much as I could, but I had only gone one time before I took Leo. Once he grew up and understood everything, he had asked me, and I would not say no.

I had been certain the allure would not transpire. Perhaps

the laws of time wouldn't allow me to go through it again or the compulsion was not strong enough anymore. Maybe nothing was calling me back since the man I had fallen in love with no longer existed.

Or would he *now*?

I couldn't have known. Life loves to play the trickster, and time is unpredictable. I only knew I had been given a chance to seize the day. *This* was my chance to change everything. If I could.

No matter if I can, I have to try.

The roof of the villa emerged from the high hills, and I stopped to catch my breath, inhaling the fresh air. I took in my surroundings, and then my eyes followed the dirt trail that appeared from the clearing and stretched all the way as far as I could see. Everything was all land. The green grass, weeds, and flowers covered the ground for miles. I was back.

But *when* was I back?

Gazing onward at the place that changed everything, my happiness outweighed the troubling thought of whenever I stood, as long as I hadn't traveled back to before I even met Armond, or I wasn't too late.

I shook my dubiety away and kept my feet on the move, holding my purse close to my side. The trek was tiresome, but I imagined it would be worth it if I could at least *see* his face once more. I ran and walked for what felt like hours until I finally nearly made it to the end of the long trail, entering the villa gardens.

My ears perked up as low, hurried voices caught my attention. I crouched down to hide in a patch of tall weeds, spotting Bartoli's hardy guards at the front entrance. Albertinus, Gerbrando, and one other I did not recognize. I only knew they would not be speaking during their duties unless something was very wrong.

Listening carefully, I made out Gerbrando's next reply. "I

swear I heard something approaching the gardens," he whispered hastily, becoming impatient.

Damn his good ears!

Afraid to present myself in worry of being killed, I had to sneak past them. They could mistake me for someone else or not recognize me if we hadn't met yet. I wouldn't get anywhere if I died. I groaned, beginning to army crawl through the grass slowly, calculatedly. I tried my best not to make too many rustling noises loud enough to further alert them. I reached the dark stone wall covered in vines and carnations, then made my way around to the left corner of the seemingly never-ending wall. Our bedroom balcony would be visible on the other side of this wall ... once I climbed over.

Heh heh. The things I would do for this man, the far lengths I would go ... God help me

Shaking my limbs out, I took a deep breath.

Do things with fear. It's different to be bold and undaunted than it is to have courage, a loud voice inside boomed. *There is no courage when doing things recklessly, without reason.*

Think of it as rock climbing, Lavinia. Don't focus on the fact you could slip and possibly fall to your death.

I wrapped my hands around a thick vine and stepped my feet onto the others, climbing my way to the top. I grasped hold of the edge, lifted my upper body weight, and hooked my leg over the top of the wall to hoist myself completely up. With this view, I could clearly see into our bedroom window. A soft glow of light appeared and moved away until it disappeared. What was he doing awake?

The guards began shouting, and it sounded like they were coming in my direction.

Carefully but quickly, I lowered myself, jumping down from about a quarter of the way above ground. I sprinted to where I knew a door was hidden, one that I'd hopefully be able to enter. I approached the outside wall of the villa and felt around for a crack in the exterior.

Come on, come on, come on! I know it's here somewhere ... found it!

My fingers finally grazed it, and I hurriedly yanked away the creeping plants concealing the doorway. After struggling to pry open the door, I finally rushed inside and pulled it shut behind me.

Swallowed in darkness, I trudged through the narrow passageway, using the walls for guidance. I may have known where the door was, but I had never gone through. I was unaware that the farther I ran, the smaller the space would become until I had to crouch. After not very much longer, I reached an end, but there was no room to stand. I felt around for a door and pushed on the barrier above me, popping open a trapdoor. As I climbed through, I saw what appeared to be the wine cellar.

I had never been down here, and I didn't know how to reach the main floor. As I looked around, I spotted a staircase and moved quickly and quietly up the steps. But, of course, the door was locked. I cursed under my breath. There were only two things left to do. Go back out and face the guards or bang on the door in hopes someone would hear. Before I could do either, a loud bark pierced my ears. A series of whines followed, and paws clawed at the door from the other side.

My eyes widened. *Pudge!*

I detected the sound of keys jingling before a voice I did not recognize rumbled, "We know you're in there, thief!"

Well, I was facing them either way it seemed.

Another voice interjected as the door swung open. A hand reached out for me, but I grabbed their wrist and twisted it, kicking them back in the abdomen. Several firearms were pointed my way, so I held my hands up.

"I'm not here to hurt anyone," I began in a hurry. "I'm—"

"Lavinia?"

Oh, *that voice*. The velvety tone was music to my ears. The guards parted and lowered their flintlock pistols, revealing the tall, handsome man of my dreams.

He's so beautiful.

His hair was tousled, eyes sleepy and so wonderfully green. The glow of the moon and the dim lighting gave a stunning shine to them as they filled with dismay. The drawstring at the top of his cream-colored nightshirt hung over his pants, the shirt loose and open against him, showing part of his defined chest. I was frozen with shock. The sight of him before me in real time was enough to make me die of pure happiness. I couldn't contain myself in my own skin. The tears began to fall unabashedly.

Armond lifted his hand in a gesture to dismiss the men. They left hastily, returning to their assigned guarding spots.

"Lavinia, I was looking for you. Then I heard the guards. What are you doing—" his accented voice began to ask groggily.

But I was on him before another skipping beat of my heart as I heard myself sob his name. My arms enveloped him, and I held him close, shoving my nose into his neck. Instantly, I breathed in his divine scent of pine, faint aftershave, and fresh soap. An intoxicating blend to kill for. But the sound of his voice was everything. It had fluttered to my ears and filled the hole his death had put inside me, enabling the heartache that I had pushed deep down to crawl outward from my chest so it could be replaced with an overwhelming exuberance.

"Oh ... Armond ..." My voice choked as I clung to him, and tears streamed down my cheeks. "I can't believe it ..."

"*Cuore? Mio Dio*, what is wrong?" His obvious concern was evident, and one hand cradled the back of my head while the other hugged me into him.

"Just hold me. Please," I sobbed. He said nothing and did just that. Held me close to him silently, waiting until I could speak again. "It's you. It's really you. Here with me."

Alive and well.

"Come, *cuore*." Armond lifted me by my legs, my face still

nuzzled into him. "Let's just go back to bed." His tone was soft and slightly faltered, conveying his unease with my actions. He carried me up the staircase and to our room, placing me on my feet. Armond brought my face back to look at him, scrunching his eyebrows together in confusion. "Did you have a bad dream and go for a walk?"

"No, no ... I—everything is fine now. You're not a dream. Not a ghost. You're really here." I touched his face as if I needed more reassurance that he was in front of me.

He shook his head and began speaking, but I couldn't hear him once my eyes dropped to his lips. Before I knew what I was doing, I slammed our lips together for a long and sustaining kiss. Oh, I had missed him so much. I gathered him in my arms, and he welcomed the tight hold of our lips until he slid his hand on top of mine, which was on his cheek, and pulled gently away from me.

"Tell me what's going on, Lavinia," he whispered, staring unwaveringly into my eyes. "You're beginning to really worry me."

I gasped a breath and shook my head. I couldn't speak. I couldn't think. I couldn't explain everything just yet. I only wanted him. I *needed* him.

"Please," I begged. Shaking my head again, I grabbed his face in both hands and crushed my mouth into his. He froze for a mere moment before deepening the kiss and sliding his hands around my waist, squeezing firmly through the loose blue dress I was wearing. He didn't break our lips apart even as he pushed me to our bed.

My back fell against the duvet, and he moved on top of me, the heat of his body warming me. He roamed his hands all over me until he finally found the hem of my dress. He suddenly pulled away, seeming very confused.

"What—"

"Shh!" I pressed a finger to his mouth. "I'll explain later," I whispered, guiding his hands down to pull up my dress. "Right

The Art of Bending Time

now, I just need you."

Armond groaned at my words, lifting the material over my head. He was about to continue, but his eyes immediately widened to the size of full moons at my attire underneath. "*Signore abbi pietà!* What is *this*?" he asked in outrage.

I rolled my eyes. "*This*"—I pointed to the bra—"is called a brassiere, and these"—I snapped the fabric of my bottoms back—"are panties."

He looked horrified. "Well, these garments barely cover you at all!"

"It's my underwear, thank you very much! The clothes cover me!"

"*This?*" He held up the blue dress, his voice shrilled with disbelief. "This is a nightgown! An odd-looking one at that!"

I snatched it away from him, glaring sharply. "It's a dress! Now, would you stop complaining?"

"Where is your corset? Why must you torture me by going out alone at night in nothing but a shift?"

Wait till he hears I walk around in a bikini.

"Oh, for hell's sake! It's not a shift! And that's not what I was—oh, just forget about it and kiss me, dammit!"

He growled in frustration but didn't hesitate to follow my command, connecting our mouths together again. Finally. I had forgotten what it was like to argue with him. Strangely, it was refreshing. At least he was alive to bicker back.

His tongue eventually found mine. Heat coursed through me, igniting a hot, blinding need for him. His lips moved down to my jaw and neck, leaving brands in their wake, and then caressed the swell of my breasts. I arched my back, sighing as he left more kisses there.

He abruptly stopped when his hands brushed over the bra. I squinted my eyes open lazily to see him looking at me expectantly. His eyes zeroed in on the bra, silently asking what to do with it.

I let out a breathy laugh, then pushed him back by the

chest to sit up. I grabbed his hand, guiding it across my skin behind me to show him how to undo the bra. Once it fell away and he took the silky material off, more ogling occurred. More undressing, more touching, and more kissing everywhere followed suit. Together. For the first time in a very long time.

We collapsed into each other, and I nuzzled my face in his neck, sighing and catching my breath. Armond chuckled and brushed his thumb over my cheek before capturing my lips once more. He lifted my chin so I would look at him. As I gazed back, he seemed to memorize me as if he was seeing me for the first time. The wound in my chest had never felt so painless.

"Lavinia ... will you tell me what happened now?"

I swallowed nervously.

Where was I to start? He had been dead the last time I saw him. I instantly forced away the resurfacing memories of his deathly pale and lifeless features. Instead, I focused on the beautiful and alive man before me.

I had lived years without Armond, and having him look back at me with those loving sea-green eyes again, quite honestly, was a bigger shock than his death had been. I had spent years trying to heal by meeting other people. Years that had taken a lot of effort and time. Time does heal, but your wounds turn into scars. For a long time, I had believed I couldn't mend my heart. The inner pain had been sustaining.

"What is the date?" I asked, my voice barely above a whisper.

He furrowed his brows. "March sixteenth by now. It's past midnight already ..." he replied with confusion in his tone. "Why are you asking?"

It was a week before the war. I had argued with him about fighting hours ago during my last trip to this time.

"Lavinia, what is going on?"

I shook my head. "This war, Armond ..." I began in a whisper. "It will be the death of you."

Armond's concern was evident, but his puzzlement continued to grow. "Lavinia ... I told you—"

"No, Armond. You don't understand." I had to be tough with him. I had to fight him hard on this and come straight out with the truth. It was the only way he'd listen, and so I said, "You're going to die."

"*Cuore* ..." he brushed my hair out of my face, shaking his head. "You don't know that."

"Armond, look me in the eyes," I told him sternly. He did without hesitation. The sight of them staring into mine gave me the same feeling they always did. "I do. I know it for sure. I'm serious. You will die in this war if we don't do something."

That made him pause and sit up in bed a little. His eyebrows furrowed even further. "What are you talking about?"

"I have ... I've lived through it."

I heard Armond's involuntarily sharp and barely audible gasp. He seemed lost in thought for a minute, putting the puzzle pieces together. My unfamiliar clothes, my strange appearance. Then he shook his head, only able to utter the stammered words, "You ... how?"

"You died. Years ago. I went back to my own time like you told me to do. After all these years, I finally fell through again. I think I've actually disrupted the flow of time ... which is why I had that dress on."

His eyes darted to the pile of discarded clothes on the floor, then he visibly swallowed, whispering, "Last I knew, we were beside each other when we went to sleep." He looked like he was in shock. "And I woke up from the commotion just to see you weren't beside me at all. I thought something terrible happened to you. Now you're saying my death is nigh."

It sounded crazier when I heard him say it. I sighed and looked around the room, scrambling to think of something to show him. When I spotted my purse, I jumped from the bed, fell to my knees, and clambered to find my wallet and phone.

"Look ..." I spoke. Armond glanced at the objects in my

hands and froze. "Here. This picture. It's me and our son." I pointed to the photo in my wallet. "And I'm sure you haven't seen anything that comes close to this." I held up my phone.

Armond, who had still been frozen, was more interested in the photo than the phone and slowly took my wallet in his hands. He stared at the picture with pure astonishment, which morphed into a faint grin.

"Our son, huh?" he murmured with deep emotion, chuckling. He was slightly smug. His eyes drifted back to me. "What did you name him?"

"Leo, of course," I assured him. His face broke into a wide smile. "When you were gone, I was broken. I could hardly breathe." I sighed out a shaky breath at the thought. "But I kept my word and went back to my time. You begged me to do it when you were ..." I swallowed down my thick emotion, not finishing my sentence. Armond grasped my hand. "I had Leo. Thank God for Leo; at first, he was probably the only person I wanted to live for besides some others in my family. And now I'm here. Again."

I watched Armond's eyes begin to water. "Oh, *cuore*, you're so strong."

I sighed, looking down. "It was hard to be." There was so much more to tell him. Some of it I wasn't even sure he wanted to hear. "I was barely holding on."

One of his fingers lifted my chin so my cognac eyes met his sea-green eyes. "You did better than I would have." He shook his head like he didn't want to imagine it. "I would have rather died if I was in your position."

"I wanted to, at first," I admitted. "But ... I knew I couldn't just give up. Not only for you, but for our son and myself. For the little joy and beauty left in the world. There was more for me to do."

Armond leaned his forehead against mine, and I took that as a chance to cherish the moment. I was afraid he'd be gone in a millisecond if I closed my eyes for too long. It felt real; he felt real. I knew it was real, and still, I was afraid that everything would turn out to be a dream.

"Do you see now?" I asked. "Do you see why we have to do something? I have lived over twenty years without you. I don't want to do it again. Especially now that I have you. I swear to God, if you make me, I'll kill you right now."

"Lavinia." He pushed back another hair from my face and looked at me earnestly. "I still want to fight, but I don't ever want you to be unhappy. I'll do whatever it takes."

The corners of my mouth upturned in a wistful smile as a sob worked its way out. He shook his head, then grabbed my face and kissed me hard on the lips. Our mouths crashed into each other like waves do on a beach, pulling in with the tide and drawing back to sea, to their home again. He and his soul were the life force of my world, as the pull of waves is the life force of the world's oceans.

A once fervent kiss soon turned quick and fierce. Our tongues delved and reached into each other's mouths, exploring more than we ever had. His hand curled around my neck and guided my mouth hard against his, our breaths mingling as we parted our lips to draw a single breath in. He captured my lips again in a long kiss, savoring the moment before disconnecting them to attach his own to first my jaw, then the underside of my jaw, and lastly, my neck, lingering there. His soft, affectionate kisses felt hot on my skin and reignited the flame that had died down, heating me up inside.

I was no longer cold and without him. I had to try to make sure that I'd never be without him again, at least not for a very long time. At the right time. I couldn't let him be taken from me again so soon. I was able to be with him, feel him for the first time in so long. I wouldn't let him slip through my fingers.

I lay on his chest for a while, thinking of the extremities at hand, before I felt one of his tears fall on the side of my face. I lifted my head just to see his tear stained cheeks.

"Armond. You're crying?" I kissed his face. But another tear fell. "Please don't. We'll figure it out."

He smiled softly through his tears. "I'm not crying because I know I might die, Lavinia." He caressed my face. "I don't fear death at all. If anything, I'm afraid of leaving you to your grief, maybe even more than your demise. Your pain is more abhorrent to me than my own. The fact you were in pain makes me out of my mind."

"Don't feel that way. It's not your fault."

Armond grasped my face in his large hands. "I'll do everything in my power to be certain I won't leave you again. Not for as long as I live. Hopefully, longer this time." That was what began the waterworks once more. He wiped away my own tears. "You are my lifeline, Lavinia. You have lived a life losing your own anchor. You're stronger and braver than you know."

I nodded. He kissed me, then I rested my head on his bare chest again and closed my eyes. His arm wrapped around me as he kissed the top of my head. I melted into the feeling of being in his arms. I had missed his warmth. I never want him to grow cold so soon again.

His hand traced over the skin on my back. "Lavinia ..." he trailed. I hummed in response. "Tell me what it was like. To be back. And tell me about our son. I want to know everything."

I frowned. He sounded so sorrowful when he said it. "Well," I paused. There was a lot I could say. "It certainly didn't feel like home anymore. Not without you. But I met people along the way who helped. It's much louder there. Busier. I wasn't used to it after being here where it's quiet. Complained about it constantly." I sighed. "Leo has the same green eyes and beautiful curly hair as you. The same dimples but looks a lot like me when he smiles. He has similar mannerisms and facial expressions as you do. He's married to a wonderful girl, Jules, and their daughter's name is Stella."

"Stella?" I heard the smile in his sleepy tone.

"Yes ..." I whispered. "I told Leo all about you. Our whole story. He named her Stella because I never had a girl. She's five. He was twenty when he had her." I paused, thinking about the last time I saw them. "You know, I'm really in my forties. It's odd to think of it that way ..."

"Not too strange for me. Although you certainly don't look like you are. You didn't even age a day in that ... still memory."

"Picture," I corrected, laughing. "I was still young in that one." I sighed, looking down at myself and remembering the aging my body had gone through. "My body changed during the fall here into the past. I look the way I did the last time I was here."

"That doesn't matter to me," he dismissed the idea. "I'll have you however I can, even if you do look older."

I gave a slow smile, shaking my head in awe. He could never disappoint me.

"Tell me more," he said.

I took time to think for a minute. "Leo has a birthmark shaped like a heart, like yours except it's on his stomach and lighter than his skin, not darker. His favorite food is cheese, and he loves to draw. He's good at it, too."

I smiled as I thought about him, going on and on for hours. He listened intently as I talked until the sun began to rise. I felt Armond's breathing start to slow, and I glanced up at his face to see his eyes shut and lips slightly parted. Grinning softly, I settled in close to him and let sleep welcome me, home again in the warm arms of my love.

CHAPTER 3

BREAKTHROUGH

CALIFORNIA
1991

A little over a week after my first session with Dr. Terri Fields, I made up my mind to visit her again. I arrived with my written answers to her questions and the resolution to give this a try.

Terri sat in her comfy chair, hands folded in her lap and wearing her stylish glasses. She regarded me passively through the lenses, but I did not miss the small curve of her lips. Either she was smug that I was back, or she was happy to see me.

"I'm very glad to see you back, Lavinia," she told me sincerely in a soft tone, confirming the answer to my unasked question.

I nodded. "I need to be."

She grinned and voiced her agreement. Once I handed her the papers of answered questions, she thanked me with a polite smile and briefly perused them. A few minutes later, Terri set the packet aside and dove into the session. The more we talked, the more I wanted to come back. After a month, I slowly began to feel improvement, although the pain remained the same. As I sat down in her office for the eighth time in four weeks, she naturally broke the silence.

"How are you today? Better or worse since I last saw you?" she asked.

"Oh, you know, about the same." That was the truth. I was still overwhelmed with grief, guilt, and self-doubt.

"I don't know, actually. Would you like to elaborate?"

"Something you can't perceive … That's a first."

Terri shifted in her seat with an amused look on her face. "You are quite sarcastic today."

"I am sarcastic every day, usually."

"So, you've regained the humor you said you wouldn't."

I paused for a moment to mull that over. "Not exactly."

"And that's okay, normal even. Baby steps." Terri crossed something off on her paper and tapped the pen to her chin. "Little by little, you'll be able to laugh the same and make people laugh like you always have."

I sighed and crossed my arms and legs, sinking back into the couch. "It doesn't feel that way."

"Not right now, it doesn't. Your emotions are just very downcast at the moment, probably even angry. Sometimes blameful." She leaned forward with a comforting and understanding smile. "Have you ever heard of the stages of grief?"

"Yes … There are five main ones, I believe."

"Denial, anger, bargaining, depression, and acceptance," she listed. "Where would you say you are? What is your mindset right now? Can you put it into words?"

"Erm …" I threaded my hands together and took a deep, cleansing breath. "I think I'm circling back among the middle three a lot. I lose sleep at night because I can't seem to keep away the awful thoughts, and they just bounce around the whole time."

Terri nodded. "It's important to be aware of those thoughts; you shouldn't repress them, as hard as that is."

I looked at the floor. "I know."

"And don't be ashamed of not being able to. You'll learn and find a way to free your mind eventually. Just try to focus on all of the happy thoughts, especially before you fall asleep."

I nodded. "If I ever finally do fall asleep, I usually have dreams that turn into terrible nightmares."

"Hm." She paused. "Are you reliving something?"

"Yes, they always end the same way," I muttered, swallowing.

Terri tilted her head. "Can you explain?"

"Uh …" I shifted uncomfortably. "A death. I'm reliving someone's death."

Her eyes only widened a fraction, and her face filled with sympathy. "You watched someone die?" she asked. I couldn't speak. My head only moved up and down once. "That is absolutely devastating. I can understand your pain even if I've never gone through something so traumatizing."

My hands began to shake, grasping the other firmly to cease their trembling. "It had a detrimental effect on me."

"Yeah. I don't think a robot could even walk away from that without being emotionally disturbed. And you've watched somebody you love die."

My eyes darted to hers. "How do you know I love them?"

"I assume you lost a loved one, of course; that is only what I meant by it."

"Right." I sighed. "I did."

"I thought so." She gave me another pretty smile that displayed her straight teeth. "On a happier note, I want to ask, what are you doing for Thanksgiving, hm? It's coming up soon. Do you have any special traditions?"

I was able to momentarily drift away from those taxing images as I answered. "My brother and his girlfriend are coming over. I'm meeting her for the first time. My dad used to be the one to cook, but my mom now tries her best to keep up with his recipes. We play board games and cards and watch the same movies every year." I let a smile turn up my lips marginally.

"That sounds very nice." Terri writes down a few words. "Is your father not around?"

"No ... My dad has been gone for a while now."

"So, this isn't the loss you're dealing with now, correct?"

"No, this recent loss is someone else."

She nodded. "I am deeply sorry. Losing a parent is awful enough."

I wiped my hands down my thighs nervously. "I am better now about him being gone. I just don't know how to cope ..." I swallowed. "I can't seem to find a way to cope with this exact loss."

"Hm ..." She hummed. "Like I said, you just have to find a way to come to terms with your grief and slowly pick up the pieces that are broken inside you. Accept the many different emotions it can trigger."

"I ..." I began. "How do I do that?"

"Well, for starters, try not to pretend your feelings are not there. Talk about it with someone you trust. The more you keep things to yourself, the deeper the piece of glass in your heart is going to go and the harder it will be to find and figure out. A regular nighttime routine is important. It can help fend off the thoughts that overwork the brain so you can relax. When you aren't talking to me or someone else, try ... rewriting the ending, hm? Don't focus so much on what you have seen and, instead, imagine it in a way that is happy as you go to sleep."

My mouth opened, then snapped shut at how intelligent and helpful she really was. That was an amazing idea, actually. "Okay ... sounds reasonable. I can try that."

Terri gave a slow, reassuring nod. "Now that I know you watched someone pass, I just wonder ..." She took a lengthy pause to regard my reaction. "This is touchy. Remember, you don't have to say anything. I'm just putting this out there ... Do you think you could have done something?"

My breathing quickened as his pale face flitted across my memory, a permanent scar on my brain. "I could have helped, but it was too late," I murmured.

"But what could you really have done?" she asked. "You didn't know it would happen."

"I could have saved him," I reflexively replied.

"Saved *him*?" She came to a realization, or maybe a confirmation, right then. I had let her know it was a *he* I lost. "Save him how? Medically?"

The words were immediately stuck in my throat; I couldn't say them.

Terri offered a reassuring grin. "Do you know it's not your fault? Do you blame yourself at all?"

I shook my head. "I did for a while. I've thought many times I could have done something different, but I know it's in the past." Literally. My voice choked on the last few words spoken.

Terri's head cocked to the other side. "Who did you lose, Lavinia?"

I instinctively gulped at the question and went completely silent for a moment until I built up the courage to say all but two words, "My husband."

Terri was fairly unsurprised. She most likely caught on not too long ago. Terri was incredibly insightful, more so than the others. Her compassion was stronger, and her willingness to listen was palpable. "And he's left your little one behind ..." Her low voice was kind.

A wave of emotion came over me as my hand slipped to my swollen belly. I nodded my head in confirmation. "That's all that is left of him," I choked.

"Lavinia ..." Terri began, "he may be gone, but he's always going to be in your heart."

I covered my mouth to prevent a sob from escaping, chills sweeping over me. "That's what he would say ..." I told her, voice catching. "He ..." I grasped the locket resting on my chest, about to tell her he had given this to me, about to show her the inside, the words, but I stopped myself as a hint of fear held me back. The necklace was so old-fashioned. I wasn't up for her questions. "And he is ... I know that. He's in my heart."

Her eyes became so soft. "And it's true, he is. You keep him there in order to live on for your baby. The little one needs you."

I bit my trembling lip. "That's what I keep telling myself. It's just that ..." I tried to find the words. "All the things he liked about me, I can't seem to bring out them again because it reminds me of him."

"Remember those things and remember him. It's all part of the process. You shouldn't hinder yourself by trying to forget. Don't neglect the good memories you have with him."

"That's not what I want. I could never forget him or any day I spent with him."

She nodded encouragingly at the expression of my feelings. I was shocked by how good it felt to get them out freely without judgment. It felt good to know she wasn't judging me. Lately, I had felt judged. A lot. I almost smiled at her sudden excitement, but it slipped, and I began staring at the floor in thought. I wondered what Armond would think, wondered if he was watching me at the moment. I would have given anything to be able to read his mind.

"Of course not," Terri whispered. I swore her eyes were glassy, but she smiled. "What is his name?"

Is.

One little word, but so significant. I was used to people using "was" when referring to him. What *was* his name? What *was* he like? Dead people still have a name. Why do we feel the need to use past tense?

For the first time in months, I spoke his name in a breathy sigh, a cry flying up my throat. I couldn't care what I'd look like in front of her. There was no holding back the sobs that wracked my body in a storm of heartache as they fell into my hands. I shed my tears freely for him because he deserved every single one.

CHAPTER 4

THE PLAN

1848

I was exhausted after our long discussion that night when I returned to his time. I drifted off into a deeper sleep than I had gotten in a while, comforted by the feeling of being in his arms again. My mind dreamt up wild possibilities. The look on Armond's face if he could meet our child all grown up. Building a beautiful home on the coast somewhere. Growing old together ...

I walked alone on a battlefield, sword in hand, taking careful step after careful step. The blood-soaked ground beneath me saturated my boots as I watched the sun emerge from the horizon. I gazed at the colorful glow, mesmerized as more and more light gleamed down on me by the second. I lost grip on my sword, and my hand reached out to the sun as if I could grasp it.

Heavy footsteps caught my attention, steps that were not the sounds of my own because I had stopped moving sometime along the way. The hairs on my neck rose before I built up the courage to turn around. Nothing ... until a shadow appeared, towering over me.

I was not alone.

I gasped awake, beads of sweat on my forehead. My cheek was still lying at rest on Armond's chest. I slid my arm across his midsection and brought him closer, drifting off again into a seemingly dreamless sleep.

When I woke, there was sunlight falling on me, and I felt more refreshed, more recharged than usual. I was almost too scared to open my eyes because I might find that Armond was not beside me. But the familiar warmth of his body pressed against mine was enough indication that he was real. I rolled over to face him, and his arm fell off my waist. The bright sun cast light onto his curls, revealing the pecan-like lightness and darkness of his hair. I brushed away a strand and twirled the piece around my finger before putting it behind his ear. Then, I leaned in to plant a soft kiss on his mouth. His lips instantly cracked a grin.

"You seem to gradually care less and less about that," he whispered in his husky morning voice, startling me.

I sighed softly, shaking my head. "About what?" I asked wonderingly.

"Morning breath, of course."

I rolled my eyes, and his own fluttered open to look up at me, eyelids lifted indolently. I had missed the unique green color and the way a golden ring encircled each of his pupils. His focus fell to my chest.

"You still wear this ..." Armond whispered thoughtfully, grasping the heart locket resting on my collarbone.

"Of course," I murmured, a smile playing on my lips. "I never took it off. I wore everything I had left of you. Even your ring ..." I nudged his finger. "Which isn't on me anymore now that I'm here with you."

A soft grin graced his face in return. I switched my focus to our bay window, looking far out at the high green hills of Rome. Everything was already set in motion for change. I had woken up to him sitting by the bay window the last time we had lived through this day. We were soon on our way to the battlefield. Many changes would occur. But I anticipated the difficulty and the aftermath.

"What are you thinking?" Armond all of a sudden asked me.

My eyes fell back to his flushed face. "I'm thinking that this is going to take a lot of thought and planning."

"Preventing my death?"

I nodded. "And what you said about still wanting to fight ... we have to anyway. I did a lot of research and training in my time, and this is something we'll have to face head-on."

"Did I hear you say 'we'?" he asked, his brows nearly raised into his hairline.

"Yes, we," I enunciated. "I've gone over this for years. I've had this plan in mind for a long time now."

He blinked and swallowed. His eyes were wide awake from the thought and drifted to the hardwood floor, fixated there. "What plan?"

"To fight alongside you."

"I apologize, *cuore* ... But how would you do that?"

I watched him for a moment, cocking my head to the side. My silence caught his attention, and slowly, his eyes moved to look at me. I reached out and twisted his arm behind his back, then hauled him against the headboard, eyeing him fiercely.

I hummed, caressing my mouth gently over his ear. "I think you'd be surprised."

I let up my grip on him a little, and when he faced me again, his eyes hurriedly searched my face. His eyes were narrowed into slits. "I know I didn't teach you that."

I laughed dryly. "You taught me a lot. But not enough to do what I want. I know more now."

He gave me a lopsided grin. "Is that so?" His hands slid down my figure, but I snatched his wrists to pin them away.

"*Sì, Signore Cavaliere*," I whispered. He chuckled with amusement. I loosened my hands on him, moving them to his face. "I can do it. Let me show you."

He sighed defeatedly with a slightly encouraging smile. "How did it happen?" he asked, catching me off guard.

Terrible flashes made my teeth clench. I leaned away from him and closed my eyes. "Who killed you, you mean? If someone did?" I asked.

Armond propped himself on his elbows and gave me a solemn head nod, then grasped my hands to stop their incessant wringing. I relaxed significantly and opened my mouth to speak.

"The only thing I know is that you fell off your horse and hit your head. I wasn't sure I could take knowing what else had happened." He sighed heavily and grasped my hand tighter. My words came out slowly and hesitantly. "You … You had a brain bleed. You didn't tell me you were injured until it was too late."

Tears welled up in my eyes at the memory, but I had to ward my thoughts away from that fateful day and focus on what was ahead of me. His death wasn't going to happen again. I wouldn't have been given this chance otherwise, right?

Armond swallowed visibly and closed his eyes as he took the news, shaking his head. "I'm so sorry, *cuore*."

"Don't apologize, please," I said, grabbing his face in my hands again. "I'm going to do whatever it takes to save you."

He engulfed his hand over mine and kissed my palm gently. "I know you will." His smile was faint. "But what if … what if I'm fated to die?"

My heart panged in my chest, replying with a question of my own. "What if it's my destiny to change that?"

He watched me for a moment passively, sighing deeply. "You have a point. But fate is fate."

"At least I would have tried."

His face formed a deep frown as he swallowed. "We'll do everything we can, Lavinia. You can lock me up here if it makes you feel better."

I smiled softly and lightly kissed him. "As much as I want

to, that wouldn't be the best idea. That could cause more trouble."

He huffed in disappointment. "I was looking forward to being your prisoner." I shook my head at him with an eye roll as he asked, "What happens with all you left behind?"

I pulled away and sighed before explaining. "It will seem like I never left them. Time doesn't stand still when you aren't present. We were on a family trip. I didn't go there with the intention of time travel. I didn't think I could. But when I saw you in the painting ..." I stopped for a moment. "All the memories just came rushing back. And so did the guilt and the blame I had for not being able to save you ..." My face screwed up in pain. "I wished to change what happened as I touched your face in the painting, then ended up here." I scrunched my brows. "That must be it."

"You made a wish?"

"I did ..."

The fortune teller, Krysta, had warned me. This was what she had meant by interfering. She had said I had a strange fate. Had she granted my wish, or did I have that power?

I looked down. "I shouldn't have gotten mad, Armond. Knighthood is your life. I knew the day would come when you'd go to war. I am sorry I upset you."

Armond immediately shook his head. "I understand the unpredictability of war and how scary that is for you. I only expected more support."

I frowned. "I know. You told me that, when—when we woke up. And I had said you will have me as your backbone for life, which is true. You will always have my support. I just had a terrible feeling. And I was right. I've spent so much time kicking myself for not fighting you harder on it. I wished I hadn't gotten so mad." I sighed, and he frowned with me.

"Oh, cuore. Knighthood may be a big part of my life, but you are everything to me. We can't let trivial matters overcome us."

I nodded, agreeing. "It's all behind us now."

He gave a low-spirited smile. "Or ahead of us."

He had a point. I absently worried my lip. "There's a lot you still don't know."

"Please, by all means, tell me." He shifted into a more comfortable position. "You know I could listen to you for hours." He chuckled.

"And you've done it." I offered him a smirk, but my lips flattened as I turned serious, coming straight out with it. "I had another encounter with the lady I saw before I met you. Her name is Krysta. She gave me a reading and talked to your ghost, which was amazing, but …" I had an impending feeling deep inside me. "She also gave me a warning of a consequence for interfering with something. And I gather it has to do with being here before your death and the possibility of changing your fate."

"You'd alter time by keeping me alive. I believe a lot could go wrong with that."

"My fear of that doesn't outweigh the fear of losing you again. If your death really is inevitable, it's not happening without my best fight for your life."

I only hoped it wasn't the consequence of a life other than Armond's being taken. If it was my life that I was risking, I didn't mind much, but if it risked his brother's life or another's, I wasn't ready for that.

"And there's something else I found out from my mother after bumping into Krysta." He noticed my body tense ever so slightly, anticipating his reaction to what I would divulge. He rubbed his thumb in circles over my skin to calm me. "I … I wasn't born in 1969 like I thought."

Armond was completely still, speechless, and most likely, lost in thought.

I continued when he didn't reply. "I've just found out that I was born in this exact century. In 1828."

"That's … a year after me." Armond became even more riddled with shock. "But … but how?"

"Apparently, my mother is a time traveler as well," I blurted. The gears in his mind seemed to turn. "She came back to my father." I paused for a moment so he could gather his emotions. "And my father ... Well, he went by Tony Melrose. But his real name is Antonio Melrossi."

Armond's eyes were immediately the size of dinner plates, and he struggled to find a reply for once. "Antonio—Antonio is Giuseppe's—"

"Brother, yes. Giuseppe is my uncle. That's where the resemblance comes from."

"Lavinia ... Lavinia, this is—this puts together everything we've wondered about!"

"I know. According to my mom, they had trouble with Calabrese, too. He betrayed my father somehow, which I'm eager to get to the bottom of. When I caught the measles, they needed to time travel to the future in order to receive proper medical care."

"I don't want to think about you being sick so young." He suddenly sounded stricken, his memories of Della probably resurfacing. His eyes were wide. "June sixth, 1828. This means Antonio didn't leave for America with his wife, like he claimed. His children—you and your brother are his children. And that also implies ..." I saw tears forming in his eyes. "He is dead."

I frowned, feeling an ache in my chest. "Oh, Armond ... how close were you?"

He sighed and secured his focus on me. "Antonio was more of a father to me than my own. When he left, it broke me, and—" He cut himself off, deep in thought. "Giuseppe stayed, as you know, to keep on the royal line. Antonio held you both in secret; only very few knew you existed. Giuseppe was the one who told me about his brother's children, much later."

"So, you didn't know of us until ..."

"Until a few years ago, before I met you."

More silence ensued. All the new information stirred around in my brain as my eyes drifted from object to object in the room, taking everything in. Then, I remembered something. I flew off the bed and quickly reached underneath it to pull out the box of my clothes.

"What are you doing?" he asked.

"I'm checking for ..." I lifted the lid and frowned when I didn't see his letter. "It's not here."

"What isn't?"

"Your letter."

"How'd you know I ..." he trailed off, then his eyes widened. "You read it, didn't you?"

I nodded. "I haven't read it in years."

Armond gracefully slipped out of the bed and went to his desk to retrieve the sealed envelope from the drawer. "I didn't know where I was going to leave it for you until last night. You knew exactly where I had in mind."

"That's where I found it before I left."

He walked toward me and silently handed me the encased letter. I took it in my hands and ripped the envelope to read it twice to myself in my head. I folded the paper back up when I finished.

"Armond, did you ... expect to die?" I asked.

He was momentarily stunned by my question before he replied, "I didn't know what was going to happen. I put it there for the time you would need it and open that box again, whenever that would be."

I nodded and held it back out to him. "Well, it's beautiful. I never got to tell you that."

He gave me a slight smile. "Keep it with you." He pressed it against my chest. "I wrote it for you."

Armond and I spoke for a couple more hours before we went down for breakfast. We had woken up early despite staying up all night, but I was glad we had time to talk more.

As I walked through the familiar halls of my home, I was met with overwhelming happiness. And nothing could have prepared me for the strong pang in my heart when I first caught sight of Armond's sister.

Chiara had waltzed up to me like any other ordinary day, but of course, it wasn't that for me. My grin was wide as I ran to her and took her in my arms. She froze for a moment before her arms reciprocated around me. I could sense her throwing Armond an odd look over my shoulder. I pulled back from her with tears brimming in my eyes and quickly willed them away.

"*Oì*, Lavinia. Are you quite all right? You act as if you haven't seen me in forever." Chiara laughed awkwardly.

I shook my head with a small laugh of my own, then gave her a nod. "Uh ... well, I have a lot to tell you. It can wait, but not for long. It's important."

She tilted her head in question. Her eyes darted to Armond, then back to me. "Should I be worried?"

"Oh, no, please don't," I said. "Let's just enjoy breakfast together."

"All right, then." Chiara sighed gently through her nose. "Come, everyone is waiting."

The mention of them almost brought tears to my eyes again. "Armani's here, isn't he?"

Chiara smiled brightly, a light in her eyes I've seen in mine while looking at my reflection. "Yes, how did you know? He's visiting."

"Just had a feeling; you seem extra happy," I played it off.

With a tilt of her head like a confused puppy, she turned around and headed for the dining room, not questioning me like I knew she would later.

I followed her to the table and felt Armond's hand wrap around mine before he pressed a kiss there. I gave him a soft smile as we walked hand in hand. The sight of Carmela, Bartoli, Giovanni, and Armani sitting around the long table sparked warmth in my heart. I had missed this. Missed them.

"Good morning, darlings," Carmela greeted us with a gentle smile.

Bartoli was slurping his cup of coffee loudly at my entrance.

Nothing had changed, it seemed. Giovanni smiled at me as Armani told me, "Good morning."

I tried to act normally and not like I hadn't seen them in ages. Inside, the joy was hard to contain.

Armond pulled out a chair for me. I gave him a quiet thank you, then sat down. He joined us at the table next to me, and the footman came to pour us coffee.

"We'll be leaving in a few days, son," Bartoli said to Armond. The same words I remembered him speaking before. "Be ready."

Armond glanced at me quickly, then looked at his father. "Actually, Father. Not only me. Lavinia will be accompanying us."

Before, Armond hadn't brought up the fact that I was coming until we were about to leave. Bartoli had not been thrilled and, of course, had advised against it, but he had not fought us too hard on the decision the last time around. However, it was apparent by the look on Bartoli's face that mentioning it during breakfast this time put him on the verge of exploding.

I flinched at Bartoli's coffee cup slamming against the saucer, nearly cracking both china pieces. Coffee slapped over the sides and seeped into the tablecloth. "She what?" he sputtered in annoyance.

"She's going to war with us. We've decided," Armond told him without wavering.

"Lavinia, darling, why on earth would you want to do that?" Carmela asked softly in concern.

Seeing my loss for words, Armond responded for me. "I don't reckon it's an adequate idea to be away from Lavinia, her being with child and all." He paused to grasp my hand and threw me a reassuring look, but my heart stopped at those words.

My hand slipped away and found my belly. It hit me that I wasn't even pregnant anymore, but Armond had not put that together yet. He wouldn't get to hold Leo as a newborn and watch him grow ... at least as far as I knew. Armond's following words became unintelligible while my thoughts ran wild. He detected something was off and placed a hand on my thigh, bringing me back to the conversation. "I want to be beside her at all times. I wouldn't want to leave her right now. Besides, she wants to ... help."

"Help?" Bartoli threw sharp daggers from his eyes and probably visualized sticking them into my face. "So, this is your influence, I assume. You can't handle being on your own. I should have known."

"No, Father. Have you not been listening? Lavinia is the strongest woman I know. That's not the problem. I already told you the reason; don't twist my words."

I placed my hand over Armond's on my leg, and he visibly relaxed. I watched Chiara sip from her cup with interest. Her eyes looked over the rim, moving back and forth between Armond and Bartoli. She thought this was entertaining, no doubt.

"Are you really going to disrespect your father at the breakfast table, Armond? Careful," Bartoli said slowly, hissing. "That's what you're trying to hide. Don't tell me I'm wrong."

"Yes, you're wrong. You're always wrong," Armond retorted. "I'm not changing my mind, so accept our decision and start acting like a grown man."

Bartoli's laughter was manic. "You're the child here. I always knew you were soft, but this? Where is your strength? Better yet, your sense?" He raised his hands in front of him, shaking them furiously at me. "And you! Shouldn't you know your place by now?"

My blood had begun to boil more furiously with every word he uttered. I couldn't hold it inside me any longer. I was done with him demeaning everyone in his life. He needed to stop.

"You shouldn't speak about strength and sense when you have none," I snapped. "You only want to show off Armond like one of your ponies and don't care if your own son dies!"

Armond's hand, which I had let go of during my rage, pressed on my thigh. I turned my head to see him giving me a soft look, attempting to calm me. It hardly worked. I was past the point of placating.

"Watch your mouth, young lady," Bartoli hurled back. His tongue had always been sharp, but so was mine. "Of course I care for my child. My youngest daughter, Delfina, has passed on, and I've never been the same!"

"Yes, I'm very aware, and I'm sorry," I said in a quieter tone, but just as firmly. "But that should help you understand how much it would destroy me to see him dead. Clearly, you don't have any idea how much I love your son, though. Armond is my life. I am always going to stand by him. I want to be the last person he sees when he draws his last breath, if it comes to that."

I could feel the tension in the room intensifying. Everyone shared strange glances and had hardly touched their food. My words only worried them more. I swore if they watched me any harder, their gazes would bore holes in me.

Naturally, Bartoli ignored most of what I said. "Don't be melodramatic, dear. He'll do just fine out there. He did learn from the best." He gave Armond a quick and disturbing wink.

"Let me remind you that I know things you'd never think I would." More wide-eyed looks were exchanged as Bartoli's face lost some color, but I didn't let that stop me. I raised a condescending eyebrow. "Armond will be able to handle himself, always could. But even the strongest people end up dead. He might not be so lucky as to come out alive." My voice cracked a little. I swallowed before continuing. "It's much weaker and easier to prey on others rather than not react badly when you've been hurt in life. There isn't any excuse to treat your wife and children like the dirt under your shoe. You've treated them that way since even before Della died. So, I don't know what happened to make you this way, but we've all been dealt tough cards. Not just you. You really need to get your shit together and be a better person."

I visibly saw how much my words got to Bartoli; his lip curled in annoyance, and his fists clenched so tightly his knuckles whitened. I hadn't meant to curse, but I was fed up with him. I knew I had hit a nerve when he stood abruptly, growling low in his throat, and stomped out of the room.

Armond looked nothing but proud. Armani had wide eyes. Carmela was shaking her head and sighing. Giovanni was quiet and contemplative. And then there was Chiara, who looked at each of us remaining at the table with a mouthful of food, smiling with her lips sealed before she swallowed. "Well, that went well, didn't it?" she said, full of satire.

Carmela scowled in Chiara's direction, then began to rub her temples, showing how inappropriate she found the comment. I had sunk in my seat and then pushed my food around with my fork, embarrassment replacing my anger. I didn't say another word for the rest of breakfast. Nobody really did.

"I feel terrible for yelling, but I couldn't help it," I said apologetically to Armond as I sat by the bay window, looking far out at the cypress trees that marked the trail to the forest. He came up behind me and rubbed my back gently to comfort me.

"I understand," Armond replied. "Although, it's about time someone said it. He needed to hear that. I think you rattled him nicely."

I gave him a wry smile. "Rattled, yes. Nicely, no. He was so mad."

"Oh, beyond mad." He chuckled, but I could hardly laugh with him. "But his anger will dissipate, Lavinia. There's nothing he can do."

I nodded, and my focus dropped to my belly. "You said something earlier, and it made me realize …" I glanced over my shoulder at him. "Leo was already born. I'm not ... pregnant anymore."

Armond swallowed. The warmth of his hand vanished as it fell to his side. "Oh ..."

"I'm sorry." My heart ached for him. I could see the longing clearly on his face at the realization. "I can follow through with my plan easily this way, though."

He looked back at me, scrunching his brows. My heart forbade me to let him go off and die, but I was afraid interfering would only make matters worse. My mind pushed the idea to the forefront of my brain.

"Armond ..." I trailed off. He raised a questioning eyebrow. I barely let out a laugh. "Look, I was serious when I told you I had thought this through. I'm going to fight."

Armond's face contorted. "I don't know, *cuore* ..."

I shook my head, turning to face him head-on, my features becoming contrite. "After you died, I was very depressed and angry. I blamed myself so much it was unhealthy."

I took a deep breath, eyes closed in remembrance of all the times I had screamed and cried. Those sobs still echoed in the walls of my mind.

"I visited many health professionals in order to heal, but I had to control that anger somehow. I started by punching a heavy bag in my mom's basement. When I realized how much it helped, I couldn't stop. My therapist encouraged the idea of training. But the reason I did it wasn't to balance my emotions. I obsessed over becoming strong enough to come back and save you. I trained for a long time and never truly gave up. I worked until my trainer deemed me unstoppable. Not only am I an expert at swordplay and weaponry, but I also built enough mental resilience to fuel my empty tank. I know I can do this."

He watched me thoughtfully, eyes intensely roving over my features before letting out a pensive sigh. "Lavinia, I ..." He threaded his fingers through his curls and shook his head, green orbs wild with fear. "I don't want you to be the one who ends up dead or hurt. I can't let you die in place of me."

"Hey, I won't let that happen."

"No," he said, stepping closer to me. "*I* won't let that happen."

I searched his eyes as if I could dive deep into his mind and hear what he may be thinking. "I know," I breathed.

"Anything could happen, *cuore*."

"Yeah, it happened to you!" My voice broke when I said that, causing his features to twist in pain. I swallowed down the ache building in my throat. "I won't let it happen again. Unlike your demise, we don't have to worry about mine. It's not written in the stars for some time now. Krysta confirmed that."

"I don't care. You will injure yourself. It's just a matter of how severely. I don't want that for you."

"Getting hurt is a small price I'd willingly pay," I said firmly, not backing out. He watched me dubiously, silently. "We need to formalize a plan."

"*If* you do this."

"I'm doing it, Armond. If there's any way that I can prevent this, I'm going to try. You can't change my mind."

He let out a hardly amused breath and looked downward, shaking his head. Then, he pinned his stunning eyes on me. "Indeed. You are more stubborn than I am."

"I can argue that."

He smirked. "What first, then?"

"Your family …"

"Will you tell them?"

I nodded. "Chiara could knock any minute now. I'm just unsure how to break the news to them."

Armond was still slightly brooding and finally relaxed a bit. "You're going to tell them you're from the future?" he asked.

I nodded again. "And how I know you're supposed to die."

We were silent a minute before Armond spoke up. "Once this is all over … what if we just leave here?"

"Leave?" I echoed, furrowing my brows. "And we'd go where?"

He hesitated a moment before saying, "To your home. Your time."

My eyebrows raised in surprise. Leave Italy? His home? His family? Was he really willing to do that?

When I didn't answer and remained silent, he sighed. "I want to see the world you come from, and more than anything, I want to meet our son."

I softened. "Armond, I ... Okay, but I don't want you to feel like that's the only option. As I said before, I could—"

"Lavinia"—he took my hands in his own—"I'll do whatever it takes to keep you happy. I'd do anything for you. If we must leave here, we'll do it."

I frowned. "Then you must understand I'd do the exact same for you." He stared at me for a moment and eventually nodded. There was just one problem. "Your family, Armond. What about them? And your home?"

Armond's lips turned downward. "I don't know ... I will miss them. But they will understand." He offered the slightest of smiles. "Anywhere is home with you. We'll build one together."

"Armond—I ..." I whispered, pausing and tightening my grip on his hands. "I want you to take time to think about this some more before you make your final decision. This is a big move. Literally It's a big jump forward and a difficult change."

"I know," he agreed, raising one hand to caress my cheek. "But we don't have much time to think. I want us to be somewhere safe, away from war and the place that has caused you pain. I want to build a new life with you there, build us a home. I want to see my son and raise a baby together. We'll live till we're old, just watching the sunset from our front porch. I'll admire the gleam in your eyes because you'll be so happy." I felt an overwhelming need to cry as he said that while caressing my cheek. "You won't be without me this time."

Those final words sparked tears in my eyes. I could only hug him, with my words lodged too tightly in my throat. I hoped he was right.

A knock was heard, and Armond allowed the person to enter. Chiara was peeking through the doorway with a wary look on her face. "There was something you wanted to tell me?"

CHAPTER 5

TELLING MY STORY

1848

My jaw locked in place as Armond and I both stared at Chiara, who was waiting for one of us to speak patiently. Neither of us did. We didn't know what to say, how to begin. Armond shared a long gaze with me, and then, slowly, we fixed our eyes back on the curious girl ahead of us.

"Is … is everything all right?" Chiara asked warily.

I gaped at her, lost for words, and Armond assured her everything was fine. Chiara hesitantly entered the room when he grasped my hand to coax me into speaking. I pressed on his hand for a short moment, then lifted my eyes to Chiara's.

"It's not just you who should know. This is important. If you could inform your family, I'd appreciate it. We'll meet in the drawing room around noon."

"Oh, my!" Chiara exclaimed. "Have you finally decided on names?" she asked enthusiastically, hopping on her feet a few times.

I frowned deeply. Her excitement fizzled to none as I shook my head and exchanged a glance with Armond, who was pretty blank of emotion. "This is different … Urgent."

Chiara's features instantly became worried; she spoke in a hurry. "Oh … Lavinia, whatever it is, I shall inform Mr. Benicio to gather everyone straight away!"

I smiled softly. "Thank you, and, oh, Chiara … I'd like Dino to be there. Please send a message that I need him and that time is of the essence." I missed my grumpy friend and was anxious to see him again. I would need him for this.

Chiara raised a confused brow but nodded firmly, probably more earnest than I had ever seen her, as she slipped out of the room quickly on her feet.

Armond let out a long sigh, echoing the one that I was still holding compressed inside my lungs. I couldn't have known how telling my story would turn out. The person I was most worried about already knew my secret. Only, Bartoli didn't know the most crucial issue. Acceptance was all I had ever gotten from most members of Armond's family and counting. So, I assumed everyone would accept the truth eventually and was optimistic they would believe me. But there was always going to be an overwhelming amount of hyperactive, disquieting thoughts bouncing around in my brain. Thoughts full of doubt that I hoped weren't true and didn't want to believe. Thoughts I asked and couldn't answer until I acted and found out for myself.

Time travel was unbelievable enough. Telling them I knew Armond was soon fated for the grave, in just days, was a whole other level of incredible, and so was thinking I had the ability to interfere and successfully save him.

"Are you certain about this, *cuore?*" Armond questioned, thankfully interrupting my musings. "Are you ready for my family to know who you really are?"

I swallowed and gave him an unsure look. "There's no time to wait, let's hope so."

My feet nervously shuffled down the hall to the drawing room as Armond's hand gently rested on my lower back. I moved quickly, even though I was incredibly apprehensive. I believe what made me pick up one foot after the other was the thought of seeing Dino again.

"Is Lavinia all right?" I heard his familiar gravelly voice ask just as I was about to enter the room.

Nobody could seem to answer him.

It didn't matter, though; he'd find out for himself. A few short moments later, I was finally visible to him. A small noise of excitement shot out of me, and then immediately, I was by his side, my arms wrapping around his largely built frame. Dino surprisingly stumbled back a step but didn't protest my hug. He instead held me to him tightly as if he knew what I needed. Minutes went by, then he chose to speak up.

"What is it, little one? What happened?"

I shook my head against his chest. "It's a long story you all deserve to know," I muttered. I pulled back and slapped his arm, saying quietly, "You didn't tell me you knew me."

Dino's expression was a bit confused until smugness curved his lips for the first time in forever. "Oh, that. Yes. But how did you …" His eyes slanted.

"That's part of the story." I glared at him. "There's so much you never told me."

He shrugged. "If I had told you we met, you would have done things differently. You aren't smart to mess with time, Lavinia." He said that last part very softly so others wouldn't overhear.

I swallowed harshly. His words only made the knot in my stomach become even more tangled. I felt Armond behind me, and I turned to see him completely serious, expression impassive. He waited for me to drop the awful news on Dino.

My whole demeanor drooped. "Dino, there's a problem …" I drifted off, then started again, lifting my eyes from the floor.

"I'm afraid we have to mess with time whether we'd like to or not."

Dino instantly looked worried after I finished speaking. His eyes darted from Armond's impassive face, him at a loss for what to do or say, to the trembling of my hands.

"Tell me everything," Dino said.

I let my gaze wander across each person in the room. First Carmela, then Giovanni, eventually Chiara and Armani, regretfully Bartoli, and finally Dino, who smiled gently. Their expressions varied. A few were flat, some worried, but most were eager and curious. The sight of several people in front of me willing to listen was a rush, but a rush I couldn't hasten. My story had to be thorough and convincing. But the only way I could begin was by being blunt with the truth. There was no time to dilly-dally. I cleared my throat, even though it was impossible to quiet a room of people who were already silent and staring at me.

"Everyone," I began, gaining their full attention, "thank you for being here ... I just want to say: be ready to hear the impossible because you are going to hear plenty of inexplicable things." I wrung my hands nervously. "A few of you already know about the real me. I just ask those of you who don't to really give me a chance to tell you everything, and you will understand."

Chiara immediately spoke. "What—what do you mean, Lavinia?" she wondered aloud, brave as ever. "What do you mean, the real you? I know who you are just fine."

I frowned at her. "I'm glad you asked, because the things you don't know about me don't change who I am," I said and threw a glance at Armond, whose stare never wavered from me, so I was able to drop the bombshell. "The biggest inexplicable thing about me of all ..." I paused, choosing my words wisely. "I can say truthfully ... one of those things is that I am from somewhere else in time."

If it was possible, the room was further put to silence.

They were so still that nobody seemed to breathe, and most were confused beyond belief. Bartoli wasn't surprised at all, but I half expected him to rudely interrupt. Dino, of course, wasn't shocked, but how he managed to hold his stone face was always going to bewilder me.

Only one dared to speak after that.

"Somewhere else in time?" Armani echoed.

"Yes," I replied, barely smiling. "I am not just from America. Many of you have probably wondered why I am so different, and if so, you'll hear the reason when you listen." I swallowed my heart down, then went on to explain further. "I'm going to just admit to you all now that I have lied. I despise myself for it. But I didn't lie about my name; I really am Lavinia Melrose. I lied because ... well, I had to in order to protect myself."

I straightened my back and continued:

"I arrived here the day before you found me. How could you forget? I was wearing clothes you assumed were men's attire because they are clothes you've never even dreamed of." I laughed to myself quietly. "I know things you can't even begin to understand because time has allowed humans to evolve in ways you've never thought possible. You constantly hear things I say that confuse you. There are many reasons I say it so entirely unlike all of you. And the truth lies in the fact that I traveled to here, in the past, from the future. This time is a century before the one I grew up in." I gave them another moment to mull that over before I blurted the words, "I am a time traveler."

No one spoke at that time. Everyone just listened, more and more stunned by each word I uttered next.

"I know this is a lot to take in, but it is the truth. I'm sorry I have lied, but you can believe me when I say this. The rest is a long story, and it's hard to explain, but I will do my best to try."

And so, I began my story again, saying things I hadn't known when I was here before because I had been naive. So naive. I'd had no idea what I was in for once I returned to this time, had no idea what I was capable of even as I poured my heart out to them.

They listened, all of them. Most of their eyes were bugged out, and a couple had their mouths agape at my every word. Chiara was the most eager. She was in awe that time travel was the reason I was so strange. She and Carmela, Giovanni, and Armani had many questions, and I was willing to answer them to the best of my ability. I gave each of these people a chance to understand me, and I believed they heard me. My largest hope was that I was heard by the man I assumed didn't want to listen, their brutal father.

Oddly enough, Bartoli kept his trap very tightly shut, probably to the point his teeth were gritting, but at least his mouth didn't open. He was still brooding, I assumed. He remained off to the side, sitting contentedly on his wingback chair. Why he was content not to interrupt me, I wasn't quite sure, and honestly, it was a little concerning.

The hardest part of all was telling them Armond's fate. A confession that was the biggest ticking time bomb of all time. Essentially, that was Armond's situation. A ticking time bomb was bound to go off, and it was pretty unstoppable. But I would die trying to get our happy ending. We deserved nothing less. I would save him if it was the last thing I ever did.

"And there's just one more thing, a big, terrifying thing ..." I paused hesitantly. I eyed each of them with caution, gulping down my nerves because there was no other way for the rest of the truth to come out. "Armond will die in this war if we don't do anything to stop it."

CHAPTER 6

TIMING CAN BE EVERYTHING AT TIMES

**CALIFORNIA
1993**

The historical research library was one of my favorite places to clear my head. The convenience of it being on campus made my life easier. One day, I'd just wandered in to take a look and loved it ever since. I'd study there, work on projects, or read, and the hours would fly by for some reason.

It was one of those days when I needed a quiet space to begin my schoolwork, away from the classroom buildings. The library was a perfect escape. I was stressed about due dates and sleep-deprived while raising Leo, juggling homework, and grieving. The occasional nightmares had started to get out of hand. So, on the weekend, I'd be content to stay at my mom's. My roommate had always been concerned until I switched dorms. Too many questions were arising that I couldn't bring myself to answer. Nobody could mind their own business. I understood some people were worried about me, but most of them I didn't know well enough to give them an explanation.

Except for Serena and Wren. Serena had become one of my best friends a year before Wren did. Serena was probably one of the few who didn't pester me about my sleep troubles. She had transferred to my college after being at the local community college, and we were inseparable within months. I had switched my dorm to be with her the year after I met her. Not only had that made things easier, but her company was also the best.

I had met Wren one night while I was out with Serena the next year. She was a beautiful Japanese woman with the shiniest long black hair I had ever seen. She was also the funniest girl I knew. Wren was a drama theater student at the University of Southern California and wanted to be a Hollywood star, which I already knew would come true. She had the determination of a bull. We all love each other and have always gotten along, but I was closest to Serena since I saw her much more.

I had been glad to have her around because when my mom or brother couldn't be there, she always was.

The grand entrance of the library welcomed me as I walked inside. I was met with the seemingly endless walls and aisles of history books. Books about all kinds of history. That was what I needed. That calming atmosphere and ambiance. And, of course, my favorite librarian, Mrs. Jones, a middle aged Spanish woman who spoke with a lovely British accent. Her father was British, hence the last name, and her mother was Spanish. Mrs. Jones had been born in Spain and moved to Yorkshire, England, when she was just three years old, then had moved to America in her thirties. So, Mrs. Jones spoke in her wonderful Yorkshire accent, and she definitely had the best British humor. I enjoyed all the times she tried to make me laugh, and it was interesting to hear about her mixed-culture background.

"Ah, good afternoon, my lovely!" I heard her gush enthusiastically before I even saw her. Her dark curls hung just below her shoulders. "How are you? I was hoping to see you today."

She waved me over from her place at the book check out.

As I made my way to her, I replied, "Hey, Mrs. Jones. I'm glad you were expecting me. I've been wanting to see you." I usually came in on Fridays or Sundays, and it was Friday that day. "I'm doing okay."

She sighed wistfully. "Oh, dear girl. Lay all of your troubles on me. Not all of them, I know. But what you can."

"It's just my lack of sleep and heavy workload. I have an art project due next week."

"You must be overwhelmed." Mrs. Jones didn't know about my nightmares or that I had time-traveled into the past, but she did know I raised a son as a widow and that he was running me ragged no matter how well-behaved he was.

I barely put on a smile. "A bit, yes. It's more so that I'm tired."

"I understand, darling." She was sympathetic; she had kids of her own. She would know. Although my nightmares had been occurring less and less frequently, she understood having weird sleep patterns because of my loss. "How is your baby?" she asked, smiling widely.

"He's an angel," I said in reminiscence, thinking about how much I wanted to go home and hug him. I'd visit him soon. I had to do it every weekend, at least. I was close to home from college, about an hour. But I always missed him too much. "Always is. I just miss him. All I want to do right now is go see him, but I need to work on this."

"Oh, goodness. I know. I can't be away from my kids for too long." She laughed, and I offered a faint grin. "When was the last time you went out, darling? You deserve some fun."

"Eh …" I screwed my eyes shut in thought. "A month ago?"

"Dearie, no! Go out for a change. Meet new men." She wiggled her brows.

I laughed awkwardly. "No thanks. I'm just trying to get through school."

"Oh … never mind then." Antonella Jones had a sudden

weird smirk on her face.

"What?" I asked, lifting a curious brow. "What is that face you're making? And why? I know you."

"*Querida*"—she was looking more mischievous as the seconds went by—"have you run into the new male employee yet?"

"No ..." I trailed off archly with a slight question to my tone.

"Didn't think so." She let out a strange, hearty belly laugh. "His name is Luca."

"I haven't heard that name around here, but I might have met him. I see a lot of people."

"Oh, no, sweetheart. You didn't. You would have remembered him."

I blinked. Once. Slowly. "Uh—what?" I thought about what she was insinuating, and I was not about to jump on top of that.

She giggled. "It's just that he is very handsome and likable. Foreign, too."

"Oh," I muttered, then scratched my head awkwardly. She was a tiny bit disappointed by my disinterest. Unknowingly to her, though, the word "foreign" had slightly caught my attention. Slightly. "Well, I'm going to get started."

"Oh, yes, yes"—she gestured for me to go ahead—"I don't mean to keep you. Let me know if you need anything."

I expressed my thanks and settled at a table in the corner near the front windows with everything I needed in place. My notebook. Pen and pencil. And ... I unzipped the main part of my backpack and looked inside to see my sketchbook was not there. My eyebrows furrowed, panicking as I began searching for it frantically.

Damn, where are you? Please be here!

I rarely forget my things anywhere. Strange. It couldn't fit anywhere else but in—

And there you are. Phew!

The fairly large, old blue sketchbook was found in my second zippered compartment. Not where I usually put it.

Oh, well, I thought. *I must have mindlessly stuffed it there on the way out.*

I shrugged and got to work.

My project was a figure drawing. The only rule was that whoever I drew had to exist at some point. I could not draw from my imagination. Looking around for inspiration, my eyes roamed the shelved old books, my thoughts straying back to when Armond had read to me from a couple of books in his time.

I smiled as an idea came to mind. I began with the eyes, forming their partially hooded shape. As I really started to make good progress, something strange happened.

"*Lavinia ...*" a deep and blood-curdling, disembodied masculine voice whispered from the ceiling, a draft of chilled air creeping down my spine.

My skin crawled, my bones immediately aching from a sudden overwhelming exhaustion. I clamped my eyes shut and tried to shake the feeling away, but the sensation wouldn't dissipate because this voice wasn't the one I wanted to hear.

No ... no ... Not this again!

I shivered as more chilly air snaked down my shirt, my hand squeezing the pencil in a Godzilla grip. The coldness intensified marginally, and I wasn't imagining the feeling either. Others rubbed their arms to warm up. Continuous freezing-cold chills swept over me.

"Go. Away," I barked slowly. "I don't want to hear that. I can't handle hearing you right now. Let me work in peace," I hissed.

"*No!*" another voice cut in, a pain-filled harrowing sound. It was distant yet just out of reach and so jarring. Very familiar.

My body stilled on instinct as my heart plunged deep into my stomach, farther down than it had ever been before. My free hand crumpled up the corner of the page in my notebook involuntarily. I hadn't realized the harsh pressure I was putting on my pencil until the tip snapped against the paper and poked through to the next page.

A crackling in the air seemed to echo like a radio tuning in a song while the room seemed to grow empty. It wasn't a vacant feeling of being the only one in the room, no. Goosebumps raised on my arms, the hair standing up like grass. A presence seemed to be with me, a person I missed so much was suddenly right behind me. A feeling I can only describe as sentimental washed over me. My eyes immediately became dewy-eyed.

"*Lavinia*," he whispered in a muffled echo. I swear I felt the sweet caress of his breath on my neck. "*I'm here. He's gone.*"

Suddenly, this rare occurrence turned out to be more wonderful than strange. In fact, I hoped it would be the start of the second round of visits from him. The man I still considered my husband. I hadn't heard my name called in that chilling yet silvery other voice in such a long time. Hearing it again, now, after having known him and his voice so well confirmed it had been him, years ago, in that hotel room all along. That voice was unmistakable.

"*Lavinia ...*" There, my husband spoke again.

At that moment, I knew I was not imagining the sound. I had not heard his voice in so long. Not while I was awake, only in my dreams. Not as a ghost, either.

"*Follow my voice, Vin ...*" His whisper caressed my neck once more.

I jumped out of my seat to leap forward much too quickly and tripped on the leg of the chair. Before I could fall, a forceful and cool blast of air hit my face, steadying me backward. Then, a slight burning heat encased around my wrists, pulling me upright.

"*Careful*," Armond muttered swiftly. I couldn't see him. I merely sensed him. He said more softly, "*People are suspicious ...*" It was barely a whisper, firmly spoken. "*Pretend you were about to grab the thick red book on the shelf over there to your left. Then sit back down."*

I had totally forgotten that anyone was there. I was too shocked. Too shocked to speak or comprehend properly. Even to move like he had said. Was I in shock?

I discreetly glanced out of the corners of my eyes at the bystanders around me. Two girls about my age gave me wary looks, and as soon as I noticed, they darted their heads back down to their books with wide eyes. Were those girls' eyes bulging because they had just seen me teeter forward and backward like some sort of Cirque du Soleil show? Or were they embarrassed I had caught them staring?

Another thing occurred to me, something more crucial ... Was I the only one who could hear him?

"*You're all right, cuore. Fortunately, sì, it's only you who can hear me.*"

A slow grin lined my face. I could finally hear him! My smile only grew at the full heart-stopping realization he had always been there, lurking like an invisible shadow. "Armond," I choked out, stumbling forward. "It's really you. Again." I held back the tears.

"*Sì. It is me,*" Armond confirmed.

My bright simper remained as I walked toward the bookshelf to pick out the thick red book like he had suggested. I grabbed it without reading the title, then looked around, twisting in a circle. "Why can't I see you?" I asked him in a hurried hush. "I want to see you."

"*I shouldn't show myself,*" he whispered; the distant sound made it seem like his voice drifted away.

"Don't go," I rushed out. "Please," I begged.

I miss you so much, I thought.

"*I know.*" I could sense him nodding. "*Do not worry; I won't,*" he told me, pausing for a moment. "*I can't leave, really. Not yet.*"

I smirked. "Using English this time now, are you?" I

mocked playfully, marching back to my seat. "You were just being dramatic before, weren't you?"

I had cracked a joke for the first time in probably two weeks. And I actually laughed to myself afterward.

"*A bit, yes,*" he answered truthfully. "*You were being very stubborn. As usual.*"

I glared at nothing as I sat down and rolled my eyes. If he kept this up, I might have actually been able to live with him just visiting, even if I couldn't see him.

I could get used to this, I thought.

"*Don't.*"

I frowned. It was concerning that he didn't want me to expect him to visit regularly.

"*I always visit,*" he corrected. "*I won't always make my presence known.*"

I couldn't ponder that for long. *Wait a minute, are you answering my thoughts?*

"*Of course ... sì.*"

And he did it again. No way. He had once jokingly spewed out about the possibility of reading people's minds when we were by the waterfall. Who knew he was right on target with that one!

"*It's not quite like telepathy,*" he was quick to reply. "*And I'm not ... alive.*"

"What do you mean?" I asked. What else could he do? "You're literally answering my thoughts."

"*No time to explain,*" he responded abruptly. "*Follow. My. Voice.*"

I sighed with slight disappointment. There was a long pause as I contemplated how to answer. "Just don't make me look insane," I decided to say. That was a significant concern for me.

"*You do that all on your own anyway, my love,*" he teased lightheartedly. I heard the playfulness in his easygoing tone as I scowled with amusement. I was about to make a clever remark, but he was back to business in no time. "*Now, dai. Follow me.*"

I puffed a few of my stray light hairs away from my eyes, noticing how my hair was growing slightly darker in tone. Then, I squinted forward at the absent space where his voice traveled. He was being cheeky, and he knew it.

Annoying, I thought

"*Always.*" His voice echoed its way to me like he was even farther away.

I couldn't fight my smile as an idea popped into my head. I straightened my spine and crossed my arms.

Armond … wait! I mentally exclaimed to catch his attention, careful not to yell while others were watching. I already looked like I was talking to myself.

"I will." I said and then paused with a little hesitation. "But only if I can see you."

I would only follow him if he appeared to me as a ghost. Even though it was likely that I would follow him anyway, I was dying to see him. I could sense his loud sigh even if I really couldn't hear it.

"*After …*" His accented voice sounded a bit faltered, and that bothered me.

"After what?" I asked, a little confused but mostly concerned. The tile lights flickered above me when he did not reply, but I was not unsettled by it. "You're beginning to sound like Dino with these short answers."

The mention of my friend made me melancholy. I began to think of everyone else I had left behind, and I had to brush it off quickly, or I would have cried. I didn't want to cry in front of him at the moment, but that hardly mattered. Armond understood what I was thinking … or maybe it was a feeling. Maybe he didn't need words. But, for once, I found myself happy to merely speak with him.

"*We're communicating,*" he specified, as if there was a difference somehow. "*Not necessarily talking to one another.*"

I scrunched my eyebrows, completely and utterly muddled by his words, which only intrigued me. But more pressing than any other thought in my mind was whatever Armond wanted to show me. All worries that I had about school, work, or Leo vanished.

Armond was probably still rolling his eyes at my Dino remark. "*After you follow me,*" he said earnestly. He would not elaborate more. He was in a rush for some reason. "*I promise.*"

I trusted his word on that. He was good at keeping promises. Better than me. He never broke a single one. Even in death. He once told me he'd always protect me. And his way of protecting me was sending me back to the future. I didn't think I would ever have to follow through with it ... but here I was, *communicating* with his ghost in the 1990s.

Even after his last breath, I had known he would watch over me. And I was right. I felt him everywhere. He was always there watching, just as he had said.

"*And don't forget it, cuore.*"

My heart skipped a beat, then picked up speed. I had missed him calling me that. The way he spoke the word still did all kinds of strange things to my heart.

I sensed his smirk. "*Now follow ... Please.*" His velvety voice drifted down the aisle closest to me.

Dead silence ensued, which was sort of creepy, though not as creepy as before. I quickly sprung from my seat again, steady on my footing this time, and hurried my way down the aisle that his voice was leading me to.

"*Dai. Over here.*"

His accent came from the left of the aisle around the bend. I followed it, determined. My steps were confident and long while I passed the back row of books against the wall. I tried to act natural, not to draw unwanted attention to myself. As I approached the end, I started to worry that he would leave when I heard him again.

"*This way,*" Armond finally whispered faintly.

I quickly stopped in my tracks and whipped my head around. I had missed the aisle that his disembodied voice had sharply turned down, so I veered in that direction instead. As I reached the other side of that aisle, he told me to go down the next one. I abruptly slid out of the way of a woman entering the aisle that I was exiting and widened my eyes, saying a quick and polite, "Excuse me."

I kept maneuvering to the sound of his voice. In that amount of time, two older men, a young man, and a young girl had time to come through the entrance of the library. When I saw the familiar bookcases I liked to visit to be with nineteenth-century history again, I spoke up.

"Are you taking me in circles, Armond? What is this?" I whined in annoyance.

"*Sorry,*" he said, chuckling, "*I had to be certain of something before I led you to the correct location. Keep following.*"

I sighed with an impatient laugh, but did as he said, not questioning him. I only became more eager and filled with anticipation once we entered another aisle I recognized, section 913, the Ancient World shelves.

"*Lavinia ...*" he called unexpectedly. His voice hovered over my head as he said, "*This is it.*"

I glanced at my surroundings once more. "Err—Armond ... I have to say, I was expecting something much bigger to happen."

"*It doesn't get much bigger than this. Trust me.*" I heard the hardly contained amusement in his tone.

"You sound more American and more from this time the more you talk to me."

I actually heard him sigh that time as if he was very close to me; it was nostalgic. "*I listen to people's chatter all the time now. It's difficult for it not to rub off on me.*"

I giggled. "I can tell. You understand me more now, don't you?"

"*In certain ways,*" he replied ambiguously, and then I imagined he shook his head to clear his train of thought for his following words. "*Look above you. Do you see the large aquamarine book on the second shelf down from the top?*"

I craned my neck upward and spotted the book that stood taller than the others, slightly tilted from its heavy weight. The color was close to cyan, blue with a tint of spring green, and reminded me of the sea, a bit bluer than Armond's eyes. The spine was thicker than the width of the red one I had picked up earlier, about the length of the two of them put together. I squinted in an attempt to read the fancy script on the side and failed. The book was so high up that my head hung back almost horizontally.

I leveled my head forward again. "Are you kidding?" I asked with hilarity. "I can't reach that!"

"*Step to the side,*" he commanded. "*Please,*" he added more gently.

I paused for a moment with hesitancy before stepping aside like he had told me. Another moment passed before the book suddenly moved, seemingly nudged, really. My eyes widened when it was nudged again, with more force that time. The book came barreling down to the hardwood floor with a loud smack, a cloud of dust shooting into the air. I instinctively jumped further back and waved the puff of dust away with a cough. My head whipped from side to side to make sure nobody had seen the book fall or had heard the loud thud. No one was there.

"Oh my—" I gasped, placing a hand on my heart and cutting my words short, too stunned to speak. I focused my laser gaze on the book, slowly raising my stare upward. "Armond," I hissed quietly to the empty space. "I could have asked for a ladder! How is this discreet?"

His response was quick:

"*There's no time.*"

Again, what does that mean? No time for what?

"*You'll understand soon.*" He was still being vague, which irked me. "*Now read the title.*"

Were you always this demanding? I thought in irritation, bending down to reach for the book.

"*I can think of a few times I was, sì,*" he told me playfully. "*Particularly when—*"

"Oh no you don't, Sir Armond Alessandro," I interrupted, lifting a finger. "There's no time." I wagged my pointer finger.

"*You are finally catching on,*" he said teasingly, sarcastically. "*Now, read the title.*"

My eyes reached the ceiling again. They were on a roll, and so was he that day, apparently. I scowled at the air as I lifted the big, heavy book.

"*What do Americans say?*" he asked with a pause, feigning deep thought. He was definitely tapping a finger against his mouth; I could picture it. "*Oh, yes, sì. Sassy. You are very sassy, Lavinia.*"

I was going to reply, "And you are the most frustrating being I've ever met," when the title of the book I held like a baby caught my attention. My brain already knew exactly what it said with just that one glimpse.

"*The Gift and the Curse,*" Armond and I whispered in unison.

Chills instantly raised goosebumps on my skin. The name at the bottom read: Guinevere Powers.

I furrowed my brows at the bizarre name. When I lifted my gaze from the aquamarine cover, I'd done it so fast that I swayed slightly, almost dropping the bowling ball of a book in my arms.

"Um—what ... is this?" I asked, full of scruple, voice wavering.

No response at first. Ten seconds went by before he finally instructed, "*Just open it, Lavinia.*"

Was the silence he gave me good or bad?

"*Depends,*" he whispered, then encouraged me to open the book again.

His answer was ominous. *The Gift and the Curse*? What gift? What curse? Was this said gift good and the curse bad? Or was it the other way around? And why was I so worried about it? It wasn't happening to me; this was just a book. A book that had no place in a history library.

Unless it wasn't just a book.

With that thought, I gathered the courage to shift the book to my right arm and open the book with my left hand. My hint of fear switched to complete astonishment as the pages turned without me touching them. I let out a loud gasp, then coughed up the dust that flew in between my parted lips. I almost dropped the book on my feet after reading the heading at the top of the page. I didn't have enough conviction in me to scold Armond for doing things people could see. My sense of intrigue was through the roof.

I read the first line, the words so tiny in comparison to the big and bold letters of the heading.

The Time Traveler

For centuries, humans have perceived time travel as wildly difficult or absolutely impossible until they experience the phenomenon for themself. The void carefully chooses the beings pulled into its web. Time is so far beyond its measure that comprehensively laying hold of that is onerous.

A forceful shiver wracked my body as Armond explained to me. *"The responsibility of knowing the ramifications of time can be burdensome. The consequences of interfering are at times unwelcome."*

"What the hell?" I asked slowly, freaked out. "What the actual hell?" I was about to hit the ceiling and lose my mind.

Armond chuckled at my thoughts, and hairs raised on my arms again upon hearing the deep sound. *"I haven't heard that* expression, *cuore*, and I hear quite a lot. Especially in the last hundred years."

A hundred years. He had been ... dead for longer.

I snapped the book closed, my arms shaking. "Why are you showing me this? I already know I am a—" I didn't say it aloud, fearful of people hearing and questioning.

Time traveler, I mentally finished the thought for him.

"*Sì, you are.*"

"Armond ... how am I talking to you?" I shook my head abruptly, realizing my mistake. "Communicating. How am I communicating with you?" I sensed his smirk as the book forcefully opened in my arms. I caught it before it could hit the floor. "Armond," I spat, berating him. "Someone is going to see sooner or later!"

"*No need to fret about that. I sense when people are coming. About ten have passed us already without you noticing.*"

A smile crept onto my face. "You really are my protector. Or should I say my Alessandro?"

Alessandro does mean "defender of men."

His low laughter made my heart sing, dance, and ache all at the same time. "*Lavinia,*" he whispered, chuckling. "*Look down at the book. The answers to your questions are there.*"

I sighed, and pages flipped further into the book, landing on a page headed:

The Gift

I froze at those two words, the ones that were in the title.

"What's ... 'The Gift'?" I asked slowly, cautiously.

"*I think you should be saying,*" he began, and my heart almost gave out when he said, "*your gift.*"

I stumbled backward from the blow of the truth, my vision blank and unfocused until blackness consumed me.

CHAPTER 7

BLURRED FIGURES

CALIFORNIA
1993

"Lavinia." Armond's compelling, deep voice tickled the edges of my mind. "Wake up."

A hand shook me firmly to consciousness, startled gasps erupting from my chest. I moaned at the pain in my head and blinked my eyes open, seeing a hazy figure of a man with dark hair ...

"Armond?" I asked in a croak, failing at my attempt to sit upward as my heart kick-started and attacked my rib cage. "Am I dead?"

"Who?" a different voice asked, the same hand that shook me awake lightly pushed on my shoulder to keep me lying on the floor. "No, you are definitely not."

My vision finally focused, disappointment stinging my eyes. It was not Armond hovering over me but another man instead. Several other people stood around me, including Mrs. Jones. The man shooed everyone away but her and told them to give me space.

"Are you all right, darling?" Mrs. Jones cooed. "What happened?"

"I—I don't know." My eyes bulged as far as they could go, watching the unfamiliar man warily. "W—what? I—who?"

The man chuckled with only a smidge of amusement. His next words sounded full of concern. "I think you hit your head. You should go to hospital ..." He had a foreign accent. I had barely noticed it before that moment. An Italian accent. "I never forgive myself for not making sure you are fine."

"That's a great idea," Mrs. Jones chirped.

I pinned a narrow-eyed stare on her. I wasn't going anywhere with a complete stranger.

"*She's just fine ...*" I heard Armond snap at them as if they could hear. "*Trust me, cuore. I am certain. You don't have to go.*"

Armond, don't start, I thought so that he could hear me secretly. *There's nothing to be jealous of.* I wasn't planning to get checked at the hospital anyway.

He sighed as if I didn't understand. "*I'm dead, cuore. He is not. He could give you what I cannot. I have a reason to envy him.*"

That really put me off track, and chills raised the hairs on my skin.

"Did you hear me?" the man with curly dark hair asked me. His voice was now tuned in like I had been in another world just a second ago. This man's hair was a little shorter than Armond's natural, loose curls. "You just went into a zone."

"Uh ..." I shook my head. "No, I'm sorry; what?"

"I said"—he paused seriously—"I can take you now if you'd like to make sure you are all right."

"*No need!*" Armond exclaimed, and I winced at the ferocity behind it. He lowered his tone when he spoke again. "*Her head isn't even bleeding—*"

"Armond, shut up for a moment," I hissed aloud accidentally. "So dramatic."

"My name is not this Armond you speak of, but I do tend

to be dramatic at times," the man joked. A snort came out of me despite my minor annoyance and slight disorientation. His lips stretched as he gave me an odd, half-hearted smile. "All right. Up you go. I'm taking you to hospital." The man had his hands out to reach under me. He raised a brow, silently asking if he could lift me.

"I can stand on my own," I insisted, shifting to my knees.

"Wait, easy," the Italian man said, his accent very thick, as he assisted me to my feet with a hand in mine and another light one on my back. I gulped at the feeling of a different man's hands on me, only wobbling slightly. "Oh, I ... I was going to carry you to my car, but you do seem fine." He seemed a bit disappointed.

"Yeah, I am," I told him, nodding more firmly, and instantly slipped my hand out of his to rub it down my side awkwardly. "Thanks for the offer."

"*Sì*, of course," he said. "I mean, ye—"

"I am fluent in Italian. I'll understand anything you say."

"Oh my," he whispered with a light and shocked laugh. "That is *magnifica*. But I better use English for practice."

I grinned softly. The man stood there smiling at me like a goof from a height a few inches below Armond's.

He cleared his throat. "I haven't caught your name. What is it, *bella?*"

I tried not to roll my eyes at his smoothness and pursed my lips. I decided to be a little playful. "Tell me your name first."

His mouth popped open with surprise to speak, but I did not hear his reply as I found myself comparing him to Armond.

It was obvious to me he was boyish. From the beginning, I had known Armond was the opposite, wise. His eyes had conveyed a worldliness that this man's did not. The young man before me had slanted eyes the color of lightly roasted coffee, inviting and radiant. I recognized an impish look in them, but sensed kindness beneath the facade he carried. His hair was darker, a lot darker, actually, and shorter, in tighter curls.

There were no dimples in his cheeks, but when he smiled, tiny marks indented the area around his mouth. He wasn't an expert at English like Armond but smarter than he gave himself credit for, I imagined. Clearly, he was a charmer in the way he easily spoke without pause. Although Armond had easily charmed people, he had done so unwittingly.

The Italian man had an undeniable light in him, a brightness I had seen in Armond's painted eyes, though this man did not stir my soul quite as much.

Still, he was pleasant.

"Did you hear me?" he asked with a mirthful smirk, snapping me back to reality. "I said my name is Luca. Are you sure you are all right? You keep staring into space. And ... I don't need to repeat the rest. I don't know why I ramble so much." He grunted in annoyance to himself. The fighting thoughts in his brain were clear as day on his face. He put on an awkwardly wide smile. "I don't usually do that," he muttered, his grin dropping from being so embarrassed.

My heart jumped as I remembered something, followed by a harsh pang. "Wait—your name—your name is Luca?" I stammered.

His tone was comical as he questioned, "*Sì*, why?" His tongue pushed out his cheek, even more amusement lighting his eyes

Great, now he thinks I am stalking him!

"Oh." I blinked, then shook my head. "No, reason. I just knew a Luca once," I lied, laughing under my breath and brushing the subject off. I couldn't lie and say he wasn't handsome, though. Mrs. Jones was right about that.

He seemed skeptical but didn't question me. "So, will you tell me your name now?"

"Oh ... I'm—" I was distracted when I looked down at the floor and noticed the big aquamarine book was not where I dropped it. "Oh no! Where is ..."

"*On the shelf and back into place, cuore,*" Armond reassured softly, sounding a bit downcast.

I frowned. He was off, and I knew exactly why. It was difficult for him to watch this play out, as much as he wished me happiness.

"Where is what?" Luca asked, furrowing his brows.

"Never mind. I ..." I tried to think of an escape. "I left my stuff on a table, and I need to grab it."

"Oh, all right. I can walk you back. Do you need help looking for anything?"

"Uh ..." I paused, leading him to the table. He followed hot on my tracks, hands in his pockets. "No, no ... I was about to leave. Thank you, though." I gathered all of my belongings and rushed to shove them into my bag.

"Okay ..." I could hear his disappointment. "You never did tell me your name."

I sighed and turned to face him. His look was contemplative, his stance nervous. I wondered if that was because girls didn't always brush him off so easily.

I offered a faint smile. "It's ... Lavinia," I told him.

"I'll remember that." He nodded with a smile lining his lips. "I look forward to seeing you here again, Lavinia."

"Don't hold your breath," I said teasingly and tossed my backpack over my shoulder. He pouted playfully. "I might not be back as soon as you think."

"I hope it is sooner than you plan." His smile was charming as he took a step back and winked, turning over his shoulder to help another patron.

My lips quirked a little in amusement as I strolled to the front of the library. At that moment, I wanted to know him and thought that I might like him. Maybe even love him. But I'd fall slowly and not as hard as I had done for Armond. I only knew for certain that my love for that green-eyed man would never die.

I pushed open the door to walk out, then paused as a

thought came to mind.

Armond, you never ...

When I took a step back inside, I froze at the sight of Armond's glowing figure standing tall ahead of me. He waved and blew me a kiss. Of course, he hadn't broken his promise.

"Our son is beautiful, my cuore. Take care of him for me," he whispered thickly.

My lips trembled, his apparition blurring from a tear forming on the rim of my eye. He disappeared in a blink. The lone tear escaped and joined the earth as I left.

CHAPTER 8

FORGIVE BUT DON'T FORGET

1848

I stepped outdoors onto the balcony and tightly wrapped around myself the blanket I was holding, letting the gentle morning breeze calm me. I needed peace after baring my soul to Armond's family. They had not taken my bad news well, and it tore me up inside. It was almost worse than the looks I remember so clearly on their faces when they had realized Armond was gone when I was last in this time.

I pressed my hands to my face and just let the waterworks come freely. Was I wrong to tell them? Should I have waited? Should I not have told them at all?

No, I convinced myself. *No, you did the right thing. They deserve to know so they can do something about it.*

I had broken when Carmela fell to her knees and bawled her eyes out. It had killed me to see Chiara look at me as if she couldn't talk to me. I had wanted to run at the sight of Giovanni so still and blank that it had been terrifying. I had been more than surprised to know Bartoli had something other than anger in his eyes, which was, in fact, fear.

He might have cared for his children in his own sick, twisted way, the only way he knew. There was no other way he could show his adoration. All Bartoli must have known of love was brutality. That was all he had been given. All he had been shown.

I kept telling myself they just needed a couple of days to process everything. A couple of days, and they'd run back to me, ready to do all they could to help me prevent Armond's death.

I hadn't slept through the night like I did the first time I traveled back in time. My worry kept startling me awake. I finally gave up and decided to get out of bed, feeling tired as I sat hunched over the edge. I had looked back at Armond, fast asleep, and realized I was the one more likely to wake earlier than him. It didn't matter if I went to sleep late or how badly I slept.

I sighed into my tear-filled palms, then raised my glassy eyes to the skyline. The sun was just rising above the horizon, a bright orange-and-red glow overpowering the sky. Armond would wake soon, in the next thirty minutes or so. I wiped my cheeks and stared ahead, continuing to let the beautiful view put me at ease.

"You're different," I heard Armond acknowledge from behind me sooner than I had expected. He was close, but not close enough to touch me. I turned my head and looked over at him leaning against the railing, and he smiled softly. "In a good way, of course. There are many things I have noticed. Some small. You're not so still in your sleep anymore, for one. I remember I'd have to make sure you were breathing before. You were such a quiet and immovable sleeper." He chuckled, and I melted. His words would always continue to melt me. "Now, I feel you shift every few hours and hear you muttering to yourself in your sleep."

"Yeah …" I paused. "I started having nightmares after

you … died. It took a huge toll on me, and I knew the stress wasn't good for the baby."

He frowned at the knowledge. "Did they ever stop?"

"Eventually, yes." I nodded. "When I finally found peace within myself. When I decided to let myself remember our wonderful memories instead of keeping them back to numb the pain. I realized not accepting that you were dead was my eternal battle, and it was causing nightmares." I barely smiled. "But having a kid is really what changed my sleep. A child will change you in ways you never knew …" I began to say and stopped short because I didn't want to upset him.

He just gave me a soft grin. Who was I to doubt he'd do anything but smile? "That's the other difference. You're even wiser. You've been through so much without me. I can only imagine." He became melancholy.

"Yes, I did have help, though. From others and our son."

Armond's lips lifted in the corners slightly. He ambled over to me and slid a hand around my waist, tracing the inward curve softly with his thumb. "This time, I can be here as someone for you to lean on every step of the way."

I noticed it wasn't exactly a promise because he could not keep it for certain.

I grabbed his hand firmly and pressed my head to his chest, not being able to look into his eyes as I said, "You don't know that for sure."

I heard his gulp, but his words comforted me like they always did. "You may have the ability to give me the chance, Lavinia. If anyone does, it's you. You take my breath and breathe life into me just by looking my way." His arms enveloped me, and he planted a kiss on my temple. "I do know that my love for you is strong. So very strong. I'm just as determined to change my fate for you as you are to change it for me. I can't bear the thought of really leaving you alone in this world again. We have to go on thinking the impossible is possible."

I brought my eyes up and grasped his angelic face, speaking slowly to him. "No matter what does happen, I'll just be glad I had this time with you, even if it is only for a short time."

"There won't ever be enough time in the world." He tucked my hair behind my ear. "We may well not grow old together. We may only spend very little more time together. But one thing is for certain: we will both die one day. And once we are both gone, we will be together again, one way or another. I trust we will always find each other. That I can *promise, cuore*."

My breath hitched, and I lost the ability to talk as my heart softened into mush. I could only hug him close. His hand rubbed circles on my back as his cheek pressed against the top of my head.

Another thing was for certain; we had the choice to die for each other. I would die for him, and I know he would, without a doubt, do the same for me.

"You are worrying," Armond said. "I can practically feel it. Tell me what I can do."

I sighed. "Your family despises me now. I don't know what you can do."

Armond lifted my eyes to his with a hand under my chin. "Not at all true. They could never despise you. They adore you for reminding me who I am every day," he uttered softly, touching my heart with his words once again. "They are only upset. Give them time."

I shook my head. "We can't wait long."

He nodded, eyes falling to the ground. "As I said, no matter what we try to do, there's not enough time for everything in life."

Those words couldn't have been truer. I had lived to see that through, after all. And he had known it much earlier than myself, I was certain.

"I'll speak with them," he added in a whisper, stroking my cheek with the back of his hand. "Don't be bothered by their reactions. Just remember how it felt to think I was gone and never coming back."

I tightened my eyelids shut, sighing dejectedly. I couldn't help but know I was his only chance at living a full life. His words only had me contemplating whether or not life had declared he had already lived and loved enough. Armond's life might already be over. He could be dead no matter how many attempts I made to save him.

And be gone forever.

Bartoli didn't attend breakfast, which was unusual. I noticed maids rushing to bring food to his room on my way to the dining room. By lunchtime, he had canceled the luncheon. He made a point of wanting to stay locked in his bed chamber. Bartoli was always irritated when someone missed a meal, even part of it. I guess it was only acceptable when he did it, being "the man of the house" and all. He must have really been rattled by my story.

Throughout breakfast and dinner, Carmela could barely look at me. Chiara picked at her food, and Giovanni only politely offered me a few glances. Honestly, Giovanni took the news best, but he wasn't the blameful type. I didn't think any of them exactly blamed me for telling them what Armond's future held, but maybe they would have rather been kept in the dark. I just knew how they felt. They must not have known what to do with themselves. I could only guess that Bartoli's missing presence meant he took it the worst.

I thought for certain he planned not to show himself at all for the day until I had nearly finished my food during dinner.

"Lavinia," Bartoli muttered so softly I hardly heard it. I didn't ever expect his voice to speak that gently, and I was shocked at the seriousness in his tone. I hadn't even noticed him coming, he had approached that quietly. My head turned in his direction at the foot of the table with his hands behind his back. "I'd like to speak with you in my study."

I instinctively looked to my left at Armond, who stood up abruptly. "What about, Father? Anything you have to say, you should say to me."

"This matter isn't between us, my boy."

"If you must speak with her, I must be present. You're not conversing alone together," Armond rumbled, his fists clenched by his sides defensively.

I sighed defeatedly. "Armond, I can go by myself," I assured him, engulfing his hand with mine, feeling the tension there relax in my touch. "It's all right."

His head slowly veered to face me. I tilted mine to the side, trying to convey with my eyes that I really could handle Bartoli. He swallowed with a reluctant head nod and lent me a hand to bring me to my feet. "Can I please walk you there, at least?" he asked.

"Relax, son. She'll leave perfectly unharmed. I only want to talk."

Everyone was silent with shock. I noticed Carmela watching him closely, eyes squinting in suspicion. But I had listened carefully and didn't detect any malice in Bartoli's unusually honeyed tone. He seemed sincere for once, and I discerned that by the less-than-confident look in his stance. I didn't know if I should be bothered or relieved. Bartoli was always overly sure of himself. If he wasn't, he was triggered. Either I really scared him, or I made him question himself on a deep level. Possibly both.

"I think it's okay this time, Armond," I murmured.

He raised a stubborn eyebrow. "I'll stand outside the door, just in case."

His father started to say, "There's no need—"

I threw a sharp look at Bartoli, and I was surprised to hear him stammer into silence.

"I'll allow it," I whispered to Armond.

"Therefore, it's final," he grumbled curtly, glaring daggers at his father.

"Erm—I only meant to say…" Bartoli struggled to continue. "There's no need to fret, but if you'd like to, erm …" He waved a hand in a gesture for someone to finish for him.

I had never heard or seen him this way; it was nerve-racking. The whole Alessandro family, including me, was bewildered by his compliance.

"Be certain you won't go behind my back and hurt her again?" Armond said as a question scornfully.

Bartoli winced but sighed, seeming vanquished, and nodded. I saw deep exhaustion for the first time in his face. His pain was no excuse for what he had done, but his sunken eyes and the unusual paleness of his complexion were hard to miss, along with his twisted features. He actually allowed himself to show his true feelings. Shocking … Before, his walls were well guarded, and then, all of a sudden, they were crumbling little by little. He constantly replaced his pain with anger, his rage so untamable that it was all he could feel. His wrath was real, yet it was a mask.

"I won't hurt her," Bartoli said promisingly, "as much as she vexes my spirits."

Armond scowled fiercely and scuttled his way to him, towering over Bartoli as he stuck his nose in his father's face. "And she maddens me at times. . Still, she will always utterly outweigh any disagreement we may have, even if it makes my head spin. There's no valid reason to beat that out of her," he snapped. "I mean no disrespect, Father, but I don't think I could ever entirely trust you. You best not hurt her. Don't even look at her for too long."

Bartoli nodded, unphased but not about to bite back. "Understood, son. Understood."

Armond stilled for a moment, probably just as stunned as me by his father's submission, then glanced back at me. "Go ahead, Lavinia. I'll be right behind you."

I nodded and stood, walking around my chair and then over to the two men. I didn't pay Bartoli any attention as I continued my way toward his study. Bartoli stepped inside the room after me. I caught Armond's perturbed look before the door shut, then patiently folded my hands against my front.

Bartoli stared at the floor for a long while until he leveled his gaze upward, avoiding my eyes with caution. "Please have a seat, Lavinia," he instructed politely, addressing his arm out toward the chair by his mahogany desk. I was struck by his soft tone and the fact that he had called me by my actual name.

My eyes remained on him even as I slowly approached the more-than-comfortable seat. Then he followed suit, gracefully sitting down on his fancy, tufted, swivel-tilt, brown leather chair.

What a mouthful.

He steepled his fingers, pressing them against his lips. I waited for him to speak first, but our exchange of looks became a staring contest instead.

"Are you ever going to speak?" I asked impatiently, crossing my arms.

Bartoli grunted and rubbed a hand down his face nervously before leaning back in his precious chair. "When shall Armond's demise take place, Lavinia?"

As per usual, he didn't feel like beating around the bush.

"The very first day he fights, within a couple of hours. Sometime between three and four in the afternoon."

"That is quite a big chunk of time, Lavina. There are many seconds in an hour, and it only takes a few to cause major damage. Are you positive?"

Never mind, he was back to himself.

"I'm well aware, *Barti*," I mocked. "You don't even *know* how *aware* I am." My eyes narrowed. I could have done major damage to him if he had given me a reason. "If you're going to criticize my answers to your questions, don't expect me to speak with you."

Bartoli's face slackened, and then he began to chuckle before putting a finger in my direction. "You think yourself quite funny, don't you?"

"This isn't the time to be funny. I'm serious about what will happen to him. Now, if you can't find compassion in that frozen heart of yours, please excuse me." I began to stand.

"Sit down, Lavinia. Would you please hear what I have to say first?" he entreated.

I pursed my lips in annoyance, then reluctantly followed his order. He had said "please." I hadn't thought that was in his vocabulary. Plus, the anxious way he clenched and unclenched his fists made me uneasy.

"So Armond will die …" he started in a mutter, "unless … we do something."

"That's what I've been telling you."

"Then … that is why you don't want him to fight in the war alone."

"Evidently, yes."

Bartoli rolled his eyes at my reply, but he must have seen the grave emotion on my face because he sighed dejectedly. "The last war I ever fought, I shattered both of my kneecaps. They were almost certain I would not survive once I had a fever. But eventually, it broke, and my knees healed. Not completely, of course. But I was very lucky. Unfortunately, the doctor told me I could never participate in battle ever again unless I had a death wish."

"I'm sorry. Yes, there's a risk of *infection* with any open injury. That's why you had a fever, and most people die from fevers during these times. Is there a purpose to this story?"

"I am not entirely certain what you are maundering about, but yes, I always speak with purpose."

My eyes reached the ceiling. "I could argue with you on that and probably win."

He scowled at me, wishing an ugly death on me before he

sighed. "You won't believe me when I say this, but ... I cannot—" He closed his eyes, and my brows furrowed at the raw emotion he revealed, clear as the day. "I cannot lose another one of my children. I cannot ..." He paused, breathing deeply. "I'll do anything I can to help you keep him alive."

I gasped gently, astonished and speechless.

"Therefore, I shall fight along his side as his shield."

"Bartoli ..." I swallowed. "I do believe you. I ..." I straightened my spine, laying a careful hand over his trembling one. "Losing a child is unimaginable. I am deeply sorry you went through it. I will do my best to save you more heartache as well as my own. I don't think—I know you should not risk yourself like that. But I do appreciate you willing to sacrifice yourself for the man I love."

"He's a good man with the heart of a saint. He has his mother to thank. He doesn't deserve death. I will do it."

"You made him an amazing knight despite your poor parenting," I admitted.

He shook his head. "I have made too many poor choices to count and have been wrong a lot of the time. Especially about you, Lavina."

Goodness me, he would never let that go.

I smiled faintly, pressing his hand before pulling away. "Thank you."

He nodded once firmly. "You are undeniably the right woman for him. I wish I had seen it sooner. I am ... sorry. Very sorry for all I have said and done to you."

My eyebrows shot up, reaching for the ceiling. He was apologizing. I almost wanted to hug him. "It means very much to hear you say that." I paused to exhale a long breath. "I forgave you a long time ago, Bartoli. That's just what you have to do in life in order for your emotions not to consume you in a destructive way." I shrugged. "Apology accepted."

"What?" he sputtered in shock.

I smirked. "Just know that if you ever again do anything

like you have, you won't be so hard to stop. And I think you'll lose your son."

He glanced downward at his hands contemplatively. "Forgive and forget?" he asked.

"Yes ... but you can still forgive if you can't forget. You can remember and learn from your mistakes."

He nodded. "*Sì*, yes. I understand. I will try."

"That's all you can do." I offered a faint smile. "But I think your family are the people who really need your apology." His face fell as he pondered that. "I am curious, though. Why the sudden change of heart?"

Was it really Armond's fate that had caused him to spiral?

Bartoli shook off his thoughts. "Armond reminds me of my younger self. I was a soft boy. Determined. Stupidly fearless. Unusually strong. The same as Armond." His mouth curved into a fond smile. "But I was always told softness means weakness. I shouldn't want to be the weak link."

I frowned deeply. By his long and tired face, I sensed a story coming.

"When I was very young, I lost my whole family in a home invasion. All murdered before my eyes. Except for well ..." He shuddered. "Calabrese. He is the one I wish had been there when it happened. He only made my life that much harder, and so did his father. My mother and father were everything to me, and my brothers and sisters made me whole. But they were gone. I was forced to accept Calabrese's father as my guardian and have him and Calabrese live with me in my family home because they were all I had left. I would have rather lived on my own." He looked away from me as I listened. "I was treated as I was, the child of an unfaithful woman, not his son. A 'harlot,' he'd say, and things much worse than that, of the woman who bore his own son, too. I was not his child. I was unacceptable to him.

"Calabrese wasn't always cruel to me, but he had always

been meddling in matters he shouldn't. I followed in his footsteps; at least he wanted me around while he created conflict. Until he didn't." Bartoli sighed, full of tension. "I was sick and tired of both fools, so I went on a journey one day and stumbled upon an old man." He actually smiled. "He trained me as a knight at eight years old. A year late, but he always told me it was never too late for anything. After years of his influence, I was just beginning to become unstoppable. But ... he died suddenly when I reached the age of fourteen from *angina pectoris*."

"Heart attack," I murmured.

Bartoli's eyes finally met mine, but he was silent for a while. Emotionless. Still. Until his eyes lost their blank look and brightened. "Then, I met Carmela. I had thought she was the most *bella* woman in all the land. I didn't think she'd ever want someone miserable like me. Only she did. She had the power to make me less miserable no matter how terrible I acted. And I still could not make her as happy as I wanted. When we wed, I focused too much on becoming the best *cavaliere*. I was successful, yet my marriage declined. I became worse than Calabrese's father the second I realized how similar Armond was to me. I thought I was doing right by him. I thought I made him tough by hurting him like that man hurt me. Turns out my own son is stronger than I ever was."

He put his face in his hands shamefully. "The day my daughter died, I didn't think I could handle any more. The more loss I had to bear, the less and less of me I was able to recognize. I'm not proud of my choices. The worse I became, the worse my decisions were. I was more and more ashamed of myself every day." He bowed his head when he finished. "It is hard to ... forgive myself."

I let him think for a moment before I spoke, hoping I could console him.

"I'm so sorry," I said genuinely. "I can understand your pain. That's horrible but eye-opening. As you can see, how we deal with what we are given in life determines how we go on."

He nodded once firmly. "I realize it more as I grow older. I've tried to ignore it."

"Then don't ignore the pain. Take it and use it."

"I don't think you've ever said anything that makes more sense, Lavina."

I glowered at him for both the nickname and insult, even though his tone was light. "Lavinia," I corrected.

He chuckled wickedly. "I like Lavina more."

"Well, I don't."

"And I don't care."

My scowl was immediate, and he gave me a chilling smile. I guessed some things would never change.

"Lavinia is frisky and heedful," he said, then added with a chuckle, "Lavina is ... plucky and a bit ... brash."

I rolled my eyes and hummed in annoyance. And some things would change.

"Do you think ..." I began in a stammer, my voice hardly above a whisper. I couldn't believe I was asking him this, but I did anyway. "Do you think they will ever talk to me again?"

Bartoli raised an eyebrow. "Do you really believe they could ever shun you?" He shook his head. "You're the best thing that has ever happened to my son, and you have made their lives happier ever since you arrived."

For a second, I thought my ears stopped working because I didn't believe I'd ever hear Bartoli tell me anything close to that. "Are you actually being genuine?"

"This would be the time to laugh in your face and make you feel more insane than you are, but I'm not doing that today. I am trying something different for a change."

I couldn't hold back the patronizing laugh under my breath. "Not just today. Not ever again."

"Si ... not ever," he admitted slowly. "I'll talk to them," he added.

"Are you sure that's a good idea?"

"No, but I said I'd try."

I nodded in approval. "Armond told me he would as well … We don't have much time."

He nodded, too. His panic was visible. "What are we to do?"

"Well …" I paused. "I plan to protect him. I can save him."

"*Protect* him? *Save* him? *You?*" His eyes bulged. "How?"

I paused, weighing my words. "I'm going to fight in the war with him."

Bartoli stared at me, and his expression changed to completely bemused. "I'm sorry, you are going to do what?"

"I'm going to fight in the war and prevent his demise," I repeated, this time firmly.

Bartoli's head was shaking. "I said I'd go. You are a woman with no training experience. You'll be killed!"

"I am a woman with almost twenty years of experience. You forget where I have been all of this time." He looked baffled as I stood to my feet. "We'll both go."

This plan was the least risky, even if it risked a lot. And by a lot, I really meant everything.

I continued, unwilling to back down. "Not facing this head-on could cause a whole ripple effect of disaster, more disaster than we will actually face. So, it's final." I turned on my shoulder to march out of the room. "I'm finding out who the hell thinks they can do this to Armond."

CHAPTER 9

THE GIFT AND THE CURSE

1993

The last I heard and saw of Armond was in the library, disappearing faster than my own blink. I went back the following weekend, eager to get my hands on that book again. If I was being honest with myself, though, I hoped more that he would make another appearance.

He didn't.

I went to my mom's and nearly punched a hole through Dan's heavy bag in the basement that night. Then proceeded to fall into a ball of tears. Still, I was determined to try again.

As soon as I entered, I noticed Luca speaking with a patron. I meant to quickly pass without him seeing me, but he acknowledged my presence not a second later.

"Lavinia, you are back."

I stopped quick in my tracks and dropped my head back in defeat before turning to face him. He sent the patron off and then approached me.

Luca laughed. "Wanted to see me again so much, eh?" he joked.

He saw me running away from him, didn't he?

"Sorry, I came back for a book. I ..." I wouldn't tell him the whole truth. He would assume I was on drugs. He looked nothing but amused as he waited for me to continue. I said with a little laugh, "This is a library, you know."

He put a hand to his chest, looking offended. "Ouch, you wound me."

"Hey, don't be so quick to assume then," I attempted to tease, meaning for my tone to be light, but it came out a bit clipped.

Those words coming from my mouth that way kind of surprised me. I hoped I didn't sound rude. My disappointment was seeping through me. I had been hoping Armond would have spoken already, but he had told me I shouldn't expect his visits to be frequent.

I was relieved when Luca chuckled, then tried to hide my embarrassment by starting on my way to where the book was located. The floor creaked behind me, and I furrowed my brows at the fact Luca followed me.

"What are you doing?" I asked.

He smiled widely. "Making an effort to talk to you."

"That's sweet. I won't be here long, though. I have to go see my son after this."

I knew Luca had immediately stayed in place because his steps ceased. I stopped to face him, offering a small, polite smile. Yeah, conversations with guys usually ended when I mentioned Leo. Honestly, it had slipped out that time.

"You have a son?" he asked quietly. He wasn't rude about it at all. He didn't even seem disgusted, which I appreciated. Only shocked.

I nodded shyly. "Yes, I do."

"And ... does that mean you are married?" He was hesitant, glancing at the ring on my left hand.

I instinctively grasped my finger and gave him a more awkward smile. "My husband is no longer with me, unfortunately. He passed."

"Oh." He frowned deeply. "I am sorry. You do not deserve that pain."

I looked down at my shoes, fidgeting. "It's definitely always going to be there."

I sensed he was still frowning. "Lavinia, I feel like a … like a jerk. "

My eyes lifted to meet his brown ones, barking out a laugh. "That sounds funny in your accent," I told him, giggling like a schoolgirl. "How are you a jerk?"

Luca grinned. "Because I was going to ask you out."

"Oh …" I paused and swallowed. He was certainly forward. "I just don't think—"

"No, you are not ready. I understand."

"Yes, it's not that you … I don't—"

"I know." He nodded knowingly, which confused me.

I stared at him for a moment silently, then asked, "Hey, could you—um—help me a second?"

Luca grabbed the aquamarine book from up high for me. He read the title aloud in a puzzled tone and handed it to me with a raised brow. "I don't think I've even heard of this one before. Would you mind if I took it to the front desk after you are done using it?"

"Oh … I can when I check it out." I didn't mention most people probably never heard of it. "But you're new, right? Maybe that's why you don't know about it."

"*Sì*. Maybe." He didn't seem too convinced.

I shrugged. He stepped forward, nudging my shoulder playfully, then continued on his way to help another patron. "I'll see you around, Lavinia." He went to answer a woman's question as I sat down with the book, turning to the beginning.

Introduction

The universe is full of stories and the unknown. The space between the earth and the stars may seem incredibly infinite, but nature always has its limits. Observable eyes have only seen a certain extent of what is really out there.

A bunch of questions tumbled around in my mind as I kept reading. I settled on one: What really *is* out there? Apparently, time travelers and odd old women who steal money after telling someone's "fortune." But there was almost no explanation of that. After mulling over some things for several minutes, I looked for a specific page. The book was worn with creases, and I turned the delicate pages carefully. Strange, almost like it was a couple of centuries old. I brushed off my feelings again. Strange was becoming my normal.

Once two words came into view, I unintentionally sucked in a breath.

The Gift

The Gift of falling through time is rare. Only a select number of humans are given this ability. Usually, an existing object, whether it be an antique, special item, or heirloom, brings the traveler to a different time in the past. The traveler has a deep connection to this object. If they shall come into contact with it, they travel to their destined time. Traveling to the future is more complicated. The only way to travel into the future is to hold on to something that will exist in the future. When you travel back in time what you really do is jump to a different reality where what you did has changed history, but you come from a universe where nothing was done, so your memory of that history remains the same.

That explained a whole lot. The second Armond showed me the book, I knew it wouldn't be some phony load of information. He would have had a solid reason for telling me to read it.

"So, what's the curse?" I asked aloud, but stumbled upon a different page.

A Time Traveler's Soulmate

The whole reason a time traveler goes back in time is to find their destined soulmate. The traveler is called by the other, compelled and swept through the void. They are bound to each other by a power that was split and yearns to join again. When these two souls meet, there's a certain familiarity. They'll feel close from the beginning and form a connection so strong that they're drawn to one another in a way many people don't experience. A love so deep and complex is shared between them that it is doubtful they could love another with the same totality. Strangely, one can feel the other coming.

The Curse

The Curse of time travel is unfortunate. Once you're in a different time, you cannot go back until your time there is finished. A time traveler will know when it is time to go back to their original era. If a traveler ever attempts to go back before their time to do so, it could put too much strain on them, leading to faintness or even death.

My mind flashed back to when I had tried to go home. It had been so painful. This book was right, or rather, the author was right. Knowledgeable even.

I kept reading the other part of the curse.

Time travelers only have a short time with their soulmate. The number of years a traveler has with them varies, hence the curse. Their time together is limited, as is any death ultimately assured, but their life is taken early. Eventually, they pass through some means or another. However, if the traveler never went back in the first place, then they wouldn't have found the love they were looking for.

Made sense, but that didn't give me much closure at all. My eyes drifted over the next line, which had me internally screaming. Whether it was in a good or bad way, I didn't know.

Although, that doesn't mean they cannot find love again, if only a different kind of love, if it's one not so consuming.

I slammed the book shut so fast and held back the tears threatening to fall. My glare could have burnt a hole through the front cover. I was never going to see him alive again, was I? I buried my face in my hands and frustratedly wiped away the tears that brimmed my eyes.

Only minutes later did I find the strength to read on. I kept on reading for longer than I had anticipated. I thought learning all of that information at once surely should have blown me to pieces. I found more and more surprising information that made sense and, at the same time, didn't. Although it was a lot to take in, it was refreshing and, I would admit reluctantly, addictive. I must have spent a couple of hours sitting there on a reading spree.

"So, what is ... *The Gift and the Curse* like?" I suddenly heard over my shoulder.

I snapped the book shut in a frantic manner, startled, and spun around in my seat. Luca had spoken, of course.

"You certainly seem very invested," he added, leaning against a bookshelf.

"Erm, what?" I muttered. "No—I ... I just have no other choice."

He cocked his head in suspicion. "How is the book?" he rephrased his first question.

"Oh, it's fine." I sighed and shook off my alarm. "Lordy, do you always sneak up on people?" I asked lightheartedly.

"I'm not a lord, but it's very funny that you think so." He giggled at me, and I rolled my eyes. He nodded his head in the direction of the book. "What do you have to hide from me, Lavinia, hm?"

I sighed again and removed my arm away from the title. "Uh—nothing—I'm just a very ... private person."

"So am I. But people say I'm forward."

"Well, you definitely do let people know what you're thinking. You say that like it's a bad thing."

He smirked, but my mind quickly drifted. All my thoughts had fallen on Armond, how he'd always shown me his vulnerable side from the moment I met him.

"Hey, are you okay?"

I hadn't noticed how upset I must have looked until I saw Luca's genuine concern.

"I *will* be okay," I answered honestly. "And, uh—the book is ... informative for sure," I added to answer his earlier question.

He chuckled and nodded in approval. I laughed a little, and then an awkward moment ensued. He looked like he was scrambling for something to say.

"I thought you were not staying long," he finally blurted.

"Yeah, well, I can really get my nose stuck in a book sometimes. When it is interesting, I lose track of time." I checked the clock on the wall instinctively. I had to leave in ten minutes at the most.

"Hey," I began, "do you happen to know more about the author of this book?"

"Let me take a look," he offered and sat down next to me, reading the name. "Hm, Powers? Nothing comes to mind. I can do a little research for you. How old is this book anyway?

By the structure it looks to be from the nineteenth century."

I opened the book back up and flipped to the front. "It was originally published in 1652, and this edition was published in 1845."

"*Oì*. All right. I will do some research on the name for you. It should not take long. Wait here."

"Thank you."

"Anything for you," he assured with coquetry. I shook my head at him, letting a laugh escape me. "I will be back soon."

I nodded, facing the book and resuming my place, a certain word catching my eye. Chills immediately racked my body.

The Seer

The Seer is a kind of time traveler that has more power than an ordinary one. Seers do not always have premonitions and predict the future. Usually, their ability is solely to see, hear, and feel the spirit world. They can often communicate with spirits and shadows, benevolent or malevolent, and celestial beings, including the Soulmate. The spirit world appears objectively outside of their mind with open eyes, as if they are in the same room. Seers can hear from the person in spirit talking inside their head and even sometimes hear thoughts that might sound like their own. In rare cases, Seers with the most strength can hear voices outside of their head. These Seers can use this gift without having any visions. However, they might see or have a clear vision of the past, present, or future …

Rarer are Seers who can also feel the emotions or pain of other spirits, which usually coincides with the presence of their Soulmate. They feel the message the spirit wants to convey and can sense what they feel in general …

Sentence after sentence made me furrow my brows more. Completely sucked in, I turned the page and kept reading.

The True Gift

The True Gift goes far beyond just the gift of time travel. If one can change the curse of having the gift, that is even rarer. There is only one every seven generations given the chance to go back before their soulmate's death and successfully avert it. However, interference comes at a price. It is impossible to twist the fabric of reality without having the consequences ricochet. By altering time, one can inevitably alter one's own memory of what happened, ultimately leading to different decisions. The traveler must find the will to remember their duty as they create change.

For any ordinary traveler altering events impacting their own timeline would automatically fail.

Travelers lose their power to time travel once the Soulmate is dead.

True time travelers commonly end up being centuries old, as they can travel back as far as they know. Physically, they will look younger, only as they grow older ...

My mind had been completely blown by that point, the information compacting into my brain until there seemed to be no room left. But out of everything I had read, one point attracted me the most.

I might be able to go back. I might be able to see him again. I could change everything!

Was this really true? No. That just couldn't be. I didn't know if I was one of those lucky time travelers. For all I knew, I was stuck with the curse.

"Lavinia."

I jumped out of my skin again, of course, Luca was back.

He chuckled at me. "Sorry, I couldn't find much. I am going to take more time on this. Can you wait a little longer?"

"I—no—I ..." I stumbled out of my seat, grabbed my things, and rested a hand on his arm. "I really do have to go now. There's something I have to do, and my son is waiting."

"Oh ..." He nodded in understanding. "That's right. Of course." He put on a little, kind smile. "Your son is your life now."

I frowned. There was a time when a man was my life, too.

I barely smiled. "You're right; he is my life. I don't know what I'd do if I didn't have him."

His smile was glum. "Don't let that stop you from having a life outside of him, Lavinia." He lightly touched my shoulder, and my lips parted in surprise by his words. "Come back soon. I will have everything ready."

I told him I would and said goodbye. To my shock, I was a bit disappointed to leave so soon. I did enjoy his company and wanted to know more about this book. But the need to reach my mom's house was more pressing.

"Mrs. Jones! I'd like to take this book home, please."

"Of course, come right on up, darling!" I did as she said and handed her the book. She immediately seemed muddled and gaped at the dusty old thing. "Oh, dear me, where did you get this?"

I shifted my weight onto my other foot. "I found it on a high shelf. Why?"

"Vin, this—I've never seen or heard of this book before. There's not even a barcode. It does not—it should not be here."

"Well, I found it. Can I still take it?"

"Honey, as much as I want to say yes, I can't let you do that. Somebody might have left it here by accident, and it somehow got thrown up there. And if so, they are probably looking for it. I'm sorry."

"Right—um—that's okay," I stammered.

"She's wrong ..."

I could have sworn I had actually heard those words. A soft and faint whisper of an accent, almost as if my conscience was speaking to me in *his* voice. My heart began to thud in my chest.

"Would you hold on to it for me anyway? It won't hurt to read it if no one claims it, right? I mean, who would leave an old book like that lying around?"

She hummed. "All right, Lavinia. I supposed I can do that. I trust you. And you are one of my favorite people who visit here."

I thanked her, rushing to exit the building. I caught her by surprise with my abrupt goodbye and hardly heard what she said in reply. Driving like a maniac to my mom's and Dan's house, I eventually burst through the front door crazier than a wild banshee.

"Ugh," I groaned as I stubbed my toe on the way inside, breathing heavily. "Guys! It's a curse!"

"What is? School?" a voice other than my mother's answered, not to my surprise. "It definitely can be."

Dan.

I rolled my eyes at the joke. "Yeah, not this time," I played along, then sighed. "Leo isn't back from his play date yet?"

"No, your mother said she will pick him up."

"Is she still stuck at the hospital? I will pick him up now. I'm not making him wait on one of us."

"Nope." He grinned. "She is on her way home!"

"No way! She is?"

"Yes, she could be getting here as we speak—"

The sound of the front door creaking ajar distracted us, followed by my mom's shout: "Hey, we're home!"

Leo came strolling into the kitchen on his chubby little legs and jumped right into my arms when he saw me. "Mommy!"

"Hi, my sweet boy. Did you have a good day?" I asked.

"Yeah! I went swimming at Billy's," he whispered like it

was a secret, with a grin so large it almost split his face.

"That's great, buddy. I'm glad you had fun."

"Vinnie, you're here," my mom said as she entered the room.

"I'm more surprised that you are." I gave her a hug and pulled back. "There's a lot I have to tell you."

"School is a curse or something," Dan filled in.

Mom gave me a look.

I rolled my eyes again and shook my head, becoming serious enough for them to know this was important. "Leo, would you like something to eat? And maybe watch some television?"

"Sure!" he chirped.

I kissed him on the head, then made him a sandwich, and he ran off to the family room.

I sat down at the table to join Dan and my mom. They waited impatiently for me to spill the beans. "School isn't the curse," I muttered. "Time travel is."

"Oh, honey ... don't feel that way," my mom comforted, eyes softening.

"It's not a feeling. For real, it's most likely a curse. I found this book at the history library about time travel. I was reading for a couple of hours." I spoke super-fast. I was sure they could barely comprehend. "And apparently, time travelers are cursed to have only a short time with their soulmate."

"Soulmates exist, you think?" my mom questioned.

"On a much deeper level than we think, actually. Armond was mine. It's like in lycanthropy when werewolves have mates. The connection is instant, and you are destined to be together. But the curse is what brings them death."

My mom glanced at Dan. I didn't miss the glossy look in her eyes, something unspoken communicating between them. She shook her head, not speaking a word.

"Vinnie, this is pretty crazy to hear," Dan said.

"It's not that much crazier than the concept of time travel, is it?"

The Art of Bending Time

My mom sighed. "You're right. But this is a book; how do you know what it says is even true?"

"Almost everything I've read so far has already happened to me. It even says some time travelers are haunted before they go through and can communicate with ghosts. Doesn't that sound familiar? The book calls them Seers."

They both shared a look. "Like a psychic medium ..." Dan trailed off.

"Yes," I agreed. "And guess what? It happened again."

My mom's eyes were wide. "You heard him?"

"Not only heard. I spoke to his ghost in the library. We had a real conversation. He ..." I swallowed. "I saw him. He appeared just as I was leaving."

Dan didn't respond. He couldn't. Just blinked at me as if I had five heads. But my mom immediately walked to me and grabbed my hands. "Oh, Vinnie. Are you okay?"

I looked down. "I think so. It was kind of ... nice."

She smiled faintly and pulled me close. "I don't want you to think I don't believe you. I do. Knowing a book about time travel exists out there is the insane part." She pushed away and looked at me. "What else did it say?"

I hesitated. I wasn't sure I could divulge everything, at least not yet. "Well, what I've told you so far is not even the craziest news yet," I muttered.

"Then what is?" my mom wanted to know. "What did Armond say?"

I sighed, preparing myself. "Armond is the one who led me to the book. He wanted me to see it. Communicating with ghosts is the least of my worries." I sighed and turned away from her, watching Leo with his eyes glued to the screen. "Sometimes ... you can go back and change everything."

"I was afraid you'd say that," my mom whispered. I frowned and turned to face her. "Vinnie, I think this is a trap. I know you wish you could save him. *If* that were possible. But if so, you must remember there could be serious problems down the line if you were to go back and change things."

I looked away from her and back at Leo. "I know."

"Things you'd never see coming, more things you wouldn't want either. Something … much worse."

"Since when did you become an expert on time travel?" I asked, a bit snippy. I didn't mean it, but I was annoyed. "What could be worse than death?"

She sighed, looking back at Dan, then returning her eyes to me. "Who knows? Time is a funny thing, Vin. That's all I am saying."

I shook my head, silent. Dan was slowly backing away, trying to remove himself.

"Dan, do not think you can get out of this," my mom snapped, eyes in the back of her head. He reluctantly stayed, and she continued. "Lavinia. Promise me you won't do it."

"I don't really give a damn if time shouldn't be messed with. If I know for sure it's possible, I'm going to try," I rebelled.

"Vinnie, please … you know your father never liked it when people curse," Mom scolded me.

My sigh was softer than my tone. "I know, Mom. I know. I'm sorry."

My father had despised cursing and always joked it hurt his ears. But sometimes the words slipped out, especially at times like these.

"Vinnie, look at me," she beckoned. I begrudgingly brought my teary eyes to her compassionate ones. "As much pain as his death has caused, he was meant to die, and there is nothing you could have done. Divine intervention is a thing, but don't think you can play God in this situation."

More tears welled up in my eyes.

Who knows what I would have to face if I should have the chance to go back? But I hardly cared. That book had given me hope. I wasn't worried about the ramifications. If I had the chance to prevent his death, I had to do everything in my power to try.

CHAPTER 10

WE STAND TOGETHER CALMLY

1848

As soon as I opened the door to walk out of Bartoli's study, Armond pushed off the wall and rushed to my side, checking every inch of me. He was more shocked to see my content smile.

I explained to Armond what Bartoli had told me about himself. Armond said he never knew anything of his father's family. Bartoli had always been vague about his past. Armond only knew it hadn't been pleasant. He had never pressed since he had no interest in knowing anyway.

The next day, I walked into the dining area to find almost everyone standing up the second I entered. Carmela encouraged me to sit and join them, and I slowly approached my usual place at the table.

"I apologize sincerely, my dear," she began in an earnest whisper. "Forgive me. The thought of my son dying is just too painful. It is not your fault. That never will be. I can't imagine having that weight on your shoulders. I thank you for telling us the truth."

"We all do," Giovanni said. "We are sorry for our unforgivable reactions."

"It's all right. It's not unforgivable. I understand."

Armond's hand rubbed my thigh comfortingly. When I glanced at him, his gaze was soft and reassuring. His eyes read, "See, I told you they would come around."

Chiara stared at me as my eyes drifted to her; she couldn't hold back any longer. "You can't save my brother alone, Lavinia. We'll figure out what to do all together."

"Lavina already knows exactly what she is doing," Bartoli assured them. "Go on, tell them." He sipped his coffee forcefully, receiving eye rolls from me and Chiara.

"And you approve of her idea?" Carmela asked, bewildered.

"Approve? Probably not, darling. Although, I do think it's a good enough plan. No matter how agitated the decision makes me."

"Because he doesn't like the thought of me saving the day," I muttered in annoyance and didn't miss his short glare. I gave them a moment of silence before I said, "I'm going to fight in the war, disguised as a man."

I couldn't miss the intensity of their stares at me, frozen with shock. I wasn't surprised even a little. Armond's head had immediately turned in my direction. He opened his mouth to say something, but I continued over him.

"I'll be by his side the entire time, shadowing his every movement. I'll watch out for him when he needs me the most. He's taught me a lot, and I trained for years in my time. I can protect him and stop this."

"Lavina is a fierce protector of those she loves," Bartoli said, catching my attention. "I stand by that. You can count on me being there as well, son. I'll watch over both of you."

I couldn't believe his change in behavior. I had bigger problems than Bartoli, it seemed. War and death.

Armond's expression filled with shock and appreciation for his father. "You would do that for me, Father?" His voice trembled, and my heart swelled for him.

Bartoli shrunk in on himself as embarrassment was coloring his cheeks. "Oh ... yes! Do not make things uncomfortable for me!"

"We will protect you, Armond."

"As will I," Giovanni assured. "And Armani."

Armond nodded firmly, sighing gently. Then, his eyes flitted over my features. "Lavinia, I—" he started to protest.

"Armond, I want to do this. Let me. Please."

He gave me a look that said it wasn't so easy for him.

"Darling," Carmela caught my attention, speaking to me. "Are you certain? War is ..." She couldn't settle on a word.

"Yes," I responded. "I know it is best. I think it is what I'm meant to do."

There was a long pause of silence, then the noise of Armond's chair backing against the wood floor.

"Excuse me," Armond muttered in a strange tone and left the table in a rush.

I watched him exit the room and vanish, and then my gaze wandered back to Carmela. "I'm sorry. I better go see what's wrong. Excuse me."

"You're excused, dear. I already know what's wrong," she told me, shrugging. "He's afraid for you. But he'd do the same for you. He should remember that."

"I've tried, Carmela," I murmured hopelessly. I swallowed.

She grabbed my arm as I passed her and gave it a gentle squeeze, nodding her head in the direction he left. "Make him understand this time."

I nodded and stalked out of the room. I caught Armond charging toward the front entrance. I thought I should leave him to his own mind but thought against it. I didn't want to waste any time if it was the last days I'd have with him.

"Armond!" I shouted and chased him in a sprint, catching the doors before they shut. I saw him enter the gardens but lost him. I searched and searched for him, coming to almost every dead end in the maze of flowers. "Armond, where did you go?"

I was beginning to worry he went far when finally, I found him standing by the fountain. He gazed into the rippling water as if it would tell him his fate, his tall figure swallowed in darkness, apart from the outdoor gas lights illuminating the outline of his figure.

"Armond ... What is the matter?" I asked, eventually capturing his attention.

He spun around with one of the most fervent stares I had ever seen him give me. My mouth went agape. Before I could think twice, he strode toward me. I remained still, waiting anxiously. He took the breath out of my gasp when he clutched me by the face and kissed me hard on the mouth. My back rammed into the nearest wall of flowers from the force, and he held me there until we couldn't stand not having oxygen anymore.

He pulled away, eyebrows pinched close. "What's the matter is you are the most frustrating and stubborn woman I've ever met, yet I love you to death. You astound me."

I grinned with pride. "Well, maybe we can die together," I said, only half kidding. "Or we can die for each other. I don't care either way."

He didn't take it as a joke, though. "I'm not letting you die."

"Good, I'm not letting you die either."

He glared at me for a solid minute, communicating all his worry, love, and ... fear. But, as the quote says, "There is no courage without fear." We needed to use our valor to our advantage.

Finally, he sighed defeatedly. "You want to disguise yourself as a man, eh? You have no shame."

I gave him a toothy grin. "You betcha."

He shook his head with a chuckle at the strange word usage. "But not just any man, *cuore*." He smirked. "An important one. You'll be disguised as a real *cavaliere*."

"There ..." Armond said as he placed the helmet on my head, the final piece. I tried on armor before, but this legit armor felt like dragging a ton of bricks. "Are you all right? How does it feel?"

"Like I'm wrapped in a steel blanket."

He chuckled. "You look like a true warrior to me."

I laughed at him. "I think you mean you do."

He smirked. "Well, see for yourself."

I turned to the full-length mirror, seeing my tiny figure covered from head to toe in armor, my face totally concealed. Although this would not be the attire for war, it was entertaining to see the whole getup on me. Hopefully, nobody would ever know I was a woman.

"I'd like for you to practice in it today. It will make having modern battle armor on feel light," Armond told me from behind, resting his hands on my shoulders comfortingly. "I hope you're ready, *cuore*. Mentally prepared, that is."

I swallowed, shifting my eyes to his sparkling ones in the mirror. "I may be prepared to fight, but I don't think you can ever be ready for war, Armond," I replied.

I removed my helmet and shook my head to let my blonde waves free, staring deep into the cognac irises that appeared back at me. For once, they didn't look afraid. They held a certain strength I never had before, the strength I needed. However this was destined to end, I couldn't be scared of death.

"But the war is in days," I whispered, looking off to the side. "We have to be as prepared as we can be."

Armond took me out in the woods to watch me "practice"

weaponry. The arrow I shot stuck straight through the bullseye again. For the fifteenth time. I looked back at Armond to see his lopsided grin. I could tell he was more impressed than he expected himself to be.

"Now gunfire," he instructed.

I pranced over with a smirk to grab a pistol about thirty feet away from the bottles he had set up earlier. I positioned myself to aim, hearing him come up several feet behind me and feeling his hot stare on my back. Not seconds later, I fired the pistol off quickly and deftly reloaded each time before I hit every bottle without issue, the glass shattering into hundreds of pieces. After I was satisfied, I flipped the gun and held it out for Armond to take with the same smug face.

Armond's pure shock was priceless, but I could tell he was prouder than anything. Armond disregarded the pistol as he approached me, pushing it away. "I wouldn't want to be on the other end of that barrel, *cuore*, that is for certain."

I laughed. If he knew the way I had trained for years after he died, his jaw would be on the ground. I became mightier than the sword I wielded, and defense was like second nature to me. All I learned was ingrained in me. I trained for the day I could save him, and that day was coming.

"Show me what else you can do, *cuore*," Armond whispered, wiggling his brows. "I won't hold back."

I wrapped my hand around his own and caught him by surprise as I yanked him down with me to the ground, resting a hand on the sheath of his dagger. He raised a brow at me that said he was asking if that was really necessary. I hummed my agreement. "You better not." My smirk was so full of smugness. I could tell he noticed by the way his head shook slightly when I confidently climbed off him.

Armond reached to his side and unsheathed his sword, handing it to me. "Take this. I'll use the shorter sword."

My smile was devilish. "Oh, no ..." I stepped forward, laying hold of the hilt at his side, and pulled. I positioned the tip of his smaller blade at the edge of his chin and slowly backed him up into a tree. He swallowed, but not out of fear. "This one will do just fine."

His own returning smile was just as fierce. Then he raised his sword, and I blocked it with mine, steel clashing against steel. We both dodged and blocked every swing or stab. I knew he detected my significant improvement since the last time I had seen him because he was struggling to even keep up.

Unfortunately for Armond, I disarmed him and had him on the ground on his front within minutes, holding his head back with the flat of my sword brushing his neck.

I placed my lips by his ear. "How'd I do?"

I felt his grin, his breathing quick beneath my touch. "That is quite a new trick. It appears you are lethal with whatever you wield."

I discarded the blade, still straddled over him, and he relaxed under me. "I'm ready, Armond."

He was still, pausing in thought before he rolled me to my back. His eyes searched mine for a moment. "Almost." I tilted my head in confusion. "You trained to defeat the enemy, but you're not acquainted with war and its evils." He frowned. "But I am, and I do know who has been. There's one thing I'd like for you to do."

The next day, Armond woke me up extra early and told me to meet him at the stables in my armor. I walked out there wearing everything except for the helmet. Armond stood with our horses, ready to leave. Pudge was waiting beside him with his tongue out, tail wagging in excitement for whatever adventure Armond had in store. He wouldn't tell me, but I thought I would try asking again.

"Where are we going?" I asked. I pet Patches lightly on his face and smiled at him, speaking to him in a coo.

Armond sighed, mounting Midnight. "It takes away the whole point if I tell you, *cuore*. You just have to trust me."

I squinted at him. "Good thing I do."

He smirked. "Now mount Patches and ask questions later."

I rolled my eyes and did as he said. I recognized the path he took, but along the way, he changed course and stopped at a clearing with no trees for at least an acre. The grass was tall with dandelions, nutsedge, and alexander grass. Tall enough to hide behind.

"You brought us to an empty field alone?" I asked, confusion in my tone.

"We're not alone, *cuore*." Armond brought his fingers to his mouth and blew a whistle.

I watched in shock as a line of men appeared, some on horses and some not. One man on his horse dominated everyone with his presence in the middle of them all. And next to him stood a familiar big, muscled man who had to be Dino.

"What is this?" I slowly asked.

"Practice," he said nonchalantly, like over fifty men weren't going to devour me.

"Is that ..." I narrowed my eyes and blinked because I thought I was seeing things. "You actually got Bartoli to do this?"

"Dino and I convinced him, *sì*." I was in awe as Armond dismounted and came to stand by Patches. "We're going to practice combat in war. Us against them." He pointed in the direction of the men, then reached up and motioned for me to get down. I did with his hand resting on my back. I turned to see him smirking my way. "You will protect me as they go after both of us, mainly me. You won't let them put a finger on me, understand?"

I nodded with a smirk of my own. "Yes, Sir Armond Alessandro. I will protect you."

He narrowed his eyes at my smart tone and reached into his bag on his horse to pull out a few things. "Then we shall begin."

CHAPTER 11

MYSTERIES

1993

I didn't know how I would look my mother or son in the eye to tell them I planned to leave. The last time I had gone through the painting, it had been as though I had never left. Time kept moving. I had remained in the present in spite of only being consciously aware of living in the past. My mom had given me a fair warning not to mess with time, and the book had told me of the consequences. But I had to find a way to go back to him. Once I was gone, as far as they'd know, I never left. They didn't need to know a thing.

The minute I made it back to my dorm, I rushed inside and called Serena. She may not have been aware I time traveled into the past, met a man from the nineteenth century, and fell in love with him, but I still needed to talk to someone. I had to unload the weight on my shoulders without telling her the exact reason, and she was just the person. She always knew how to take my mind off things.

I went to sleep late and woke up early the next morning to visit the library and have a look at the Yellow Pages for self-defense classes and a trainer. Before I did anything rash, I needed to conduct more research and prepare myself physically.

And mentally.

I had to do what I never had the chance to do the first time I ended up in the past.

Plan.

I pushed open the library door, the bell ringing as I entered. The Italian man I was growing fond of looked up at me from a book he held in his hands to inspect. He quickly shelved it as soon as he saw me, then turned to me with a warm smile.

"Lavinia. You are here again," Luca said with a chuckle, shock in his tone. "Miss me that much, eh?"

"It appears I missed you a ton," I murmured with a quiet laugh. "I'm here to look at the Yellow Pages."

"We do have those," he said, pointing to the left around back. "Back there."

I thanked him even though I already knew where all the phone books were located. The footsteps behind me confirmed that he followed.

"So ... I did research on this Guinevere Powers that you asked for. Didn't find very much."

"Really?" I stopped in my tracks and faced him. "What *did* you find?"

"Among other things, first ... this book doesn't even belong here."

"That's what Mrs. Jones said," I whispered, furrowing my brows.

"The title is a giveaway enough. But there's no record of it ever being here either. I really don't know how it ended up on the shelf. The weirder part is that Powers was accused of being a witch and was treated horribly. As soon as I researched the book, I realized why. Her book is all a theory of time travel. What are you trying to do, Lavinia?"

I gulped, not finding the words to answer that. I told him to show me everything he figured out before I thought about telling him a word. He accepted. Apparently, Guinevere

Powers' cause of death was unknown. She had gone missing a year after her book was published, and she had never written another in her life. Just that one. She had lived in a quaint house in Pennsylvania on a private plot of acres of land with her brother. She had lived modestly up until she disappeared, of course. The reprint had sold many, many copies.

People had all made a mockery of her. They had thought of her as having a wild imagination and believed she made it all up. I knew differently. I wouldn't be surprised if she was a time traveler herself.

"She was called a witch and most likely condemned to die. That must be why she disappeared," Luca told me while scrolling on the computer with the mouse. He turned on the chair he was sitting on. "I can see why you find this interesting."

I swallowed and gave a shrug. "Yeah, all interesting theories," I muttered.

He tilted his head at me. "Except they are not to her. Powers writes it as if it is real."

"I know," I whispered, looking down and trying not to give anything away.

"Are you trying to find out if it is?"

My head snapped up fast, wondering why he would even ask me that question. I shrugged. "Something like that ..."

He shifted back into the chair he sat on, crossing his arms. "So, you want to time travel."

I stared him straight in the eye, not wanting to break contact. *Be calm.* "Well, a lot of people wish that. But it's all in theory, no matter how cool it sounds," I played along.

"Of course. If I could, I'd go back to the Middle Ages or the Victorian times ..." His eyes widened. "Oh, you want to make sure your husband never dies, am I right?"

Damn it. He's smarter than I gave him credit for.

"No ..." I shook my head, and he narrowed his eyes in suspicion. "No! That's ridiculous!"

And completely correct.

His eyes remained squinted. "But the thought had to cross your mind," he assumed. I gave nothing away and only shrugged. He shook his head with a smile, seeming nonplussed. "You are by far one of the strangest yet interesting people I have met."

I offered a dry laugh. He had no idea.

"But if you are thinking of looking for evidence, I must help you," he insisted.

My lips slightly parted, and I leaned forward to whisper. "Why would you help someone go down the rabbit hole, especially if that meant I could drag you down with me?"

"I'm not quite sure what you mean, but why wouldn't I want to help you?"

I shook my head. "Oh, right, you're not American; you wouldn't get the phrase," I muttered. He didn't know what he was getting himself into by helping me. "You actually think it could be real?"

"Who knows? Probably not. But technology improves every year."

If only he knew time travel had nothing to do with technology.

"You don't think this is the craziest thing you've heard?" I asked.

"Crazy, maybe. But it is absolutely something worth researching. When it comes to science and reading, I can't resist anyway."

I smirked. "Are you a nerd, Luca?" I teased.

He chuckled and looked down, a bit embarrassed. "Just passionate about literature and physics. And I might have a tiny fascination with chrono physics as well."

I raised my brows. "Do you study it?"

"Just literature, but I love physics and the concept of time travel. History is not so bad, either. That is simply why I work here."

I smiled inside. Maybe letting him help me wasn't such a bad idea.

"History is my thing," I said, then looked down. And recently, so is time travel. I swallowed. "Luca, you wouldn't happen to know the consequence of changing history, do you? Theoretically, of course."

"You mean playing with life and death? So, you can keep your husband alive?"

I rolled my eyes. "No matter how much I wish I could, I'm afraid I can't."

And that was the truth. I was scared I wouldn't be able to succeed.

He hummed in deep thought, contemplating my answer. "Well, time is hard to understand, really. It seems like everything is already set in stone. But there are movies that contradict the theory. I'd say if you could go back to a certain point, knowing what you know, it could be reversible. But yes … I think a change of events would change a lot. Your life could be very different to what it is now if you were to do so. And maybe you do not want it to change."

"What if the change is for the better and I do like it?"

"Theoretically … is it for the better?"

That ticked me off. "If you knew him, you wouldn't be saying that," I whispered harshly.

He frowned. "I only think if your husband died, he was probably meant to die. Fate is fate."

My throat closed up and filled with bile. "I work alone," I said stiffly, then stood up. "You should be working too, anyway."

I felt his eyes follow me as I went toward the back of the library, far away from him.

When I sat down, I flipped to the back of the phone book and sought out the best place to learn self-defense with the most well-trained instructors. I found a few places that seemed fitting and wrote down numbers to contact them. Only one number went to the answering machine and didn't call back, which was disappointing. The rest didn't live up to my standards. I couldn't let that deter me. I would find the right place eventually.

I ended up calling Dan to ask if he'd take me to a shooting range. He didn't even ask me why; he just agreed. Shooting a gun turned out to be something I had a knack for. Dan said I might even be lethal if I kept it up.

The next week, when I saw him, Luca apologized for upsetting me. He was a convincing and stuttering mess. I let him help me, but he couldn't help me all the time while at work, and everything was just theoretical to him. He had no clue that time travel was even real and that I had done it myself.

I spent a lot of my days in different places and libraries, trying to get to the bottom of everything. Even when I found answers, more questions were raised. I took in every detail of that time travel book along with many others, reading about events before the war and the ones following it as well. I needed to determine whether it was really possible for me to see Armond again. Between that and college work, I barely managed my time, but I wouldn't give up.

I still hadn't heard a word from Armond. He was quiet, yet I felt his presence more strongly than ever. It wasn't often that I didn't. I felt him everywhere, as if he was my shadow. Sometimes, I thought I heard him whispering my name, and I'd freeze and look around, just to see nothing. Every time, I was left empty. He really had no intention of speaking to me again, did he?

My visits to the history library became more recurrent. The more I was there, the more I was used to spending time with Luca. I found myself looking forward to seeing him. We decided it'd be easier to meet at a diner one day to talk more in depth, discovering things about each other I had never expected. We had a lot in common. I couldn't have been tired from our conversation if I had even tried. After the first meeting at the diner, we did our best to eat and talk there at least once a week. He was becoming a good friend to me.

On one regular Friday, I came to the library to work on my new art project and didn't see him anywhere, didn't even hear his voice.

"Mrs. Jones?"

"Hm?" she hummed, looking up at me.

"Where's Luca?"

"Oh, didn't you know? He won't be here today."

"No, I didn't." I furrowed my eyebrows. "How come?"

"He's taking a personal day, dearie. He didn't say anything specifically."

"Bummer. All right. Thank you."

She nodded with a soft smile as I walked toward a table, setting out my books. Reaching inside for my art book, I realized once again it was not where I kept it. My neck hair stood on end, and my body shuddered from the coolness that suddenly surrounded me.

"You know, I'm upset that you've stopped painting ..."

I completely froze, eyes darting around frantically for a sign of who spoke.

"I like your drawings, but I miss your elegant skill with a paintbrush."

"Armond?" I gasped, suddenly breathless.

A long pause, then, *"Who else?"*

"I thought you weren't going to do this."

"I shouldn't do it. But, well, your boyfriend is not here."

"He's not my boyfriend," I said slowly and defensively in annoyance.

I only heard his long sigh.

I began firing off questions. "What do you mean by he's not here? Have you been the one stealing my sketchbook?" I spewed at him.

"I look at it from time to time, yes. That's not stealing."

There was a pause. *"And he isn't here, so I'm taking advantage of that."*

"Why are you avoiding me when he is around?"

I heard a dejected sigh. *"I'm trying to leave you two alone."*

"Why?"

Immediate silence ensued. He wouldn't answer that one.

"But, Armond, I ... I'm lost without you."

"You're not," he assured me. I could sense his sad smile. *"You're going to be fine, cuore. You're on the right track. Just hold on."*

I shook my head. "Hold on to what? I hardly know what I'm doing."

"I wouldn't say that ..." he trailed. *"What have you found so far in your research?"* He pointedly ignored my first question.

I shook off his vagueness. "I have not been successful in finding anything about your death or burial." I continued in a whisper. "But the book speaks of preventing you from even dying. Could I actually do that?"

"Find out for yourself. Keep looking."

I sighed, shuffling my books around. If Luca were with me, he might have had an idea.

"Why don't you call him? Go to him?" Armond asked.

I raised a brow. "To whom?"

"Luca," he said carefully like it was obvious.

I shook my head. "No. I don't know where he lives. Why would I do that anyway? He's dealing with something personal. It's none of my business. We're friends, but we aren't that close."

He was quiet for a moment. *"If you called, he may give you an answer, you know. Without you prying."* I paused my movements and looked up as if I would find him standing there. I let that stew as he was quiet for a long time, thinking as I read for a while. That was until he said, *"You should tell him."*

"What?" I asked, confused again.

"*You should tell him about me.*"

"*Luca?*" I scrunched up my nose. "But I already did."

"*I mean about you being a time traveler. You should tell him everything. Start off slowly by opening up about the small things he'll take lightly.*"

I blinked into thin air blankly for a moment at the space where I imagined he was standing. "Armond, I can't do that."

"*Yes, you can. He already knows about your 'theoretical' research. You can trust him. Trust me.*"

I sighed with doubt. "I do trust you. You know that. And I don't know if I really do fully trust Luca. I just—I can't."

The thought of telling another person about myself scared me, especially since I had no proof. I didn't want the friendship Luca and I had to change.

I sensed his smile, or maybe it was more of a smirk. "*You do trust him. It's all right, cuore. That doesn't bother me. Remember that I want you to trust again. You can tell him.*"

"I …" I was at a loss for words. "Not yet. I don't even really know him."

"*You will.*"

My brows shot up. "What makes you say that?"

A beat of silence went by, and he quickly changed the subject. "*You won't find my death records anywhere in America, Lavinia,*" he said randomly. "*You might not even find them in Italy.*"

I furrowed my brows, my mind completely taken off Luca. "What?"

"*I know it has been on your mind ever since you've read that book, but they aren't accessible. Don't think you'll be able to find my cause of death. Don't think you'll find anything of the sort.*"

I stopped what I was doing, frozen in place. "What do you mean?"

"*I mean, ever since you put yourself on this path, they are vanishing from existence. I don't have all the answers; you have to trust me."* A black book moved and slid in front of me, one titled *The Italian Independence War*s. *"Read this one. The whole thing. It will inform you of everything you need to know about the war and what occurred after the fact. Look on page forty-three to start."*

"That's oddly specific." His laugh followed, and then the gravity of what he said finally hit me. "So, are you—are you saying I can actually make a difference? Keep you alive?"

His voice sounded a bit faded as he replied, *"That you will have to find out for yourself. I must go back now."*

"Back where? I need to know! And—and I need you!"

There was no answer, only silence.

No, he was slipping away!

"Armond!" I called helplessly.

"Lavinia?"

I jumped and grabbed my chest, turning to see Mrs. Jones. She had spoken my name. Not Armond.

"Yes?" I whispered, rubbing my brow. She sounded worried. "What is it, Mrs. Jones?"

"Dear, your mom called and said Leo got into a small fight at preschool."

As I drove, Armond didn't say another word. His warning about not visiting often and not speaking very much was apparent, disappointedly so.

I approached Leo outside the main office in the school and bent down to his level. He had his head hung low and wouldn't make a move to look at me. "Leo. Hey. It's me," I whispered. "Are you okay, sweetheart?"

"I'm sorry, Mom," he apologized glumly. "I just didn't like what he said."

"You don't have to apologize, my love." I frowned. "Who are we talking about?"

"Slim Jim."

I held in my laugh at our nickname for Jimmy. That little troublemaker. My blood began to boil just thinking of him. "What did he say?" I asked as calmly as I could. "Did he hurt you?"

"Not really; he just said that my drawing was ugly."

I shook my head. "It's not true, sweetie. He's a young bully, and unfortunately, that's all he knows, Leo." I grabbed his chubby cheeks and brought his eyes up to mine. "All you can do is feel sorry and believe in yourself. All people like him know is how to make others feel smaller so they feel greater. Bullies don't know better. When their worth feels threatened, they say mean words. It's a terribly sad thing."

"Feel smaller?" he questioned.

"Less important."

"Threat-tened?"

"Well, he kind of fears you is what I mean."

"Why would he feel afraid of me drawing a picture?"

I gave a little smile, thinking back on tiny me once asking the same things. "Because you are good at it, sweetheart. He thinks he isn't. Maybe drawing isn't his thing. And let's be honest, he isn't better than a professional like you, is he?"

He gave me a bashful smile in return before pouting. "But he said it was ugly."

"He said it was ugly because he wanted you to feel down, not know how amazing you are."

Leo slowly began to form a grin.

"Did you sock him right in the face?" I asked, anticipating his answer with a squinted eye.

He looked ashamed. "Only when he pushed me. My butt kinda hurts."

I held in my laugh and tried to remain stern, but I couldn't help praising him. "I'm proud of you for standing up for yourself." I ruffled his hair and he smiled, all dimples. "Just don't hit, okay, buddy? Don't make it a habit. You can't just punch people all the time. And I shouldn't have to remind you that you don't hit unless someone is trying to really hurt you."

He nodded quickly.

"Okay," I said, looking to my left and seeing the grumpy little dark-haired boy, Jim. "I'll be back, Leo. One second."

I sauntered over to the boy and lowered myself in front of him. Slim Jim's already crossed arms seemed to hug himself a little tighter as his eyes slightly widened. One of them was forming a purple shade and slightly swollen shut.

"Hey, there, Jimmy." I gave him a condescending smile. "You messed with a kid who is not going to go down so easily. If I were you, I would stop. Completely. Instead of being mean when you don't like something, don't say anything at all. It's not going to get you anywhere good in life. You get what you give, you see? And don't even think about doing it again, because next time, I will be meaner. So, there better not be a next time." My eyes narrowed in a warning. "Got it?"

Jim looked like he was about to have an accident in his pants as he only nodded his agreement. The office door opened, and I stood to my feet.

"Ahem. Ms. Melrose."

"Yes, Mr. Lewis?" I crooned sweetly.

The principal tried to blame my son for that kid bullying him, since Leo was the only one who had left a mark. But guess what?

I wouldn't tolerate it.

That kind of wrong doesn't fly with me. Too many bullies get away with bullying. A bully wouldn't get away with bullying *my son*. Mr. Lewis was left stunned by my words after the comments he made, and he let me walk away while he sat there with his tail between his legs.

"So, what do you say we get ice cream?" I asked Leo as we made it down the hall to the entrance.

He perked up. "Really?"

"Oh, yeah. Whatever you want."

He giggled, jumping up and down. I laughed and lifted my chin up from looking at Leo, almost turning into a glacier at the sight of familiar short ringlet hair. Luca was about to walk out the double doors with a little boy by his side.

"Luca?" I said it much louder than I expected.

He stopped in his tracks and whipped around to face us. He recognized my voice, or he was startled by it.

"Lavy?" He was full of surprise and seemed minimally nervous as well. "What are you doing here?"

"I have a son, remember?" I walked toward him with Leo. "What are you doing here?" I glanced at the boy, who looked to be a year older than Leo.

"I'm picking up my nephew."

I blinked slowly. "I had no idea you had a nephew."

Luca stared at me for a moment. He looked embarrassed and like he didn't know what to say.

"Momma, who dis?" Leo whispered to me.

I glanced at my son, then back to Luca. "This is Luca, Leo. Luca, this is my son."

Luca, who had been looking at me, smiled down at Leo. "I've heard quite a lot about you, Leo."

Leo smiled bashfully.

"And what is your name?" I asked the boy, whom I assumed was about four years old.

"My name is Rocco," Rocco said, well-spoken.

"Rocco might be better at speaking English than me," Luca joked.

"Am I really?" Rocco asked excitedly.

"Sure, *piccolo*," Luca said, ruffling his hair. Rocco had such a bright smile on his face.

I cleared my throat awkwardly. "You weren't working today. Mrs. Jones said it was something personal …"

Luca lifted Rocco's hand, the one he was holding. "*Sì*. Does not get more personal than my sister's kid, no?"

I offered a reassuring smile. "I guess not."

"Especially when sister needs a hand and Rocco's *padre* is not around to help."

I immediately frowned. "Yes. Yes, I definitely understand."

He nodded. "I know, Lavy," he said softly in appreciation, and I smiled in return.

"I like your shirt," Rocco suddenly told Leo.

Leo grasped the Superman shirt he was wearing. "Oh, thanks. My mom got it for me. I like Spiderman too."

"You like Spiderman?" Rocco's eyes lit up. "I love him!"

"Me too! I want to shoot webs like him, and he does this cool thing when …"

My heart warmed for Leo; he was making a friend, and something inside pushed me to invite him along with us.

"Hey, do you have time to walk up to the school park?" I asked Luca. "They can play for a while. Leo and I were going to stop for ice cream. Would you—"

"Yes!" Leo and Rocco said in unison.

I looked at Luca, silently asking if that was fine.

Luca sighed in defeat. "How can I even say no?"

Leo and Rocco jumped up and down.

"We can pretend to be Spiderman and Superman!" Rocco exclaimed.

"Not pretend! We are them!" Leo told him just as enthusiastically.

I couldn't stop laughing as they made a beeline for the double doors. "Not so fast, you two! What about us?"

They instantly stopped.

"Oh, sorry, Mommy!"

"Sorry, Mrs. Melrose!"

"Mrs. Melrose, huh?" I teased Luca. "You mentioned me?"

Luca chuckled, cheeks a bit red. "It's just Miss Melrose, *piccolo!*"

Rocco looked red as a tomato, and Leo just laughed. I waved over the boys and met them at the exit.

"Poor kid," I muttered. "Just call me Lavinia, Rocco. That's just fine."

Rocco nodded in shy agreement. We walked outside, seeing the small park beyond the hill was not fifty feet from us.

"Go ahead down," I encouraged them. "We'll be right there."

"Yay!" they screamed, running to the slides quickly.

"So, does he think I am married?" I asked Luca as we ambled down to a park bench.

"He ... thinks everyone who has a kid is married. So, he considers you married, *sì*."

"He thinks you are very single then?" I teased.

Luca glared. "Now you sound like him."

I laughed. "You haven't found someone special yet?" I asked.

He looked down at me. "Well, I wouldn't say that."

I avoided his eyes, changing the subject. "If you don't mind me asking, is your sister still with ..."

"No, they are separated. Rocco doesn't know about them getting a divorce soon."

"That's sad."

"It's sad for Rocco. Better for my sister."

"Oh?"

Luca stopped by the park bench and motioned for us to sit. "Rocco's dad had a choice to stay; your husband didn't. He only wants to be around if he can overrule my sister. And he never wanted a kid."

My brows formed a frown. "What happened?"

Luca was quiet for a while, a seething look I had never seen before bordering the surface of being unmasked. "The man just isn't capable of being a father."

He didn't want to specify. I would wait until he was ready. Talking to him was enough. I wanted to enjoy his company for as long as he wanted me around. I did like Luca. He was a very good friend to me. I wanted to keep it that way between us, for a while at least, even if I wouldn't keep him forever.

CHAPTER 12

PAINT COLORS OF WISDOM

1994

I carefully stared at the blank canvas with my head cocked in deep thought. Then, sucking in one large breath, I grasped a paintbrush in my hand and gently gave the stark-white woven-cotton canvas a stroke of paint.

Dr. Terri had suggested I try painting again. I had quickly brushed the thought, not feeling convinced. But something I hadn't felt in a while had sparked inside me once I knew Armond missed it. For months, I had been trying to create another worthwhile piece. Luca was pretty convincing, as well. He noticed me working on my art projects and begged me to show him my drawings. I told him where I went to school and that I used to paint. He never let that fact go until I gave it another chance.

With no such luck yet, I let my feelings wash over me, putting every ounce of them into what my fingers created with the paintbrush. Stroke after stroke, layer after layer … the painting became … Nothing pretty. An ombre of dark colors.

Plain. No life. I hated it. What even was that? This wasn't my style of painting at all. It was like I forgot how to paint.

I tossed the brush carelessly in the cup of water, causing the dyed mess to splash onto my paint table. I groaned with my head thrown back, staring at the ceiling in terrible quiet apart from the birds chirping softly outside and the occasional car passing by.

Maybe I wasn't cut out for painting anymore.

The faint sound of the house phone began to ring in my ears, interrupting my train of thought. Yes, only one; that was the odd part. The telephone upstairs was eerily silent. I would have let it go had my mom been around to answer the call herself.

A great sigh of annoyance huffed out of my mouth before I begrudgingly made my way to the phone upstairs, where it waited on a small table. I picked it up and placed the speaker by my ear. "Hello?" I asked flatly.

The line was dead while the phone in the kitchen continued to resound through the whole house. I swallowed and slammed the phone back into place, rushing down to the other one. I yanked it from the wall, speaking in an arctic tone to whoever was on the other side. A harsh, static-filled voice attempted the English language and completely butchered it. At first, I couldn't even understand what was said.

Then, I deciphered the words.

"*Don't come back* ..." came through much clearer, still crackling and hissing its way to my ear.

"Armond?" I instinctively asked, gulping down a lump forming there. Although, this wasn't Armond's voice. He wouldn't have tried speaking to me on the phone either, I was sure. This was a game. I frowned.

"*Don't even think about it,*" seethed the deep, hair-raising voice of a man.

The line cut dead after that. I stood frozen for several seconds before slowly connecting the phone back up.

Oh, no. Please no.

The voices really were starting again. I had a feeling this ghost was actually a threat to me. It could have been the same one from the library, or maybe this one was entirely different. I only knew it was evil.

I shivered as I began to walk toward the staircase, very much freaked out. Not long after, though, did the phone ring again. I absently worried on my bottom lip, then grunted and dove for the phone again. If my mom wasn't a surgeon, I would have just ignored these calls altogether. But she receives them from patients frequently. Sometimes, they really need her.

I picked it up with a bit of angst and put it to my ear. "Hello?"

Nothing.

"Hello?" I repeated, about to hang up and a little beside myself.

"Hello!" a normal male voice said loudly. "I'm sorry, there was trouble connecting. Can you hear me?"

Instantly, I was filled with relief. "Yes, I can."

"Good. This is Garrett Anderson calling from Maki's Next Level Self-defense and Martial Arts Studio. Can I speak to Lavinia Melrose?"

I blinked. "Oh, this is she …"

"Well, Ms. Melrose. I am here to answer your questions about our self-defense center. You left a message."

"Yes!" I almost forgot I called. It had been a few days since then. I had been so busy and preoccupied with everything else. "Uh—I do have a few questions. Can I start at Maki's Next Level right away?"

"Sure. You can start this weekend with Mr. Harvey. He is our new coach for beginners and known to be—"

"I want the best of the best. Is he qualified? If this guy is new, how do you know he is worth my time?"

There was a pause, a moment of dismay most likely. "I can

assure you Mr. Harvey would be a great choice to start out with …"

"Who is your best teacher? I want them."

Another longer pause, then, "That would be Mr. Maki himself, the owner. But he isn't training beginners. In fact, he is out of town at the moment. That is why we took so long to call back."

"Who said I was a beginner?" I asked, even though that was pushing it.

"Oh … well, what is your highest level of training?"

I answered with a question of my own. "What does Mr. Maki teach?"

"Advanced techniques and concepts. It's hard-core training."

"That's what I'm all about. So, when can I start?"

"Like I mentioned, this weekend—"

"No, no, I mean with Mr. Maki."

"You'll have to speak with Mr. and Mrs. Maki first."

"Is Mrs. Maki out of town, too?"

"Well … no. But she doesn't—"

"Put Mrs. Maki on the phone, please, if she's available."

A pause followed. "Just a moment." The man's shaky voice called for her.

Voices conversed intelligibly. I waited for her to speak, then heard the phone shift from hand to hand before a falsetto female voice spoke up. "This is Mrs. Maki; how can I help you?"

"Hi, I'm Lavinia Melrose. I'm looking to train with Mr. Maki."

"Of course, but Ms. Melrose, you should know there's no training *with* Mr. Maki. He trains you."

"Right." A fake laugh escaped me. "I heard your husband is out of town. When will he be available?"

"Yes. He won't be back until next week."

I groaned, but not loud enough for her to hear. "Okay,

could I start next week then?"

"Well, are you new to martial arts and self-defense classes or familiar with them?" she asked.

I closed one eye and squinted the other, saying through my teeth. "I am pretty familiar with that form of training."

"Hm, well, we can take you in and see how you do. That will determine where you should be placed. That should be no problem."

"Oh, thank you. Awesome. That Mr. Anders was saying I couldn't if I wasn't advanced enough."

"Anderson, you mean. Well, Mr. Maki is pretty generous. I'll talk with Mr. Anderson. Let me just look at our schedule for a minute here."

I knew his name was Anderson; I just didn't care.

"Great." I momentarily pulled the phone away to laugh devilishly.

"Miss Melrose?"

I frantically brought the phone to my ear, almost dropping it. "Hm, yes?"

"Could you start next Wednesday then?"

"That ... should be fine." A class in the middle of the week was bad timing with my schedule, but I could work around it.

"Perfect. Mr. Maki trains his students in the mornings and nights. Eight o'clock in the morning to ten in the morning. And from four to five and five to six in the evenings. What time is best?"

"The later class would be best."

"All right! You're set. Good luck!"

"Appreciate it. Sounds good. Thank you again."

The smile I saw on my face in the mirror that evening was priceless. There were no scary phone calls the rest of that week or next, thankfully.

On Wednesday, I made sure I was early. Maki's building wasn't small, taking up over two thousand square feet with a very plain look. The colors red, blue, yellow, and black painted the rough-looking exterior. A black sign that swung in the breeze had the training center's name displayed with large lettering in other colors.

Shouts of affirmation and hard-core music reverberated through the walls as I walked inside. Mr. Maki's class was in progress, I presumed. Making my way down the hallways, I stopped when I came across a long glass window to look into the studio.

These *kids* he trained had fifteen minutes left. Was I going to be training with kids younger than me?

But it didn't matter, they were good. Better than good. And from what I could tell, Mr. Maki did not teach in a way that caused people to fear him, but rather made them want to stand strong alongside him. Not to fight against him but also to fight for themselves.

I swore he saw me peeking through because he held a hand up, commanded an order, and they stopped moving.

The short Japanese man didn't look that muscular, but I imagined he was stronger than a lot of people. As he went to exit the room, I remained in place, afraid to disturb him further. However, when he smiled at me and opened the inviting blue door, he didn't look so fierce.

"You must be Miss Melrose. I'm Mr. Maki. Come in, come in. Come watch." The way he spoke with his Japanese accent was endearing.

"Yes." I gave him a polite smile as he guided me into the large training room. "Nice to finally meet you. Thank you."

"My pleasure as well. First time taking self-defense?" he asked, motioning to the chairs inside the room.

"Not exactly," I muttered, sitting down on one. "I've been taught a lot, but I have never taken a class."

"What is your reason?"

I blinked slowly in confusion. "I'm sorry?"

He chuckled, rephrasing the question. "Why are you interested in taking class now?"

"Well, I ..."

"You don't have to answer." He gave me a lopsided grin. "I ask again later."

The students in the room laughed. He hushed them with one narrow-eyed look. I was only more puzzled.

"Should I be concerned?" I asked.

"Concerned? No. There are no worries for the bull. We take the bull by the horns here."

I blinked again, stunned, and he walked to the front and resumed directing the class. Most of the boys were intimidating in spite of being so young.

When Mr. Maki dismissed everyone, they all walked out, and more people began entering. A lot of them. Most looked between the ages of sixteen and thirty. I thought they were all men until a muscular woman strolled in with confidence. Her eyes immediately pinned on me. She smirked. A man smacked her arm, pulling her attention away from me. She fit right in with the guys, who all laughed together.

The warm-up was pretty tiring but not bad. Jumping jacks. Squat jumps. Bear crawls. Sit-ups. Burpees. Run in place. Planks and more core exercises. And as many push-ups as we could do. A lot of them did more than me, but I was okay with that.

He decided to put us into groups to work on different stations. He started me off with the heavy bag, which was fine with me. I had been practicing. My only complaint was that Mr. Maki always called me Melrose.

"Spread apart. Get to work!" Mr. Maki called out. "Melrose, I'm watching you."

Of course, I was first up. He waited patiently as I wrapped my hands and slipped the padded gloves on, stopwatch in his hand. The drill was to punch the bag for a minute straight without pause. I'd been wanting to get a little anger out anyway; this was the perfect opportunity.

As I began hitting, I ignored the pairs of eyes on me and focused on bashing my fists against the heavy bag, knocking it back each time. The seconds went by quickly, carried away in the thrill of it. Suddenly, I kicked it so hard it went sideways.

An arm blocked it, and I heard the click of the button as Mr. Maki stopped the timer. His furrowed brows and dark eyes scrutinized me intensely.

I swallowed. "Oh. Thanks for that. I could have been a pancake against the wall right now," I deadpanned.

That was dramatic; of course, I could have caught the bag on my own. My first instinct when things like that happened was to make a joke, especially when I felt dumb in certain situations. And yes, I felt very stupid.

He ignored my comment and looked dizzy from my words. "Okay, woah. Take break, Melrose. Let's not punch out my equipment on first day. Next!" He told a taller and muscular young man behind me. Mr. Maki pulled me aside. "Where you learn to punch like that, Melrose?"

I sighed with slight irritation. "Please, just call me Lavinia."

He tilted his head at me, furrowing his brows. "Melrose, where did you learn?"

I swallowed my heavy breathing. "From my … husband."

"Is this man in CIA or something?"

"No, he was trained in professional combat and …" I trailed off.

"So, is he ex-military?"

"Not exactly."

Mr. Maki raised a brow.

"So, you are impressed?" I asked dubiously.

I could not read his expression, not even a smidgen at that moment. "I change my mind. We do get concerned. I'm little concerned for you. This isn't hitting; this I call murdering the bag."

"So, not good?"

"No, excellent. But the way you going at it shows you have untamed anger in you. Should be careful."

It wasn't different from what Terri once told me. "I already am aware of that. Are you my therapist now?"

I thought I saw a crack of a smirk, but it vanished. He straightened himself. "Very well. Continue, Melrose. But please take it over there." He nodded his head to the speed bag. "Know how it work?"

"Not really." I shrugged. "Lavinia is my name."

"I already am aware of that. Are you boss of me now?"

I folded my lips inside my mouth, careful not to bite a reply. "No, Master Maki. I am your lovely student."

"Uh-huh." Mr. Maki shook his head. "Good attitude you have there."

"I've been told so." I sighed, wiping away the sweat on my forehead with a towel. "I do apologize. It is hard to tame it sometimes. But I do know how."

He nodded. "Good." He began to walk off, then abruptly stopped and said, "Let me show you how speed bag work. I can't let you injure yourself on my watch."

Master Maki showed me how to work the speed bag. After many tries, I started to get the hang of it, and he left me to it. Despite me being new, he didn't focus on just me. He focused on everybody. He was a good teacher. Good for me.

Near the end of class, we stood in a circle, and students were attempting to send a strong kick to the padding Mr. Maki was holding up. Then, we would practice hitting the Thai shield.

Soon, it was my turn.

"Give it your best shot, Melrose. Aim for this and kick as hard as you can."

"As hard as I can?" I was sure to ask.

"Yes, with all your might and mind."

"Okay." I got into position. "Here goes ..." I lifted my leg and kicked the pad so hard that Mr. Maki must have felt the strength behind it because it caused him to take a couple steps backward. "Woah, there, Melrose. Are you trying to create hole through this?" He laughed, and so did everyone else, and then he became completely serious. "Do again."

When class was over, I grabbed my stuff in a sweaty mess. I felt good, though. Better than usual. A deep female voice called my name, and I turned to face her and the group of men who flanked her side. She was very muscular for a woman. Tough too. I wanted to be just like her.

She offered a faint, approving smile. "That was cool, Lavinia. You did well for your first time. Keep it up."

My smile was instant and reached my eyes. I never expected any of them to think that of me. "Oh, thank you so—"

"Yeah, yeah. Now, don't tell anyone else I said that, or I'll change my mind."

"Yes, yes. Of course," I assured.

She chuckled at the squeakiness in my voice, and they all slipped out the door. If it was possible, my grin only brightened as I tried to leave.

"Not so fast, Melrose! Come here," Mr. Lang demanded of me.

I stopped in my tracks and turned to him, approaching slowly. I kept a distance of eight feet between us.

"Closer, Melrose. I no bite," he said. I took another two steps. I swore he wanted to roll his eyes at me. "Come back tomorrow. Six o'clock."

I furrowed my brows in disappointment. Had I actually done horribly, and those people were teasing me? "But ... there are no classes with you then."

"Whoever told you that is wrong."

I squinted at him with disbelief. "Your wife did."

He softened at the mention of her. "Ah, yes. Okay. No, I don't do *classes* after six. I usually go home and let my best employees take care of it."

"So?"

"So, I want you to come to my private training room. At six."

"Private?" My eyes widened. "Where is that?"

"Behind that door there." He motioned with his head to the right, where a faded purple door was. "I carefully select ones I feel have potential to ever go in."

"Wait ... only some people will be there with me?"

"No," he told me, wagging a finger. "We train alone. Private room, private training."

My eyebrows must have been raised to the ceiling. "Just me?"

For some reason, I trusted this man, and because I was so desperate, I couldn't say no.

"Yes, just you and me, Melrose.

"So, he wants to train you privately?" Luca asked me as we ate lunch at the diner near my college.

"Yes," I said, biting into a bacon cheeseburger. It had been so long since I had eaten one, since I had even wanted to eat one. That day, I decided I would, even if it made me think of him too much.

"That's really cool, Lavy. Soon, you're going to be that karate kid," he teased, and I rolled my eyes. I couldn't believe he actually watched the movie. "Why are you taking self-defense again?"

"Just ... because I want to. You never know who is out there."

"Or what," he added, shoving French fries in his mouth with his eyebrows raised. I didn't know what to say because we weren't thinking the same thing ... but I didn't really have to speak. "Ya know," he began, changing the subject, "when I came to America, I thought you Americans so odd for calling these French fries. They are not French. They are fried potatoes ... What kind of nonsense that is?"

I laughed. "Are you pleased with the food here?"

"*Sì*, well, I try it, and some of it is so strange and so good that I want more."

"I bet sometimes you feel like you're eating a cheap Italian dish."

"*Esattamente!* Kind of."

I chuckled. "Yeah, kind of. I'm Italian too, though, and my father was a cook, so I would know."

"Was?"

I offered a faint grin. "Died when I was seven."

"Oh ... I am sorry." Luca's spirits suddenly dropped, but his sadness seemed to stem from his own more so than mine. "My mamma is gone, too. Some years back. Took my *papà* long time to remarry."

That must be why he understood my pain so well. He watched his father suffer. "My mom, too. I am sorry for your loss."

He smiled faintly. "Your *papà* was the Italian one, wasn't he?"

I nodded.

"Is that why you speak Italian?"

"No ... I speak Italian because I wanted to learn it for a trip that I ..." My voice kind of wobbled, and I swallowed my words.

"You went to Italy?"

"I did." I played with the straw in my drink. "I was in Italy to see a museum."

"A museum?" He smiled, knowing I was a bit of an artist. He didn't know I had created a painting showcased in said museum. "And I never saw you while you were there; what a pity."

"Oh, you wouldn't have found me, anyway," I whispered, looking down.

"How do you know? Where in Italy?"

I didn't make eye contact. "Rome."

"Oh, you are most likely right. I am from Naples."

"Exactly."

He hummed. "We should go," he suggested enthusiastically.

"To Italy?" I asked dubiously.

"*Sì*, why not?"

I shrugged. "You mean together, you and me?"

He nodded, then furrowed his eyebrows. "Why did you think that anyway?"

"Think what? I didn't know you were from Naples."

"I know … so why assume we would not see each other? I could have been in Rome at the time. It is not like I have never been to Rome."

I shrugged again. "I don't know, Luca. Why does it matter?"

"Because of how you are answering me."

"How am I answering you?"

"You are avoiding questions; that has to mean you are hiding something or lying."

"I wouldn't lie to you," I said.

Okay, maybe that's a lie.

But I never just lied. To him or anyone. I had the excuse of time travel to back me up … except I couldn't really ever use that excuse.

"You are right now."

"Luca …"

"So, you can't admit you lie to me? I notice. I could count how many times on one hand if I have to."

"I'm not lying now, and I have never lied to you," I told him honestly. "I've just never told you everything about me. For a reason."

"Then you are hiding from me. You always have. There's something you're not telling me. Ever since I met you, you've been doing this odd and obsessed research and don't want to tell anybody. Maybe it is not my business, but I deserve to know if this is criminal or important."

"It's not criminal." I sighed. "The research ... It's not something I can completely confide in you about. I've told you that it is personal. It has nothing to do with you or with me wanting to hide what I'm doing just to be malicious."

"So, you are leaving out the truth, and that is supposed to make it better?"

"No, it's not better; it's just what I have to do."

"Really?" Luca asked, shaking his head. He sat there staring at me, waiting for me to tell him. But I didn't say a word. I didn't know how to reply. I was shocked. I never expected my past to be brought up to Luca this way and smack me in the face so soon. "You can't trust me?"

"Maybe I can. I just don't want to risk it yet."

"What could you possibly feel like you can't tell me?" I glanced away and chose to focus on the busy workers running around the place. "This is still about your husband who passed away, isn't it? I know you still love him. But he isn't coming back. I don't think any amount of research is going to get you back to him either."

I shook my head. "Don't."

"I'm serious. Let's be factual here. Honest-to-goodness, no matter what you do, the amount of time you spend in a library doing research, I really don't know that you can bring him back. And if you did, what about the life you already have? Your son? What about me? If you are distracting yourself, I can understand—"

I slammed my fist on the table, hearing the silverware rattle against the plates. "Please. I don't want to hear any more."

He must have noticed the pain-filled look in my expression because he shut his mouth and looked guilty.

"Sí, I shouldn't have said anything. I'll just be going then."

I closed my eyes and took a breath. "Luca, you don't have to—"

"I might not have to, but I should. You don't want me around right now."

"That's not true."

"It is. And I'm fine with it." He stood up with his wallet in his hands, then threw cash on the table. "Here. Goodbye, Lavinia. Enjoy the rest of your day."

"But, Luca …"

He did walk out of there that day. He left me speechless. I had to call my mom, then I would schedule an appointment with Terri.

"So … you signed up for self-defense classes and tried to paint again, which is good, but then you encountered a strange phone call and now aren't on good terms with Luca. This man you kind of like."

I hadn't talked to Luca for a while after our argument. Not because I didn't want to, but because he made it almost impossible for us to see each other.

"Yeah, as you heard, a lot has happened this past month. But wait … Luca and I … we're friends," I reassured her.

"Yes. Right … but you like him. He likes you. And he's good to you, correct?"

"Terri, he has been MIA. I don't really know. And I can't even begin to think about dating someone right now. I'm a mess."

"Sometimes, it is what you need to get over a lover who has died. Learn to love again. And you told me Armond wanted you to meet other people, right? I'm sure he only wants you to be happy."

"It's … more complicated than that."

I'm already in the process of going back to my ghost of a husband and most likely doomed for a second love, according to the book. Stupid curse. Stupid time travel!

"Is it, Lavinia?"

"Well, if he wanted to see me again, maybe I could actually go on a date."

"It doesn't have to be him. Maybe he isn't worth it."

I sighed and shrugged. "I thought you liked him."

She raised an eyebrow. "I thought you did."

I rolled my eyes. "He's nice. But he's not Armond."

"Nobody is going to replace Armond. You're not replacing him by finding another man." She gave me a small smile and set down her pen and paper to look at me seriously. "I know you don't want to be lonely the rest of your life. Don't let his death tear you down. Go out and enjoy yourself while you are still young. You'll thank me."

I took a deep breath and thought to myself for a moment. While she was right, I didn't know how much that would work. "Yes, but I ... I can't date. Not yet."

If I really could time travel again, I couldn't play with his feelings or use him like that.

Besides, I still wasn't ready.

"That's totally fine, Lavinia. It was just a suggestion." She grabbed her pen and notepad again, back to business. "So, how are your nightmares? Are they becoming less frequent at all? Maybe less awful?"

I swallowed. "Um ... I've been doing what you told me, and it's helping a little, but ... the memories just keep coming back. And ... it's ..."

"Do you know what I want you to do?" she asked. I picked my head up, and she seemed to have a light bulb flick on inside her mind. "I think you should write to him as if he were alive. Get a journal and just write him letters. Tell him everything you would tell him as you think of it. At least once a week."

"That's ..." A wonderful idea. "Very old fashioned."

"Aren't you?"

I nodded and pursed my lips in thought. "I'll try it."

"Good." She wrote down something very quickly and

crossed a few things off before giving me a long stare. "So ... did you like the self-defense class? Are you excited to go back?"

"I ... I don't know. Do you think I should?"

"That is all up to you. But I think if it helps you and you enjoy it, then this is a great thing. I also believe it could help you take control of your emotions and get any anger out."

I tucked my hair behind my ear. "Both you and Mr. Maki have told me I am kind of angry."

She stared at me as she rolled her lips into her mouth, then burst out with laughter. "Oh, Lavinia, please tell me you did not take that the wrong way. You're not an angry person. I don't mean you have anger issues, and I'm sure that is not what Mr. Maki meant. You are just angry about a loss and haven't fully accepted it yet. All part of the process."

"Yeah, that's what everybody says."

"Well, they are right."

"But they also say loss gets better with time. That time heals all wounds. But time is what brought us together and broke us apart. So far, it has only made me miss him more. Has made it harder to live without him. I thought not being able to see him or talk to him would eventually make me used to that. But no, it's worse. So much worse." The tears wanted to fall. I could feel them forming in my eyes.

"Lavinia ..." Terri looked pained. Not just in a sympathetic way ... but an empathetic way. I wondered what that meant. "I've been where you are. I've had that exact mindset before. But you can't stay on that train, and you are the only one who is going to get you off."

"I don't know if I can."

"Of course you can."

I shook my head as a tear fell, and I swear I felt a coldness embrace me. A welcoming kind. Like a hug almost. Strange.

"Lavinia, what did you mean by time brought you two together and broke you apart?"

"Oh ..." I wiped my face free of tears. "I just mean ... I

waited for him my whole life, and he was taken away too early. Too much time, then not enough."

"Right ..." She seemed skeptical. Of course she was. Terri was incredibly insightful. "How is Leo? Is everything still going well?"

"Yes, it is so great. Other than being exhausted. But I can't even care. I love him so much."

She smiled. "Are you doing better with school now?"

"It's better. Not the best. But better."

"Hm. Okay. And your friends are still ..."

"Yeah, my friends are always good, always supportive."

"Good." She crossed another thing off. "I'm glad you tried to paint again. I'm a little concerned with this phone call, though. Have you ever had a stalker before?"

Little did she know ...

"Not a real stalker, no. Just kids in elementary school obsessed with teasing me or following me around. And people ... just being people." In other words, people not even alive anymore who were set on destroying my life.

"Well, if it happens again, you know what to do. And please tell me."

"Will do."

"So, how was painting again for the first time in a while?"

"Uh ... I'd rather not talk about that."

She scrunched her eyebrows in pure confusion. "Was it not what you thought it would be?"

I shrugged. "It's not the same."

Terri looked doubtful. "I'd keep trying." I nodded, then she smiled. "Speaking of trying ... I want to try something on you."

My eyes widened a bit. "What?"

She laughed. "You've heard of hypnotherapy before, haven't you?"

I furrowed my brows. "You're going to hypnotize me?"

"Kind of. You have complete control of the situation. I don't. You only have to relax and concentrate. So, just lie down on your back and close your eyes."

What she didn't know was that I'd been hypnotized a few times by a painting. A painting from the nineteenth century, in the years before my husband had died in front of me.

Actually, there was a lot she didn't know because I wouldn't tell her yet.

I gave her one long look before getting comfortable.

"Okay ... now just focus on my voice and my words ... and you will be pleasantly surprised."

I swear Terri did more than clinical hypnosis on me. The minute she was done and told me to open my eyes again, my body felt brand new. It felt magical. Helpful. Healing.

That night, I did as she told me. I went home, found an empty journal, and sat down at my desk with a pen. I tapped the end against the pages to think carefully about what I would say.

But as I wrote the words to address his name, the rest fell through my fingers. And so, the first of many letters to him began ...

Dear Armond,

In answer to your letter and the poem, I thank you for writing such beautiful words about me. I wouldn't have been able to put my thoughts down on paper as wonderfully as you did.

I know I'm supposed to write to you as if you are alive, but I find myself trying to remember our last of everything. The only last thing that remains clear is our last goodbye. But when was our last hello? Our last hug and kiss while you were still alive? When was our last "I love you" before we could barely find the strength to say it to each other for the last time?

I think it must have been in the tent. You entered as the light gray clouds behind you rolled in. I had been close to feeling sick again. But you strolled over to me with such confidence that screamed you weren't afraid to die, just afraid of the possibility of leaving me ... us behind. I pulled you straight in for a hug and tucked my nose in your neck, choking back my sobs as tears slipped and fell on your skin. Your arms brought me close to you while your hands held the small of my back. We had been silent. No words were said until you grabbed my face and gave me a chaste, open-mouth kiss, only pulling away to tell me you loved me more than I could ever imagine.

My response was simply that I imagine it is not less or more than how much I love you.

Three lasts, thankfully all in one. A chip of my heart cracked away the minute you walked off because I knew I couldn't predict the condition you'd be in when I saw you next. The last thought to cross my mind was that I'd see you at your worst and best moment, assuring me of your love but slipping through my fingers, literally.

I love you now and till the end of time.

Yours,
Lavinia

P.S. - I'm always in your heart as you are in mine.

CHAPTER 13

THE CLOCK IS TICKING

1994

I was late for the one thing I didn't want to miss. Two places had been on my mind, neither less important than the other. I had been greatly anticipating the opportunity to hone my skills. I should have had plenty of time, and still, I was too focused on a man that time slipped away.

Scratch that. Two men, actually.

An art gallery had accepted my art into their show. The minute I had found out, I invited Luca. He had agreed, of course, but I had assumed he wouldn't be attending since he apparently strongly believed he should give me space. I had pretty much blown our friendship, ruining Leo's chance to continue his friendship with Rocco.

I walked toward the front of the art school, my mom and Dan trailing behind. My mom reminded me, again, that we had to wait for someone she had invited without telling me, simply because I would have said no otherwise. I had only just found out on the way over. I had already flipped in the car. I couldn't do it again. I didn't want to upset Leo while we were on our way to drop him off at a friends house. And, of course,

I wasn't the kind of person to rescind an invitation.

The name:

Nathaniel Brooks. Easy-to-talk-to-about-anything Nathan.

The embarrassing and infuriating part was that he had been one of my first crushes as a young girl, and he used to be Mark's best friend. He had been adorably dorky and nice on my tween eyes. But I had liked him for being kind to me, always trying to make me laugh. The boys had included me in their inside jokes, mostly because I had always had to hang out with them when Nathan was over.

I had liked him so much that I mustered up the courage to ask him to the school dance in seventh grade. I had instantly regretted it once he told me he had already asked someone else. I had assumed he thought of me as a kid sister. Eventually, we had all grown apart, and I certainly hadn't thought I would have to face him again.

An expensive black car finally rolled up and slipped into a parking spot. I wasn't an expert on cars, but the distinctive wing doors confirmed he drove a Lamborghini. I knew his parents had been accomplished and fairly wealthy, but I had a feeling this came from his own hard work. My eyes were the size of dinner plates when Nathan appeared from behind the Lambo door.

He looked so ... distinguished. Not like the smart, cool kid with glasses. He had clearly said goodbye to having four eyes. He had probably thrown them away the first chance he had or he hardly used them, replaced by contacts for the presentable look for his successful life. Obviously, I had known he'd be all grown up, but he certainly was well-dressed and put together. Handsome even. His hair was darker than I remembered, but his smile was just as charming. The same shine in his blue eyes remained, twinkling as they landed on me.

I winced. I was a fat mess compared to him. Even if I agreed to find another man, he was way too put together and sumptuous for me.

My mom whispered, "Nathan was an architect graduate last year. He's already doing well for himself."

I rolled my eyes. Clearly! He always had been smarter than the average bear and skillfully artistic. Naturally, he agreed to come to my school art show. I really didn't want to ask what my crazy mother even said to him to convince him to go. She begged me to give him a chance while we argued in the car. She thought Nathan would be a good guy to start dating or even someone to just talk to so I could mend my internal wounds. I hoped she hadn't convinced him by telling my sob story. I had never mentioned I technically had a man in my life since I refused to talk about any man other than Armond. She had no idea I had met Luca. And I hadn't planned on telling her once I thought our friendship was over. But I sort of wished I had, precisely to avoid this situation.

Perhaps a different guy for the new me?

Yeah, I don't think so.

Nathan was different than when I had met him as a child. As Nathan walked up to me for the first time in a while, I felt in my bones something wasn't quite right, that something would be missing. He wouldn't be the perfect guy for *me*.

Besides, I had a mission to accomplish.

Nathan waltzed up with a bouquet of flowers. I had to hold back my eye roll.

"Long time no see, Vinnie," he whispered. The corners of his mouth widened to a bright smile of straight white teeth.

I think he's too perfect for me, actually.

I took the pink roses slowly, almost with hesitation. He knew I preferred those over red ones. I instinctively brought them to my nose and inhaled.

I sighed, embarrassment heating my skin when my eyes reluctantly met his. "Thanks, Nathan." I offered a faint grin. "Sorry we never stayed in touch."

Wonder why that was.

"No worries," he replied, tone easygoing. "That's life."

I nodded awkwardly. "How are you doing lately?" I asked as I turned to walk inside, and he followed.

He opened his mouth to answer, but a voice called out for me. My head snapped in the direction of the parking lot and coffee brown eyes met mine.

"Luca," I gasped.

Luca was entering the picture. Really, he seemed more like a lion entering another lion's territory with a female present. The two males pinned eyes on each other, neither afraid to fight to the death over the lioness.

Who would win?

The lioness. I would put a stop to both of them before they destroyed one another.

At first, Luca looked in severe discomfort, but he calmly came to stand with all of us despite the stormy glint in his eyes. I could tell Luca wanted to jump Nathan, just not in a welcoming way.

Luca glanced at me. "Lavinia. Good to see you again."

I nodded. I was in so much shock he had shown up that I couldn't respond. My mom only minorly saved me by asking, "Vinnie ... who ... who is this? I don't believe you told me about him. Or that he was coming." She eyed me, mouth slightly agape, conveying she thought he was a hunk of beauty.

I sighed in defeat. I already felt a disaster coming on. I rubbed my temple as I turned to Luca. "Erm ... No. Mom, this is ..." I froze, feeling ashamed. He looked so hurt. He just found out I had never told my own mom about him. That was to be expected.

"Luca," he introduced confidently, no matter what news he had just delivered. "My name is Luca. I work at the historical research library."

"Oh!" My mom showed sheer radiant excitement. "You go there all the time, Vin! Excuse her for not saying anything! She doesn't like to talk about herself or boys." Despite my mom's attempt to make things more comfortable, I hardly felt better from the comment. "Nice to meet you, *Luca*."

Luca brightened slightly. "Pleasure to finally meet you as well," he said with a smile. Luca glanced at the flowers in my hand, then nodded at Nathan as he tilted his head toward Luca. "Who's your guy?" he asked.

I cleared my throat. "He's not my …"

"I'm not. Just here for Lavinia," Nathan interspersed.

"Oh, are you?"

Nathan stood straighter. "Of course. Is something wrong?"

"No," Luca replied coolly. "I'm here for her as well."

Nathan hummed. "Your accent …" He smiled politely. "Are you from Italy or something? Lavinia, he sounds similar to how your dad used to talk." He chuckled.

"Uh …" I began awkwardly and swallowed. "Yeah."

Luca gave me a look that said he was pissed that I had known Nathan for so long. But he regained himself … for a bit.

"I'm from Naples; her father is from Verona. There's a very big difference between our spoken Italian in terms of pronunciation."

"Oh …" Nathan paused. "I apologize. I don't mean to offend."

He looked schooled and a little embarrassed. He could not have known where my father was originally from. I had never known until Luca and I had researched the very Antonio Melrossi himself, also known as my dad, but he didn't know him as my actual father, just thought my line of ancestors came from there. I had told him my father moved to America after he met my mom.

And no, that wasn't a lie. Time travel was the only part left out.

"He's just being dramatic," I said with a squeaky wheel laugh.

"Not really, Lavinia," Luca muttered tensely, not breaking eye contact with Nathan. He was currently a grumpy thing. "I am serious."

I know, Luca. I'm trying to help. Don't talk!

"Right ..." I scrambled to think of a way out of the awkward conversation. "Well, let's go inside and enjoy the show, shall we?" I asked.

Worst idea I had in years. We walked in, and I directed us to my art display, seeing people crowd around it and gasping in awe. Nathan became fixated with the painting of Armond's pair of green eyes. The one I never completed and finished more recently.

"Whose eyes are these?" he asked.

"Someone very dear to me," I answered vaguely.

"*Cuore?*" Nathan pointed to the script in the bottom right corner of the painted canvas:

L.J.M
For my cuore

"It means heart," Luca cut in, "a name reserved for ones who have a special place in her heart."

I sighed, tucking my hair behind my ear. "Yes, but I call him *cuore* for more reasons than that."

"What are those reasons?" Luca asked curiously, yet in a way that infuriated me, tilting his head patronizingly. But his condescension was not toward me; it was toward Nathan. "You have not had the chance to tell me yet."

Why did I have to bring that up?

"Maybe she doesn't want to tell anyone," Nathan budged in. "Especially right now."

"You may be right ..." Luca trailed off, muttering something under his breath, and I knew some remark was coming. "Or maybe you think you are always right."

"Boys ... Now, that's enough," my mom scolded, frowning at them, disappointed.

They hardly listened or cared.

"Quite the contrary. But I am right about this. Just look at her face. She is bothered."

When Luca stepped forward, I grabbed him by the collar of his shirt roughly. "Okay, Rocky Balboa ... You're an ass. Would you stop being an alpha male?"

"Alpha male? Who is Rocky Balboa?"

I rolled my eyes. "Just stop acting childish, and let's move on."

"I don't know if either of us can move on, Lavinia," Luca told me.

I stopped walking and let go of him. "What are you talking about?" I snapped.

"I adore you, can't you see that?" Luca ran a hand through his hair. "And it hurts to know I'll never come close to your husband."

I blinked slowly, speechless.

"Husband?" Nathan echoed. "Wait, you're married?"

I shook my head and ignored him, though I was happy to find out my mom had not mentioned Armond's death. "That's not true, Luca. You are two very different people anyway. No one could replace him, and he couldn't replace you. Now, would you keep it down?"

Luca sighed and nodded. "But I need the truth after this, Lavinia. No more lies."

"There are just things I'm not sure you can know about me, Luca." I shook my head, tears welling in my eyes.

He rubbed a hand down his face. "It's all right if you're not ready, but I could never judge you."

I swallowed. "It's not that ..."

"You will tell me eventually, right?"

"I ... maybe, Luca."

"Do you not trust me?"

I bit my lip; no words came out.

He sighed. "Okay ... it is your choice." He stepped backward, then charged toward the double doors.

"Wait! Luca. Don't do this!" I shouted. He was about to

exit, so I chased after him, running out of the building. I saw him walking away. "You are walking out like our friendship means nothing! I never thought you were a quitter!"

"And you chose not to say a word like our friendship means not a thing! So, you quit!"

"I'm not quitting! I'm not the one leaving behind a girl who cares about you!"

He stopped when I said that, then whipped around and stomped toward me. "If you care even at all, you will tell me what you are hiding and stop keeping secrets like you are some big mystery."

"But I am. It's not on purpose," I whispered. "I almost ... I almost got thrown into a mental hospital because of this secret. If not for my mom, I'd be there right now. It's not something I can trust just anybody to know."

"You think I would tell someone? You think I would think less of you? You think I care how crazy you sound? Then, you really don't know me!"

"I know you more than you think. And I know how most people react when they figure me out. It's not pretty."

"I'm not most people. Nothing you tell me could change how I feel. Not possible."

"Even if I tell you I see and hear my husband's ghost? And not just his, but dead people I used to know and ones I am not familiar with? Even if I tell you Armond is a man I first saw in a painting from the nineteenth century? That the painting is the whole reason I fell through time and fell in love with him?"

Luca was instantly silent, and his eyes slowly widened more as each word tumbled from my mouth. He was silent for too long. Too still for much too long.

"Yeah, that's what I thought." I nodded in disbelief, accepting he wouldn't take this as well as Armond had. "But there's my great big secret you so desperately needed to know and wish you hadn't heard. Goodbye, Luca. I guess I won't be seeing you anymore."

I looked down as I turned to walk back to the school.

"So, it is true, then. Time travel is real. I have a feeling there's more to this story, no?" he asked, and my feet shuffled in his direction. "Lavinia, what do you mean, goodbye? This is not goodbye. You will see much more of me. Maybe an annoying amount. I am a small bit confused. You should prepare for the questions. Did you say you went to the nineteenth century? Oh, this is the kind of madness I like."

I crept closer to him with every word and finally wrapped my arms around him in a hug. I guess Armond was right. I didn't have to worry about telling him.

"Thank you," I whispered.

"It is nothing, Lavy." He pulled away. "This really happened to you, eh?"

"I couldn't lie about that even if I tried."

Luca grinned with a nod, and I wasn't prepared for what he said next. "Then go to him."

I stared at him in complete shock for a moment, then he continued. "What are you still doing here?"

"Well, that's ... kind of what I've been working on."

Luca seemed to realize. "Oh, *si,* yes. I see. Hmm."

"Would you come back inside now?"

The rest of the evening went much smoother. Both Luca and Nathan apologized, but I did not miss Luca and Nathan's exchange of intense glances. Time went so quickly; I was not paying attention to it passing by. Luca took me back to his place afterward, and we talked all night long. I hadn't intended to stay over but ended up falling asleep there. When I woke, I checked my watch to see it was midday, and my eyes widened. I tugged on my hair and shook my head.

"Luca!" I shrieked, shaking him awake. "I'm gonna be late for my training. I gotta go." I let out a loud string of curses.

"What?" Luca grumbled. "Where?"

"East Hemet," I replied shortly. He followed me out of the house, and I jogged to my car as I reached into my purse for my keys. "I have to run home for a change of clothes first."

"I expect a call from you later!" Luca shouted.

I laughed and nodded, jumping inside my car and firing up the engine. Once I left home, I swear I was stopped at every red light before I reached East Hemet. I pulled into the enclosed space with adjacent parking where Mr. Maki's self-defense center was located.

I barged inside. "Mr. Maki! Mr. Maki! I'm so sorry I'm late, Mr. Maki. I—"

But Mr. Maki was not in the room, though I did interrupt a class. He must have heard me, too, because he came out of that secret room of his with a dramatic roll of his eyes. "I do not call this late, Melrose. You later than late. Get in here before I change my mind about you!"

"Yes, sir," I said earnestly, pushing my legs to move more quickly than they ever did, especially since every student's eyeball was on me. It felt like they all could see through my soul, which was pretty unsettling. "I am sorry. I had to be somewhere important yesterday, then I was up last night and—"

"Next time, plan things better. Toss your stuff. We have lot of work to do in very little time."

"Yes ... Okay." He shut the door behind me. "Really, Mr. Maki, I didn't mean to keep you waiting."

He shook his head as if he didn't mind, then raised a brow and motioned to me with a lazy hand. "This is what you wear to private training, Melrose?" he commented, and I glanced down at my dress. "You must be madder than I think."

"I brought a change of clothes, don't worry." I reached inside my purse.

"Oh, I'm not worried. That is why I am as calm as clam."

I refrained from rolling my eyes. "I don't need sarcasm from you right now. I said my apology."

"That not sarcasm, Melrose. I was worried. Sick even to think I might be reason you dead on highway somewhere."

I couldn't hold back my astonishment but was able to give

a level answer. "I'm very much alive. I didn't need to get on a highway to come here." I could only think of that to say.

Mr. Maki stared at me for an unnerving amount of time before he began to laugh. "You something else, Melrose."

"You thought something happened to me?" I asked.

"Not exactly."

"But that's what you said …"

"Are you going to change or not, Melrose? Chop chop!"

I sighed. "Yes, Mr. Maki. I'll be quick."

The locker room was ghastly. A mustiness and a stale odor created a heavy and potent smell in the surrounding air. I changed my clothes as fast as I could, storing my dress in a locker.

Mr. Maki instructed a warm-up very similar to the last few times. The moves were a little easier every time I did them. As I was finishing my push-ups, I collapsed on the floor and caught my breath. Mr. Maki came to stand over me.

"Good job. Need a hand?" He put a hand out for me while holding boxing pads in the other.

"No," I grumbled, standing on my own. "What are those for?"

He laughed. "Hold hands behind your back."

I narrowed my eyes but did as he said, then he walked behind me and tied them together with a bandana. "Uh …."

He hushed me and came back to stand in front of me, putting the gloves on.

"What are you—" One pad gently smacked me in the face. "Ow."

"Getting you accustomed to being hit. It will happen."

My gaze turned glacial. "And this is the only way? Hitting me in the face."

"Yes." Another blow to the other cheek, harder that time. "The only way to get used to being punched is getting punched. Obviously, I not punching you. So, this is what we do. Before you start sparring, I want you to get feel for it."

I groaned. "Can't I start to learn the cool stuff?"

He gave me a bored look. "Have you heard of patience, Melrose? Learn that first." When I began to roll my eyes, he muttered, "And less attitude."

"Yes, sir."

"You did well today, Melrose."

I smiled proudly and thanked him, walking in the direction of the locker room.

"You could be great," he told me just loudly enough for my ears to catch.

I faced him. "I don't want to be great. I want to be unstoppable."

His mouth formed a smirk as he walked toward me. "I make you that and more. You could become warrior of mind, body, and soul."

I shook my head, doubtful. "You mean like in the old days?"

Mr. Maki slanted his eyes at me, giving me a scolding look. "There are warriors everywhere, Melrose. Sometimes, they train for the day one can save own life or somebody else's. But you don't have to know how to shoot gun to be one; you don't need to have seen war and died for others or survived battle. They are not born into this life as one. Life shapes them into one. Warriors are fighters. Not always by body, but always mind and soul. You, Melrose, are fighter. I can see it in your eyes; I can see it in the way you push yourself. What have you done with your life? This talent be wasted."

I shrugged, looking down at my hands. "Painting mostly."

"You *paint*?" he asked with so much shock that I should have been offended, but I was only amused.

"I'm an aspiring artist," I said, glancing at him briefly from my hands, "who apparently has auspicious talent."

In more ways than one, according to Mr. Maki.

"I had a show last night. That's where I was," I added.

His upper lip quirked into a small smile. "Hmm ... I see. Let me tell you something, Melrose. Warriors and artists live by same code of life. They see bigger picture, see world through different eyes." I listened to him carefully, unable to grasp how he thought of me. "You are both. How ... rare."

I scoffed. "I've been hearing a lot of the word rare recently."

"That is because you are," he tried to assure me, and he couldn't have been more serious. "Why did you come here, Melrose, hm?"

My shrug was nonchalant. "I need to do something that requires a lot of skill in combat."

By the squinty eyes he gave me, I knew he thought my answer was hogwash. "What *kind* of something?"

I sighed, looking around the room. "Do you know how to use a sword?"

It took a few seconds for him to reply. "I have news for you, Melrose. I only let true warriors into this room. I hand-picked you," he told me, stepping closer to tilt my chin up. "So yes, if you accept my offer, I could make you unstoppable conqueror of blade."

I blinked. "What ... is that?" I asked in a stammer, impatiently awaiting his answer.

Mr. Maki smiled so big. "How would you like to become as unstoppable as samurai, Melrose?"

He left me speechless and told me to think about it before giving him my answer. He suggested I do some research first, but any amount of research would not change my mind. He had let *me* walk into his private training room. He had chosen *me*. He could give me everything I wanted. If he could make me insurmountable, I might even have the strength to bring Armond back.

CHAPTER 14

THE WAY OF THE FIGHT

1994

Mr. Maki taught in a painstakingly long process. And he was not heedful of injury. My body ached from head to toe every single time I left him, and I hurt myself at least once by the end of each day. The days did not get easier either. Only harder and longer. But I hardly cared. I welcomed the pain of training. Not only did the pain make me feel alive again, but it also reminded me that I was alive.

Mr. Maki was in no rush, but I was. If I was going to keep a man alive in battle, I needed years of practice, and I was impatient. His slow methods already drove me insane, but I trusted them. I anticipated the day he'd make me a force to be reckoned with.

After a few weeks of training, he asked me to meet him at a woodsy park. I didn't care where we met as long as he taught me something interesting. Only, I didn't see how bringing me to a park would make me a living, breathing machine.

"Get in, Melrose!" he ordered as soon as he rolled down his car window. When I hesitated, he added, "Lesson number two. Don't think; just do." He jabbed a thumb at the passenger seat, and then I ran around to climb inside his tiny white Volkswagen.

Mr. Maki stepped on the gas, and we lurched forward. He directed us toward the car trail alarmingly fast, and my eyes widened. "What in the—is taking the car necessary?"

"Yes," he replied vaguely, staring straight ahead. I noted to never let him drive me anywhere again. "We going where my father took me in my younger years to train. There's a fallen tree, and trunk remain level and off ground, so you walk across it."

A grin stretched my lips. "Are we going to fight on it?"

"It more balance and control, Melrose." I gave him the stink eye, and he rolled his own eyes. "Have faith in me, please."

We stopped not much longer after that. I took in the beauty of the trees swaying in the breeze and was distracted by Mr. Maki shutting the car door. I followed suit and entered the forest, hearing bees hum and birds chirp and sing in the distance. I lifted my face toward the sun, letting the light and shadow dance across my skin. I delighted in the scent of the flowers and the sound of my feet sliding through the leaves as I stalked behind Mr. Maki.

Once we began to approach the spot, the tree came into view. It looked magnificent even though it was lying horizontally above the ground, at least thirty feet from end to end. My eyes spotted where the trunk had snapped in a storm; the wood splintered skyward and in every other direction imaginable.

Mr. Maki turned toward me. "Climb up there and stand with eyes closed, Melrose."

"What?"

"You perfectly capable."

"Mr. Maki, I ... do you see ..."

The tree was fairly high off the ground.

I sighed at the stubborn look on his face. He really wasn't

budging on this part.

"Hmph." I muttered something else not worth mentioning after that as I approached the tree. Maki only laughed at me. "Don't make me use that kick you taught me to kick your teeth in!"

"Just do as I say for once."

"For once? Ha!" Once I reached the tree, I turned back to him. "You haven't seen defiant yet!"

Mr. Maki pinched the bridge of his nose and then gave me an intensely serious look. "Focus, Melrose ... tree. Climb."

I sighed defeatedly. "Yes, yes ... doing." I faced the tree again, then stared at it for a good ten seconds before bending my legs for power and jumping upward to grab hold of the trunk. But I was short, and my fingers barely grazed the bottom of the trunk. That did not work very well. I came back to the ground gracefully with a quiet whump.

"Try again. I suggest different way."

I held back an eye roll, muttering, "Obviously."

I could practically sense his mirth and feel his fierce glare burning through me as I eyed the other tree standing exceptionally tall next to the fallen trunk, disappearing in the airy mist above us. Then my eyes followed where the snap in the level tree had splintered during a storm, causing it to tip over and land in a forked tree on the opposite side of the tall tree. But not broken enough to be unstable. The tree with the fork was extremely thick and sturdy, and two ginormous rocks left about a four foot gap under the break in the tree. It held there steadily.

I began to walk up uneven, mossy ground to get to the rocks and grabbed hold of the boulder. I stepped onto a visible tree root to hoist myself up and onto the surface of that same rock. I stood to my feet and placed my hands on the trunk, pushing the weight of my body up and then on the tree. I wrapped my leg around it and brought myself to a straddle over the trunk.

A grin split my face. I threw my hands up. "Ta da!"

"Melrose, no dilly-dallying!" he scolded. "Stand up. No time to waste."

I did as he said, wobbling just a little, then catching my balance. Slowly, I closed my eyes. I teetered slightly but regained my stance quickly.

"Pay attention, Melrose. Don't open eyes," he said as he crept closer. A few moments went by before the trunk shifted under me, moaning softly.

"You're up here now."

"Ah, well done, Melrose."

I cracked my eyes open to see him much closer than I expected, almost losing my stability. He was in a crouch, balancing perfectly mere inches in front of me.

"I didn't say you could open those eyes."

I glared at him, crouching as well with my hands down. "How did you get so close without me knowing?"

"Stealth. It's all about power of observation. Once I teach you stealth and scrutiny, you know when others try to sneak their way behind you. You could fight with dirt and mud in your eyes, and you win. Or while wearing a blindfold. Don't make me use one on you."

"I won't, sir."

"I will anyway."

My jaw dropped.

He grinned evilly, then turned serious. "Close mouth and listen, Melrose." I snapped it shut, scowling slightly. "Balance is everything. *Life* is balance. It's about finding acceptance to keep stability. Only *you* can create it inside." He tapped a finger on my chest, over my heart. "Don't allow chaos in this world to disrupt your peace. If you have no balance, you fall. Always remember. Have balance. It is life."

My lips parted further and further as each word was spoken, and he pushed up my chin once he finished, chuckling to himself at my expression. "Okay. Stand up! We do some exercise for core and balance."

Mr. Maki took me back to the tree many times, as well as a lake. He nailed together planks of wood into a small square-shaped flat surface for me to balance over the water. There, he'd sit in a camp chair and watch me, again and again, fail to keep myself standing as I did core exercises. I dragged tires. Climbed ropes. Ran in sprints. Tried battle-roping and peg-board climbing. One day, Mr. Maki even took me back to his house. I thought he was inviting me over for dinner until Mr. Maki examined his curved staircase and threw me a pensive look.

"Don't give me that look," I groaned. "You're coming up with something difficult, aren't you?"

"Well, Melrose, you impress me every time we meet. But you could always build more muscle. That will help with handling weapons, especially swords."

"Okay ..." I groaned, shifting my feet in anticipation. "What do you have in mind?"

He pursed his lips for a moment, full of mirth, then blurted his inventive way of torturing me. "I want you to go up sides of stairway only using your hands and arms to hold yourself up."

"Wait ... up that side ..." I pointed, and he followed my finger with his eyes. "Then all the way to the other end and—"

"As far as you can make it at first, of course."

So, he wanted me to climb up the side of the stairs using only my arm strength.

"Won't your wife throw a hissy fit?"

"I like to see you do it first."

After my arms nearly gave out, he did have me stay over for dinner. Mrs. Maki naturally cooked deliciously authentic Japanese food. The best I ever ate. She asked me many questions about my life outside of training, and she seemed to grow downcast at the mention of my son. It occurred to me then that they didn't have children.

Once we finished eating, I offered to help clean up and wash the dishes. Mr. Maki excused himself when we were just about done. Mrs. Maki spoke up. "You're becoming one of the best he's ever taught, dear. He speaks highly of you. He tells me he's never met anyone with as much determination as you."

My lips parted in shock. "Really?"

She nodded and moved around in the kitchen majestically. "Don't look so surprised, honey. He cares deeply about you. I'm sure he thinks of you as a daughter by now. As do I. I hope you know that. We are appreciative of you."

"You ... you think of me as a daughter?" my voice faltered.

"Yes." She frowned, putting down a dish towel to look me straight in the eye. "Unfortunately, I cannot have children. I want to thank you for being the closest thing to having a child."

Her words sparked great emotion in me. "Thank you for showing me who I am again."

She brought me into her arms and held me tightly. As I peeked over her shoulder, I saw Mr. Maki had been watching us from the doorway with a rare, soft smile.

Months went by before he taught me how to fight. A few months more, and then I sparred. I fell flat on my buttocks too many times to count before I became good competition against his students. There were even times when they'd cheer me on. Mr. Maki only let me pick up a weapon when I had beat the third toughest student in his class by pinning him down. Mr. Maki skillfully showed me how to use a sword in a way I had never known. We practiced in his gym daily with fake swords until I was ready to wield a real one and use obstacles.

Mr. Maki even showed me his collection of swords at home after he had invited me over a few times. On my birthday, he gifted me my favorite antique longsword. He was probably annoyed by how much I expressed my gratitude after that.

I began to feel like a true warrior, one I strived to be every day to save Armond.

Mr. Maki and I sat outside by the lake near his house, resting from a long day of shedding blood, sweat, and tears. He broke the peaceful silence apart from the birds and leaves blowing in the gentle breeze. "I'm going to ask you this again, Melrose," Mr. Maki said as I chugged a bottle of water. "Why did you seek out a *sensei*?"

I swallowed and sighed. "It's complicated." I shifted my body to lay back in the grass, resting my eyes as the sun pierced them.

"Nothing is complicated. We are ones who make it seem that way."

"You're a walking inspiration, you know that?" I attempted to deflect, but he wasn't backing down. I sighed heavily through my nose. "Well, you're asking for the truth, and I don't know if you'll want to hear it."

"I have more of problem with liars than crazy girl like you, Melrose."

I couldn't help my laugh. Reluctantly, I spoke up. "What if I told you time travel is possible?"

He cocked his head slowly at me. "I say that is interesting notion and astonishing theory. Why?"

"It's not a theory or notion." I sat back up, folding my legs in. "It happened to me. Unexpectedly. A few years ago."

His thick eyebrows reached for the sky, and I saw his face scrunch up with mirth until he read my sincere expression. "Oh …"

"My husband died, Mr. Maki," I blurted, my voice cracking without intention. "My son doesn't have a father anymore. Except he was killed in a way you wouldn't think. He died in a war that occurred over a hundred years ago."

Mr. Maki's eyes softened with sympathy. "Over a hundred years …" he echoed, shaking his head. "I am so sorry."

I looked down at my calloused palms. "And there's no other way I can save him unless I learn what you're teaching me."

"And that is why you want to learn swordplay. You want to go back."

I nodded. "I'm going back someday when I'm ready."

"If anyone can do it, it is you," he told me.

My eyes lifted to meet his own, and I threw my body forward and gathered him in my arms.

"I've been to war, Melrose," he admitted in a whisper, and I stilled in his grasp. "Vietnam ... With how much blood war cost, there not much glory. But the glory you would feel if you were to succeed in saving your love ... I imagine that more than enough." He brought me back by my shoulders to look into my eyes. "Remember, it all in mind and spirit. Both of yours so strong. Those raised by sword not be beaten, and those toughened by fire not be burned. If you do this, you best be careful. Come out with him alive."

I gave him a wobbly nod.

Mr. Maki went on to divulge that his father was a sword fanatic and taught him everything he knew. But the one quality his father always lacked was courage. Mr. Maki learned that all on his own.

A week later, Mr. Maki called me to his private training room. He told me to lie down on the floor and close my eyes. I did as he said without question, no matter how puzzled I felt.

I listened to Mr. Maki's shoes as they shuffled against the floor, and he walked around me. "We're practicing dissimulation today, Melrose."

"Why would I have to hide under a pretense?"

"Because when you go to this war over a hundred years back, you won't be fighting as a woman. You need to always conceal yourself. Especially when enemy think you are down." I sensed him closing in on me. Hairs raised on my skin. "You will go on pretending you are. Attack where he unprepared; move when he least expect you. That when you strike."

Somehow, my hand shot out before he did without even

seeing his next move. I exhaled out a breath of shock, retracting in disbelief of myself.

His eyes narrowed, and the corner of his mouth lifted. "You are ready."

CHAPTER 15

STRANGE VOICES

1848

I told Armond I wanted to spend the day with him, knowing it could be one of his last. So, before dawn, he took me to the meadow where it had all started, to watch the sunrise. We climbed the tree together for a better view of the land and watched the sun appear over the horizon. Afterward, we lay on the grass to sunbathe and talked for hours. Then, we ventured into town. The waters were calm as we went canoeing across the Tiber, and I even told Armond about the tradition of throwing a coin into the Trevi Fountain.

Once my stomach growled, Armond told me to wait while he grabbed food. I said I'd be across the street. My eyes roamed the buildings, taking note of the differences in comparison to the modern city. I crossed the street, where I slipped into an alleyway to find a shop to keep myself busy. Only the sound of the gravel and pebbles squashed under my shoes. Strange, it was actually eerily quiet.

The hair rose on my neck, and suddenly, I felt someone behind me, watching with a heavy gaze. Hands grasped my shoulders roughly and shoved me towards the stone wall. I quickly turned my body and sent a blow to his side, grabbing the man's throat and pinning him to the wall instead.

His face was concealed by an ancient Roman mask. "Who are you?" I barked. He gurgled on his words, and I released my pressure just slightly. "Answer me."

"Nobody," he groaned. "I will leave you be; just let me go."

"That would be your best and only option," I seethed before pulling back and throwing him aside.

His mask fell to the ground. "Mark my words; I will snatch you soon, girl," he growled in a gravelly voice. I glimpsed his dark hair as he picked it up and ran off.

I stumbled out of there, seeing Armond appear down the street, both hands full. Straight away, he sensed I was off. "I bought us bread, grapes, and cheese," he said, tilting his head at me. "What happened, *cuore*?"

I rubbed my neck nervously. "I went to go inside a shop, and somebody tried to kidnap me or kill me. I'm not really sure which."

"Are you all right?" Armond asked, eyes roving my body. "Where are they? I'll—"

"Yes, they're gone now. No need."

His darkened eyes lightened only the slightest bit. "Come on, let's go eat at home."

Armond kept looking at me the entire way home, but I couldn't help my silence. All I thought about was that man's reason for putting hands on me.

Armond and I quietly sat and ate by a stream away from the villa. When he finished eating, he started throwing rocks. I watched as each stone skipped across the water, one by one, waiting patiently for him to speak.

"I'm going to tell you something my father told me when I was young and first began training."

"He has actually told you something useful?" I asked dubiously.

"Yes," he said seriously, staring off at the stream. "You're going to be under a lot of pressure, as will I. You may not be able to be by my side at all times."

I sighed. He was right; it just helped to make light of the situation. "Go on."

His gaze wandered back to the water. "It is as impossible to see your reflection in troubled water as it is hard to stay connected to yourself with a troubled soul. We can sense a lot in the silence of our own mind." He paused. "That's one thing my father told me that was worth knowing and has always stayed with me."

"Well, it's very true," I said. "Only, he didn't exactly follow what he said."

"No." He nodded. "He also told me later on that when you participate in battle, it changes you. Sometimes, not always for the better. I think a lot of us hope it has a positive impact; in a way, it can. But there is much wrath in battle, we have to be the ones to not get carried away in the fury war brings. Anger does not build. It will eventually destroy. As for what happens once we do come out ..." He did not finish that thought.

I steadied my sudden shallow breaths to relax my heart rate. "Then how do you not get carried away in war?"

"I can show you."

I stared at him for a long moment, then nodded for him to go on.

He gave a soft smile. "Come here, *cuore*." He motioned with his hands for me to come closer. I stood from a log and crept over to him, kneeling by his side. "You see yourself in the water, don't you?" I nodded. "Watch as I touch your reflection." He dragged his hand lightly over the water where my face could be seen. "It's not as clear now, right?"

"Right," I agreed, seeing where he was going with this.

"You know yourself better than anyone. You can find yourself without seeing clearly. So, let the ripples settle on their own because if you don't, and you interfere too strongly ..." He began to splash the water with his hand. "It all becomes too messy to see, and you can't find yourself. In other words, you won't know who you really are anymore if you stay vexed. If you do things that will only worsen the situation. We have to rely on our minds and hearts when times are difficult because we can lose ourselves and then have to rediscover ourselves again. Learning to rely on the mind *and* the heart, not one or the other, is important. Of course, we can't do everything on our own. But other people aren't always going to help, maybe not even be there to help. We have to find the will in ourselves to create change and keep calm in our souls. It is hard to see what lies ahead because, usually, we are blinded from seeing the future. We really show our own self the way."

I swallowed. Where had this man come from? He had never seen a movie, never had read a self-help book, probably had never even read a book that explained something like this, and he still was wiser than me in my later years. That was for sure.

I spoke seriously as I said, "When the waters are calm, when the soul is calm, there's clarity. What you are saying is we need to remain composed in order to survive this."

"Yes, exactly."

I kept nodding to myself until I looked at him. "There's one thing you are forgetting when it comes to water and ripples that also applies to us and life."

His lips formed an amused tilt. "And what is that?"

"Even a small ripple in water grows, meaning that changing what happens eventually will affect more than we think, in both good and bad ways. Especially if we manage to successfully keep you alive."

His mouth parted as he drew in a thoughtful breath, and then he snapped it shut and nodded, still scrutinizing me. "Water shapes its course, and so must we."

"But we'll cross that bridge when we come to it," I said. I sighed, and he gave his silent agreement.

The things I had read in that big dusty book came back to

haunt me. Those gut feelings wouldn't dissipate. The possibility I could forget everything I was doing and what I was doing it for hung there for dear life in the back of my mind. I had to tell Armond about my gift also being a curse and warn him of all that could change before it was too late. He saw how distracted I seemed and finally had to ask what was wrong.

"There's something I haven't told you yet," I said, shifting uncomfortably. "There's a reason I am the way I am."

Armond only seemed confused by my words. "Whatever do you mean?"

"Um, I ..." I took a long pause, thinking how I would come out and say it. "I'm not really supposed to be here ... again."

"I would believe so ..." he trailed off, waiting for me to finish. "But you are."

I sighed through my nose gently. "You are destined to die for a reason, Armond. Taking that back is defying nature, even more so than time travel itself."

"What are you saying?"

I picked at my fingernails thoughtfully. "Those who time travel are given a special gift, but that gift comes with a price. So, time travelers are bound to a ... malediction."

"They're cursed? Why on earth would someone like you be cursed?"

I swallowed. "Because time travel goes against the laws of life, and a soulmate's death is the only thing that will stop the travelers. Ergo, they go back to their own time."

"But that is—"

"I know." I nodded. "Cruel in so many ways. Sometimes, I began to believe my being here, in this time, had actually killed you. But ..." I shook my head and paused again. "There are some travelers who have the power to thwart the attempt of the curse."

"And that is you," Armond said.

I barely smiled. "I don't know yet, but so far, it seems to be coming true. The compulsion was supposed to disappear after you died. But it didn't. Only rare time travelers are able to travel more than once. Multiple times even."

"So, if you've gotten this far, then—then you must be inclined to success." He began to smile hopefully.

"I—I can't be sure. And even if I do. To go back in time before you die like I did and successfully keep you alive ... that could cause more trouble and issues than we think. I could alter the time stream significantly."

His eyes wandered to the ground and darted side and side, thoughts racing.

"But I'm holding on to hope because I can't be disappointed again. Who knows what the consequence may be? I didn't listen to the warnings before Krysta told me of the consequences. She's the one who got through to me before I met you and the second time I time-traveled. And—"

I stopped talking, realizing something. Remembering:

"These beings can deliver messages and use this gift without having any visions. Although, they sometimes do ..."

A jolt of shock went through my heart.

"Krysta ... she's ... She's like me."

"What?" Armond was completely puzzled.

"Maybe she's a time traveler, too," I muttered to nobody in particular.

"Hold your horses. You mean talking to me as a ghost is part of this gift you mentioned? Does that mean you can predict the future like her? Or say ... have visions of some kind?"

"I have yet to experience that if I can. It's all in a book; you led me to it. I spent so much time reading the entire thing. But after a while ... I just ..." I shook my head, unable to continue that sentence.

He did not question why I didn't finish speaking. "I led you?"

I nodded. "But that's a whole other story." I didn't want to bother with the details. Saying too much about his visits as a ghost might be a problem. "At the time, I thought it did nothing for me, only caused more disappointment." I thought about it for a moment. If I had not read that book, I wouldn't have worked so hard to get into shape, would not have been given any hope at all, any information. I wouldn't even stand a chance fighting in a cold-blooded war to save the man I love. I smiled a little. "In the end, that book is the reason I'm ready to save you."

That night, it poured. I watched out of the window in our bedroom as each droplet fell against the bubble glass, my mind pondering the days to come. Armond slipped into bed with me, and I sensed his gaze in my direction. "Sometimes, I want to be the rain," I whispered, breaking the quiet of the room.

Armond shifted beside me. "What do you mean?"

I turned my head toward him. "You used to say I'm like a ball of sunshine. But I've been different ever since I left here. Rain moves the world in a way the sun cannot. I think I am more like rain now. I want to be."

"You are more than rain, *cuore*." He brushed the back of his hand over my cheek. "You're stronger than a storm and grace the lands with your beautiful glow."

His words created a fire that burned me from the inside and out and melted my body into a pile of mush. "Is my storm strong enough to bring down the enemy and keep you with me?"

Armond's eyes perused me thoughtfully. "I don't doubt you for a second."

I smiled faintly, sighing heavily. "I made a promise to myself a long time ago that I'd always find my way back to you no matter how difficult. And I always will."

"And I believe you will. We have always found a way whether we were together or not."

I kissed and held him close, and his long breath danced in

a caress against my neck.

"I can understand the feeling you had when you lost me, *cuore*." I froze once he said that, sensing he was down memory lane. "I experienced it when you jumped onto the back of that horrible slaveholder. I had never met someone so utterly fearless in my life. I realized how much it terrified me that a person could take you from me in the snap of my fingers. I was never more afraid. That's when I knew I was in love with you." He pulled away with a sigh, his eyes lighting with desire and admiration. "But the first time I laid eyes on you, I knew I'd want you in my life. The first time I held your hand, I knew that I'd love you. And I knew I loved you the first time we kissed."

I couldn't stop myself from crushing our lips together. It could very well be one of the last times we'd spend a night in each other's arms like this. I held onto him extra tight as the sky darkened and the moon brightened, feeling his steady breathing as he slept soundly. All the while, I lay restless, thinking about what would be faced. My body just wouldn't settle down, full of apprehension and angst. I couldn't help but mull over what would happen if our plan did not work. It was terrifying to know someone I love could die; it horrified me to think that I could close my eyes and he'd just not be there.

I had spent the past week checking to make sure he was breathing as he fell asleep and only slept once he was sleeping. I couldn't breathe at the thought I could actually go through all of it again if I failed to keep him safe.

The overwhelming feeling in my chest intensified to the point I could not just lie there staring at the ceiling any longer. I put my hand on my heart and pressed down in slow circles as I climbed out of bed just in my slip and tossed on a robe from the bathroom.

The courtyard seemed like a soothing place to go to meditate for a while. The scene would surely calm me. As I made it out the front door to the gardens, I was immediately welcomed by the crickets chirping softly. I took a moment to gaze at the obsidian sky. The stars were bright that night, and so was the moon. No clouds were in sight. Just the pitch-black sky, shining stars, and gleaming crescent-shaped moon.

Once I felt satisfied, I finally stepped forward and began walking straight into the maze-like area, then grazed my fingers over the array of flowers that were staring back at me sporadically. I grinned faintly and took in the subtle, pleasant scent they gave off.

I took a seat near the water fountain and breathed in and out deeply, slowly drifting into another state, when a howling, eerie whisper startled me.

"Don't do it."

I flinched and whipped my head around toward the source of the voice. "Who goes there?" I asked.

Something shifted behind me and dashed across the pathway, followed by the sound of tracks shuffling in the grass. I quickly hid around the corner behind a large wall of flowers. The steps came closer, louder, heavier, and I was ready to attack when I heard a shout.

"Lavinia ... Lavinia!"

That was Armond. But that whisper, no, that had not been his voice. Someone was watching.

I could hardly be relieved, but the hopeless panic in his voice shoved that part of my thinking deep into the depths of my mind to be replaced with consternation.

I rounded the corner again to find him twenty feet away, searching disquietly and repeating my name. Sometimes under his breath and other times louder, but his voice caught in his throat every time.

"Armond!" I shouted instinctively, running to him.

He immediately stopped dead in his wobbly tracks and spun around to the sound of my voice so fast I could barely see it happening. A look I could only describe as alleviated flooded his features, and he ran to me as well, scooping me up in his arms as soon as he was within reach. I wasn't entirely sure why he was so upset, but I let him do what he needed.

Armond buried his face in my neck and puffed out a loud and shaky breath. "Oh, *grazie a Dio*, I still have you … thank goodness."

"Armond." I grabbed the back of his head and held him. "What is it? Tell me, please."

"I thought you were gone." His choked-up voice caused an ache in my chest. "I thought I lost you."

"But I'm here, I'm here. I'm still very much here. I'm not going anywhere."

"I thought—I was so worried you had disappeared without meaning to." He pulled back and grasped my face. "Why did you leave the villa? In the middle of the night of all times!"

I shook my head. "It's all right. I'm all right. I just couldn't sleep." I pulled him close again and felt his breathing begin to slow. "I was worried, too. I still am," I confessed, tightening my hold on him. "Do you know how scary it is to think I could only have one more day with you? And if we do have more, if I managed to even keep you alive, thinking you could just walk around the corner and drop dead is terrifying. I've felt this way ever since I arrived. The feeling won't leave."

"I know," he breathed, his frown deepening. "I know."

That was all he could say because, really, what could he do? What could I do?

CHAPTER 16

NO TURNING BACK TIME

1997

The ringing phone woke me from a dead sleep. Reluctantly, I rolled over to climb out of bed and enter the living room, where I kept the telephone in my apartment. "Hello?" I spoke groggily, rubbing my eyes with my free hand.

"Lavinia. It's Luca. Were you sleeping?" His voice was full of shock and confusion.

I checked the time, and the clock read:

7:54 PM.

"Uh, yes?" I screwed my eyes shut in embarrassment.

"Are you sick?"

"Just tired."

"And busy. I never see you anymore."

I sighed through my nose tiredly. "I'm sorry, Luca. I have a lot going on."

"I know," he whispered dejectedly. "You're always training."

My frown turned into a smile, an idea lighting a bulb in my brain. "You still want to take that trip to Italy?"

Mr. Maki had declared me ready. I needed a break anyway.

Luca and I flew to Italy the following week. The second my foot hit Italian soil for the first time in years, a sense of belonging rained on me heavily. I was a brand-new woman, ready for any challenge to step in my way.

Before I would go back through time, I spent those few days with Luca as if I didn't plan to travel into the past again. We rowed a canoe on the Tiber and went sightseeing all over Rome, then took a bus to his hometown, Naples. He showed me the best restaurants he remembered from his childhood and said they were just as delicious. He insisted we visit a few museums and made sure to avoid a particular one until our time together was over.

As we approached the Trevi Fountain with our coins in hand, I closed my eyes and wished a wish that was difficult to believe could come true.

"Are you having fun?" Luca asked, pulling my eyes away from the beautiful sight of the fountain. His grin was brighter than the sun that day.

"The most fun I've had in a while," I admitted, smiling in return softly.

"Me too," he murmured. "What did you wish for?" Luca asked.

"If I tell you, it won't come true."

"I think I already know anyway," he whispered, chuckling as his absent gaze drifted away from me. "I mean, that is why we are here, isn't it?"

"What?" I sputtered. "We're here to spend time together and have a lovely trip."

"That is not all." Luca finally looked at me. "You want to go back."

I swallowed. He was too insightful to hide from. "I would have gone back already if I didn't genuinely want to be here with you."

"So be here with me," he said, grasping my hands. "Stay with me."

I shook my head. "You won't ever know I am gone. That's how it works. But I can't stay forever."

He frowned. "Vin, I like you. A lot. I can't hide my feelings any longer."

"Luca ..." I gulped down the ache in my throat. "I care about you. But I'm still in love with him."

His eyes glazed over. "But it may not work. You can't chase a ghost forever."

"I'm leaving tomorrow," I said firmly, breaking our clasped hands. "My mind is made up."

"And I will be here if you don't."

I shook my head. "I need to go."

"Vin, wait—"

"Don't follow me."

My legs carried me in the direction of the museum, not thinking twice. A tour was in progress, and I quickly snuck my way over to the section where I knew my painting was displayed.

There he was in all his painted glory. Eyes glowing back at me and eliciting a feeling in me as if he was standing feet away in real-time. I rushed toward him. But as I stared into the eyes of my heart, I felt no compulsion. Nothing drew me toward him. Nothing. Even when I placed my hand over his face, hoping for something to happen, nothing did.

I kicked the wall in frustration and began making a ruckus. The guards had to remove me from the premises for touching the painting. I shoved them off me and happily stormed far away from there. From the place I despised for a long time. All that hard work, all that training and research, all of it was for NOTHING.

I'm never going back, I thought.

Before I knew where my legs were taking me, they had walked the entire way to an open field. A sign came into view not a minute later, reading:

Parco della Melrose.

"Melrose Park?" I murmured in shock.

"*Si*," a woman replied suddenly. "It was founded in 1897. Named after the royal family with the surname Melrossi. The estate where the Melrossis lived was built in 1802 and stands in Verona. The reason for picking Melrose is unclear, but as you can see, that's what it says."

"That is certainly …" Wonderful to hear. "Interesting to know. Thank you."

"Are you a tourist?" she asked. "Would you like to hear more?"

"I'm more than a tourist," I told her, and she furrowed her brows. "Yes, I'd love to hear everything." My eyes roamed over the tree. "It's still here," I whispered in awe. "After all these years."

"So, you've heard about this place?" she assumed.

I gave her a stiff head shake. "No, I've … just been here before. Enough times to know the tree has existed for a long time."

"Yes, it's been around for over two hundred years. Do you know the history of this tree? The story behind why it was not cut down?"

"There's a story?"

She smiled, seeming eager to tell someone unaware of it. "This tree was painted around 1848 before the Italian Independence Wars broke out."

"It was 1847," I corrected her, taking a step toward her, "when the painting *Non Vedo L'ora* was created."

"Oh, yes, you know your art history. Well, the man—"

"And let me guess … You're about to tell me that the man in the painting leaned against this very tree? The one with the initials L and A carved in the center of the bark, which leaves everyone to believe that this man in the famous painting is the one who signed his name in the bottom right corner, Armond

Cornelious Dante Alessandro."

"Erm—not exactly ... Yes, the man in the painting leans against the tree. But I was going to say that once the painting was released, that's when it became so well known. Eventually, the tree was so recognizable that they made this place a famous landmark, naming it *Parco della Melrose*."

"What?" My mind went wild at the news. "It was released. When?"

"1848, I believe."

"Why?"

She shook her head. "Well, I don't know. Why does any work get released? It was found on a train."

A train!

My thoughts were frantic. I didn't answer. I never released it ... so who did?

"You know, I heard he fought in the war and disappeared, along with his wife. I think that is a strange coincidence."

"Disappeared?" I squinted my eyes at her. The more this lady talked, the more mind-boggling her information became by the minute.

"Yes, they both disappeared. Nobody knows where they went. That man knew the Melrossis, so there's a lot that can be assumed. But you are right. The A in the tree leaves skeptics to believe he wrote his name to protect the artist since the first name written is Armond."

"Maybe so, but I think the artist wanted him to. Then he died in the war, and everyone was devastated, including his wife, who ran and was never the same."

She looked taken aback. "That sounds ... depressing."

"Oh, it was," I said bitterly, then cleared my throat. "It was for them, I'm sure."

The lady stared at me in a way that made me feel crazy. "Hmm," she hummed.

"What makes you think it's a coincidence?"

"I think it is weird they both disappeared before the painting was released."

"But if Armond died, why would that be weird?"

"What if he didn't die? If he did, who else knew about it? Why would the artist not have released it sooner? Either way, it is strange that he signed the painting and the artist didn't. If the artist wanted him to sign it, they must have been close, or ..." She paused, a wide-eyed look coming over her. "Or the artist was a woman."

"His wife," I said without wanting to say it. "Or the artist became his wife. So, it could have been both."

"Huh ... yeah," she muttered, rubbing her palms down her pants. "Did we just figure that out?"

"We can't be sure," I told her. "So, I'd be careful who you share that with."

"Well, I'm just a tourist who loves history. I don't have the ability to prove anything. That can't be the truth anyway."

"It very well could be," I whispered, smiling faintly. "Thanks for the info. Have a nice day."

"Oh, you're welcome. You too!"

My thoughts were scattered and in disarray. What had I just been told? What did it mean?

Little did I know I would learn everything. Just not anytime soon.

Walking over to the tree, I ran my fingers over the carved bark and sighed. "I really thought I'd see you again."

I wanted to do more things alone before I looked for Luca. I visited Armond's grave first and let my tears fall unabashedly, then visited the places Armond had taken me. I stopped by the waterfall and closed my eyes to listen to the water gush rapidly, calming my soul. When I stepped forward, I felt something hard beneath my shoe. Lifting my foot away, a misshapen orange red stone was revealed. I bent down to pick it up, inspecting it closely. It was shiny in appearance and smooth in my fingers. Translucent white eyes randomly marked the stone. I stuffed it into my pocket to research later.

Luca was waiting in our suite. He immediately stood at the entrance, coming to my side. "Did you go through?"

I frowned, and the question instantly made me lose it. Tears brimmed my eyes before they fell one by one, soaking Luca's shirt as he pulled me into his embrace.

CHAPTER 17

STOPPING IT ALL

1848

I remember what Mr. Maki had told me once, and his words would apply to the next days of my life in more than a figurative way:

"*To fight any battle, you must fight as if you are already dead.*"

I don't know who had said it first, but I couldn't spend time wondering. I had bigger things to think about at the time. I just knew what it meant; I needed to fight without the conscious thought of defeat. I had to outsmart the enemy. It was essential to win against fate, or we'd be ruined.

I did not know what would come. What my eyes would want to unsee. What countless feelings I'd be forced to withhold. All for war. The meaning of war was different from experiencing the true battle firsthand. I had witnessed the bloodied anguish before, but I witnessed absolute madness for the first time with my first lunge for the enemy on the battlefield. The following screams would never be unheard, and the bloodshed could never be erased from memory. War is like walking along some remote trail and stumbling across more than one bear.

A bear's first instinct is to kill; we have no choice but to fight back or make an attempt and die trying. The moment I began running toward my enemies, my decision to fight for a life felt like deciding to die.

Knowing who would try to take Armond's life created my worst and best moment. An overwhelming and blinding rage came over me, and soon enough, they were beyond the tip of my sword.

I would forever be different.

Hours earlier, I'd had no idea what I was in for. I had stepped off the carriage early in the morning, arriving in Lombardy Venetia. The place I swore I'd never visit again. I knew I'd be a changed woman once I left, but not how much. I disguised myself as a man under the name Luciano Ricci in honor of Luca. I had to wear Armond's male attire for the time being, until I walked away from there, if I even did. I didn't know what we would face. I just held on to the hope we would all survive.

"When we get to camp," Armond had begun to say, holding my hand tightly in the carriage since we wouldn't be able to show any affection out in the open, "I want you to keep to yourself; please do not say too much."

"I know, Armond. Thanks for the reminder, but I think I'm going to want to be quiet. Strange men I don't know aren't always comforting, especially when they are unaware that I'm a woman."

"It's better they don't know."

"It might not be. But either way, I'm capable of helping myself."

Armond's big sigh was heard. "You are more than capable. It is a bit frightening."

I laughed at him, and then I was welcomed by the noisy city of Novara. A variety of languages sparked my eardrums. I didn't understand anything but the Italian spoken.

I hadn't stuttered once when anyone asked for my name,

not even as we were granted access. We sat by a fire, and I reached into my pocket for that red-orange carnelian stone. The stone of courage. I would need courage. I took it everywhere with me once I found it. Apparently, the stone had been carried into battle by the ancient Greeks and Romans. I wanted to do the same.

An explosion pulled me from my mind.

"It's starting," Armond whispered flatly. "We must go."

He asked me to follow him and took us elsewhere to gear up. I felt many eyes on me that I knew were because I was tiny for a man. But when I glimpsed myself in the mirror that day disguised as a knight, I suddenly really felt like the true warrior Mr. Maki had made me. I didn't know how different I'd be after this, but I hoped at least that would not change.

The whole "march into battle" bit was terrifying. I entered the field on a horse, keeping my hands tight on the reins. Although Patches was my best horse, I could not have brought him along. I didn't want him to experience a place like this anyway, and he'd most likely die.

Armond never left my side. He remained there the entire time up until the point we stopped to face our enemies. The land seemed taken up by Austrian soldiers as familiar endless lines of men soon appeared over the hill. When I glanced over at Bartoli, he seemed indifferent, but I was internally screaming.

I closed my eyes, took a long breath, then opened them again. I turned to Armond and swallowed thickly, holding back the surfacing memories of his death, and choked on a gasp as I tried to speak. "I'm not going to stop until I know you're safe."

He didn't say a word, only discreetly grasped my hand for a short moment to give it a squeeze, and much too soon, it was gone. There was that moment of pause, a slow moment of near silence before the slaughter ... then the shots went off.

Italians and Austrians immediately charged toward each other, most yelling battle cries at the top of their lungs.

The first man who came toward me attacked me with a

bayonet. I blocked him with my sword, then quickly slid the bayonet away and kicked him backward, resulting in a blow to his abdomen. It shocked me at first, hurting someone like that with the intention of killing them. But I couldn't take the time to even think, as twice as many rifles were aimed at me. I kneeled and held up my shield for dear life as bullets headed my way. I pulled out my pistol and shot three men, reloading as quickly as I could each time. Then, instantly, I had to turn around before someone attempted to butcher my legs as if I were a chicken. I rolled over, stopped his sword with mine, and fired my gun as it was pressed to his chest. His body collapsed onto me; a second later, he was thrown off me and Armond was pulling me to my feet.

There was no time to speak a word to each other. I had to duck as a sword swung over my head. I butted into the man instead and knocked him to the ground, then raised my own sword, and it met with his chest. I gasped at the deafening crunch and the blood splattering on my concealed face. My hands shook slightly, but I forced them to stop, blocking out my emotions, and kept moving. I tried to keep track of Armond, but I lost him often.

A man dealt a blow to my helmet with his sword, and I stumbled before attempting to fight him off. I had been so focused on him that I hadn't seen the man behind me. Out of nowhere, Bartoli appeared and ended both of the men's lives in seconds. He had actually jumped in to help me. I nodded at him silently, showing my gratitude. He nodded back firmly.

Time went slow as gunfire whistled past me and cannonballs took out fifty men at once. Most times, the noise around me was muffled, seeming as if I was underwater. The rare times it was deadly quiet, my hearing was so sensitive that a second hand on a watch sounded like lightning. I instinctively huddled in a small ball as the ground trembled violently beneath me from another blast. Screams and yells sounded in the air. Ones of desperation and pain. All Italian soldiers.

"Help!" someone wailed, a cry that stood out from all the others.

I lay there cradling myself, torn inside.

I should not help. No, I shouldn't, I tried to convince myself. *I can't interfere too much.*

"Please! Help!" he wallowed louder in pain.

I screwed my eyes shut, trying to block it out. But I knew the sound of that cry would forever be instilled in my head. I army-crawled up the slight hill to get a closer look … a closer look wouldn't hurt. If he was Austrian, he was the enemy. If he was Italian …

Oh no … he was definitely Italian.

Spotting the man downhill, he lay in the fetal position, hands pressed to his abdomen. Beads of sweat marked his tan and slightly ashen face. Pure agony riddled his features, with blood and mud splattered all over him and his face. He seemed to be a fairly young man. He couldn't watch this mayhem without succumbing to madness and the enemy. He was poorly trained, I assumed, like most of the Italians fighting in this war for their own land. His eyes had seen enough. Alas, too much.

Unfortunately, so had I.

Heavy horse hooves pulled my attention away from him. An Austrian soldier charged ahead on horseback, aiming his pistol. I stiffened and crouched low, prowling like a lion. As he approached closer, I became certain he meant to trample the injured Italian. The soldier's face twisted in annoyance, more and more, the louder the young man pleaded for help, ready to slaughter.

"Hey, no!" I screeched, staying low. His head turned for a moment, but I wasn't in his line of sight. Intentionally. Pistol already in hand, I closed my right eye, finger hovering over the trigger as I aimed. I breathed in deeply and released.

Bam! Headshot. He was down.

I sighed sharply and ran in a crouch to the man's side.

Blood poured out of him. He was not looking my way. I do not think he even knew of my presence. All he felt was pain.

"Young man," I said, deepening my voice. I rested my hand gently on his arm. He attempted to shuffle backward. "It's okay; it's okay. I'm not here to hurt you."

His fearful eyes connected to me, brimming with tears. "My leg. My leg. Am I going to lose my leg?" he asked.

I swallowed and let my eyes fall to his lower limbs. His leg was lacerated as well.

"I can't promise that. I can promise you I have hope that you'll keep it."

He nodded firmly, shaking.

I raised my chin. "Your belt. Can I use it?"

He nodded, gasping and groaning, "Please. Just help me."

"I'll do what I can."

Suddenly, loud gunfire filled my eardrums; instinctively, I shielded him with my body. Bullets ricocheted off the ground, one bouncing off my helmet. I quickly undid his belt and slipped it out from underneath him, applying it around his leg tightly. He groaned. The blood ceased to gush.

"Okay. Let's get you away from here."

The tent wasn't too far from where I stood, but not very close. I guided him up and shifted his weight onto me, but he couldn't walk very fast.

"*Luciano*, what are you doing?"

I groaned at the name and immediately knew who was speaking. I pinned my eyes on Armond and narrowed them even though he couldn't see my expression. "He needs help!"

He watched me for a moment, defending off a few crazed men effortlessly. Deep in thought. His head shook. "I'll watch your back."

When we reached the tent, I was exhausted. The man was heavy, but I had made it. His bloody hand grabbed my arm, shaking as he did, and his deep voice gave me chills as he told me, "Thank—thank you." I ignored the cold feeling I had as a doctor took him away. He kept staring until he could not see me anymore. I pushed out the perturbed thoughts that tried to force their way inside my mind and threw myself back into battle. The doctor did not look optimistic. I hoped he was okay, but more than anything, I hoped Armond would survive the next hour.

"It's too dangerous!" Armond yelled at me as shots were going off nonstop. "Go to your safe spot and save yourself!"

"I'm not leaving your side!" The deafening sounds caused me to jump.

"I handled it this far fine before. Go!"

I didn't want to listen to him, but he was partly right. If I didn't let him take the path he took to his death, I could ruin our whole plan. Unfortunately, I had already interfered. I just hoped not too much.

I nodded and grabbed his arm, staring at his eyes under the rim of his helmet. "Stay alive, please."

"I'll do my best. Now go."

I fought my way through the woods we scouted out beforehand. I kept my guard up, finding a hideout in a large dip in the ground, and covered myself in mud and whatever else was lying there. I struggled to find Armond again, but once I did, I watched him fight someone off. I didn't doubt it was him by the way he moved.

Many minutes later, my eyes widened when a cannon went off. I instinctively ducked and laid low, feeling the ground shake and groan as the cannonball made its fall. I popped my head back up to look for Armond, cringing at every loud sound, and realized he was nowhere in sight.

I lost him.

No, no. No, no—no ... I just about had a heart attack from being so petrified.

"Armond!" I called through the fog instinctively.

Nothing.

"Armond!"

Still nothing.

I started running. I ran and ran over the grass and low hills. The incoming cannons seemed to be increasing in intensity and range; rounds were beginning to fall in the field around me.

He was still nowhere to be found.

Boom! to my left and *boom!* to my right. But I just kept running like hell. Finally, I spotted him on his horse, fighting someone on horseback as well.

Winded, I was about twenty yards from him when a round dropped to my left, far too close for comfort. The harshness of all the weaponry cut and whizzed through the air. The force of it knocked me over, and my body fell to the ground. Cursing under my breath, I got to my feet and ran again.

"Giovanni!" I heard Armond yell.

I remembered Armond saying last time that there had been an attack before he had fallen off his horse, and that made me run faster.

This was it. His killer was. This was …

As I got closer, my mind went blank, and I saw complete and utter red. *He*, the cold-blooded murderer, was someone I never thought I'd see again.

He must have been disguised before, because, at that moment, he was an Austrian soldier, no ordinary man. I watched Matvei curl his lip in irritation. He was probably spying on us the whole time. Matvei and another soldier had been going for Giovanni, but when he realized Armond was after them, Matvei changed his course of action.

But Armond was distracted by his brother; he did not see the cruel smirk on Matvei's face as he was about to strike him. I ran like lightning. As I reached them, a rage I never knew I had inside overcome me. I reached behind me for my bow and an arrow, which I nocked, and then I drew the bow, aiming it at that evil man's chest. My fingers let loose, and the arrow seemed to corkscrew through the air faster than the speed of light. There was a moment when a smile tugged on my lips as I watched the sharp tip find its place directly in the center of his chest, right where I wanted it. He clutched himself and took the hard blow, but did not crumble just yet.

I wanted to look him in the eye, wanted him to know who he messed with. I didn't care what that made me. I didn't care if that meant I wanted revenge, and it wasn't the answer. I was blinded by the emotion. All I saw was red. I was a falcon ready to destroy its prey, a primal instinct I couldn't deny.

I grabbed the hilt of my knife tightly in my hand, and I pulled my arm back before sending the knife overhand, flying ahead of me, straight for Matvei's chest again. Everything seemed to slow down for me and, at the same time, happened so fast. I witnessed the pointy knife spiral through the air after my throw, so powerful that once the knife pierced his chest, the force tossed him back over his horse.

I watched him drop to the blood-filled ground, then I tumbled out of the way. I rolled to a graceful stop, looking up to see an angry and injured Matvei. At some point, he had pulled out the knife and broken off the arrow shaft, leaving blood everywhere. Stupid of him, but I'd use that to my advantage. He'd grow weak and die much faster now. He struggled to stand and could barely swing his sword toward my head. I quickly rolled to my back and boosted myself to my feet. Our swords soon met in a cross, so I kicked my foot out and knocked him to the ground. I took that as my chance to stand above him, aligning the sharp edge of my sword across his throat. But he managed to flip us and send a blow to my midsection. I definitely felt the harsh blow, but barely. When he grabbed a hold of me and began slamming my head into the ground, I was momentarily blinded by the pain, and my body gave out. Blackness threatened to pull me under, but Mr. Maki's words rang in my head.

"When enemy think you are down, you will go on pretending you are. Attack where he unprepared; move when he least

expect you. That when you strike."

That evil man's cackle brought me out of the darkness. He may have thought I was weak and that he had won, but I had the upper hand. A blinding rage overtook my senses, replacing the physical agony. Total willpower suddenly surged through me.

I was quick to counteract his next attempt to hurt me, kicking him between the legs and skillfully robbing him of his sword, unfortunately losing mine as well. He resumed his place on his back, and I drew my other dagger, bringing it downward, but he caught the hilt.

He let out a condescending cackle. "You can't kill me, small boy!"

I smirked, fighting against him as the knife shook in our hands. "This is no boy killing a man who is already dead in my eyes …"

He was speechless for a moment, then opened his mouth, most likely about to utter his bafflement.

"This is Lavinia Melrose. You tried to kill *my* husband. I want you to remember my name as I send you to hell." I only had time to see the widening of his eyes before I, with all of my strength, pushed the dagger down and plunged it deep into his chest. His body stiffened, and blood shot out of his mouth, splattering onto me. The blood gurgled in his throat as he tried to get another word out, but I never would have been able to decipher what he said.

Something came over me, a part of me wanting to make sure he was dead. So, I pulled out my pistol and shot him once in the head.

I stayed there a moment too long, trying to process what I had just done. Not long enough for me to believe it was real. I scrambled to my feet too fast and stumbled, staring in shock at Armond's killer, who lay lifeless. Only, I had stumbled into someone without knowing it, and an arm wrapped around my neck. I instinctively turned my head so the chokehold wouldn't damage my windpipe, then grabbed their forearm with both hands to flip them over my shoulder, crushing them with my body afterward. I searched for my pistol, which had dropped on the ground, and quickly launched for it before my opponent did. I reloaded and clicked it in place, ready to shoot, but ...

"Lavinia!"

I changed focus to my left at Armond's call, and through all the smoke and the chaos, I saw him glowing like a ray of hope. He remained untouched on his horse while fighting someone off. When our eyes met, he threw me a proud look full of complete awe. I had smothered the fire, and ashes fell behind in my path, unable to stop me. Distracted, the pistol was knocked out of my hand, but I was too quick for them and elbowed the man in the face, knocking him out. I smiled toward Armond proudly and gave a laugh in disbelief, holding our shared gaze, and began to run toward him.

I did it. I had saved him. He would be alive to tell the tale. We would be free to live on together ...

Those were my last thoughts before cannonballs sailed in and landed right in front of me.

Loud booms were the last thing I heard before all I remember seeing was a blinding orange and white flash. I remember being up in the air. I felt very calm and relaxed at that moment, almost as if I were lying on a cloud. I felt ... peaceful.

Have I died? I wondered. *Was everything I did for nothing?*

I came back down to earth, hard and with a force of gravity I couldn't fathom. It was the sort of blow that knocked the wind right out of me. I had stopped breathing completely, slipping unconscious from the impact. I couldn't have known how long exactly I was out for, but it couldn't have been longer than minutes.

Eventually, my eyes fluttered open, a shrill, persistent ringing in my ears. I lay there on my back, staring into a darkening sky and gray clouds of smoke. At first, it was all a haze. I couldn't even remember where I was or what I had been doing. But I could still feel the ground trembling and distantly hear blasts and gun fires ... which suddenly made it all come back to me in a rush.

The cannonballs must've landed mere feet away ...

Was I ... dead?

Was I alive?

Was I supposed to be dead?

How could I be alive? I thought to myself.

For a minute or so, as I lay there, I really thought I might be dead until I gingerly and groggily sat up, experiencing a dizzy spell. And pain. Pain I shouldn't feel in the afterlife. There shouldn't be so much pain otherwise. Everything was spinning around me, and my head and ears were ringing like bells. A continuous ringing that wouldn't let up.

The bitter taste of gunpowder laid heavy on my tongue and in my throat. My neck was stiff and sore, but my head hurt the most. My hand went to touch it, and I groaned as the ache pounded even more, my helmet clearly missing. Slowly and painfully, I glanced down at myself. I was ... fine. Still had legs. Still had ... everything. The only thing I had to worry about was my head. I was probably concussed.

My eyes caught something on the ground near me, to my right, and looked down. Things, rather. Multiple bodies lay there, stone dead; I knew right away. They'd been traumatically eviscerated, bodies slit open like animals. Their entire stomachs and a good part of their lower intestines and colons lay in a slick, sodden, stinking heap on the ground beside them. They were all still and as white as marble.

I'd never forget the smell of the burning flesh. I'd certainly seen my share of blood, but something about seeing that and smelling the stench and splay of guts really made me sick.

But more importantly, there was Armond.

"Armond!" I attempted to yell, but I couldn't raise my voice without my head screaming back.

I tried to stand up. In three attempts, I fell down all three times. Everything was still revolving around me. My eyeballs wouldn't stop jumping, my ears still rang so loud, and my balance was almost nonexistent.

Finally, I was able to get to my feet and stay on them. I could only stand there, nearly deaf and dazed, with those bells and a high-pitched whistling in my ears, searching for Armond.

For a moment, I thought he was dead. But that was only a moment until an indistinct call sounded so faintly it seemed far away. I froze, grateful to not be completely deaf … and, most of all, from shock.

That was *his* voice.

Again. "Lavinia!"

I could barely even hear or understand the rest that was said … My brain was still a bit like scrambled eggs. I just saw him run to me.

"Lavinia?" Something else was said after my name again. His mouth was moving, but I couldn't hear a thing.

"Armond," I gasped out, wrapping my arms around him and just hung on to him for dear life, shaking severely. He was alive. He was okay.

I had saved him.

He grabbed me by the shoulders, shook me a little, and yelled right in my face, "Are you all right, Lavinia?"

That got through. I hardly heard him and had to read his lips.

"Yes … well, I'm alive," I gasped unsteadily. I couldn't even hear my own voice. It was like my ears were stuffed with corks.

He began rapidly patting me down, lifting my arms, and turning me this way and that, trying to find a wound on me.

Nothing. Not even a scratch.

"It—it was so … weird," I told him haltingly. "All of the … it must have … blown out all around me. It killed them." I pointed to the bodies on the ground. "But … none of it even touched me."

"Christ, *cuore!*" he shouted at me, hugging me close to

him. "Thank goodness you're still with me!"

I didn't answer. I couldn't really; all I knew was I really wasn't destined to die that day and Armond was supposed to be dead in a few hours. And yet ... he stood there holding me close on a blood-soaked battlefield. Still alive and well. As far as I knew, at least.

But was I really okay?

An exploding cannonball suddenly went off, and Armond threw us to the ground with me under him, shielding me with his body. The ground jumped as we were made a point to cover our ears.

Armond glanced around. "You should hide yourself." He spoke loudly enough for me to hear. "I don't want anyone to see you."

"See that I'm a woman?" I asked, feeling like Mulan.

He nodded with a sigh. I wasn't sure why I was out of breath, but I was. I looked up into his beautiful eyes and saw both relief and fear.

"You did it," he whispered, more than proud.

"I did," I muttered in shock.

I really had saved him. He had gotten distracted by Giovanni and hadn't been paying attention, and Matvei had knocked him off his horse. But instead, Matvei's death was on my hands. I had definitely changed the past into a new future. I just wasn't sure what kind of future awaited me.

My eyes widened. A flash of what I'd done played before my eyes.

I had killed people. I had killed Armond's killer.

I looked around and spotted his crumpled body not too far from us. It was a more disturbing sight than I thought possible.

"It's all right, Lavinia." His voice sounded so muffled.

I gulped. "I killed him. I have killed."

Armond didn't reply, only waited for more of a reaction, but there was none.

I had killed for *him*. There was no stopping me when it came to that. If there was a good enough reason to kill, it had to be for love. To protect not only him but myself. For this ugly war my family had to endure.

I diverted the subject with a question. "Where's Giovanni?"

"He was injured in the blast, like you said. That still happened. Armani and others took him back to the tent for help. I stayed with you. I thought …"

My one hand held the side of his face. "I probably have a concussion, but I'll be fine. And your brother's going to be fine, too," I reassured him. My other hand found its way to the little rare rock in my pocket as I said it, still magically there through everything. That had to count for something.

Armond nodded firmly and took me in his arms. We didn't stay much longer. Armond helped me to my feet, but my legs gave way as a sharp pain stabbed me in the back of my head. A sudden strong ache had returned and overtook the whole front of my forehead. I stumbled forward, and Armond caught me in his arms.

"Lavinia! What's happening?" he asked in a panic. I couldn't answer. There was no way. I stumbled into his arms, and the next thing I knew, he was carrying me. "Let's get you to safety …"

As I lay limply in *his* strong arms, looking up at the dull sky and murky air, unable to move and content with what I had done, the indistinct noise and world around me began to fade completely. I smiled and closed my eyes. I had finally found peace in the storm that raged inside me for so long. I rescued him; I just had to save myself.

CHAPTER 18

HOPE

1848

High-pitched ringing in my ears roused me awake. For a second, I believed I was deaf until the shrill sound dulled somewhat into loud whispers. The ache in my head made its presence known with a harsh pounding. I groaned and forced my heavy eyelids to lift open, complete darkness overwhelming my vision. My eyes struggled to dart around and take in my surroundings. I could see nothing but two dark outlines of figures swallowed in the night, speaking hurriedly back and forth.

"Armond, where are—" I croaked from lack of speech. "Where am I?" I tried again.

"Lavinia," he whispered in shock, quickly coming to my side. "Oh, good gracious. You're awake."

"I ..." A wave of nausea came suddenly like a tsunami, and there was no holding it back. My vision doubled, and I pitched forward to empty the little that was in my stomach onto the ground. Armond rubbed circles on my back as I dry-heaved for a few seconds, and then he eased me down onto the stiff bed again. A doctor stood over me with a rag to dab my chin. I turned my head away and groaned.

"Careful," Armond told me gently, rubbing my temple with his thumb. "You should eat something."

"Please ... no."

"Give it time. The nausea will pass," the doctor said. "Looks like you hit your head hard."

His voice seemed to echo, and my eyes felt droopy again. I was falling down the dark tunnel of unconsciousness once more.

"Rest now, *cuore*."

Complete blackness acquainted me not much longer.

A man pinned me on the ground with his hands around my neck. I gasped for air but wiggled a hand down to the gun at my waist. I aimed and pulled the trigger. Another man appeared, this one pacing back and forth frantically, his face bright red as a tomato. We both stood before my painting, and I stepped forward to touch it.

My body jolted awake, drenched in sweat and racked with shakes. I thought I had healed from my nightmares, but now I was plagued with more. The fact I had killed so many people was haunting me. The fact I didn't regret killing Matvei in cold blood made me feel out of sorts, like I didn't recognize myself.

For so long, I had wished whoever took Armond from me was dead until, one day, I had learned to forgive them and myself. I had always known that seeing that person no longer alive would not help my pain, and still, I had wished for it. As I looked at Armond sleeping soundly beside me with a small smile and color in his cheeks, I understood. Really, all killing Matvei did was assure me he was gone and couldn't do any harm again. Someday, someone or something would put Armond in a grave for all of eternity. All I had bought us was time, more time, which was fine with me. That was all I had asked for. More time. One last chance to make a difference. And I did ... almost losing my life trying, but I couldn't find in me to care. He was alive; that was what mattered.

A memory of me being thrown up in the air by the blast flashed before my eyes. I spent a lot of time pondering how I even survived. I'd never know or understand why my life wasn't taken the minute I hit the ground so hard, why I wasn't blown to pieces. Sometimes, I began to think if I hadn't been in that exact time and place just at that moment ... I would have been dead.

The only explanation my mind could conjure was that I was meant to save him, and life was not done with me. I had a greater purpose to fulfill.

"How are you feeling?" Giovanni asked from beside me, startling me as I carefully turned on my side. I hadn't realized he was awake. Giovanni was recovering as he did before, and I kept sleeping on and off, my ears still ringing continually. Armond would not leave our sides, other than the obvious necessities; he had told me he wouldn't until I was fully recuperated.

I could tell it was the middle of the night by how dark it was. Giovanni and I kept each other company, especially when we were the only two awake. Armond was asleep in a chair next to me, so I couldn't be entertained by his annoying jokes and our banter.

"Still worn out. No more nausea. How are you doing?"

"My wound still hurts. The pain woke me up a little while ago. Although it is slowly becoming less painful. I'm pleasantly surprised at how well the nurse did with the dressing. I'm grateful."

I held in my giggle, not understanding why I found his surprise funny. "I am, too." I switched my center of attention to the overhead inside of the tent.

"Hmm ..." he hummed, and I heard him groan as he shifted his position. Thirty seconds must have gone by before he whispered, "Lavinia ..." to catch my attention. I turned my head to focus on his serious expression in the darkness. "And I am also forever grateful to you. Without you, my brother would not be sleeping soundly at the moment. He'd be asleep forever."

I gulped, probably loud enough for him to hear. I nodded firmly. "Let's just hope it stays this way," I murmured, glancing at the peaceful look on Armond's face. "Let's hope air does remain in his lungs and that he'll go on breathing and living as the beautiful person he is."

"I don't have much doubt, oddly enough. We do only have our faith to rely on now."

"Yes ..." I paused to think. "You believe I actually made a difference?"

"I do, in fact." He didn't hesitate with his answer. "I don't believe you were brought here again to save the day, just to have your heart broken once more because it was all for nothing."

I quietly pondered that. I didn't really know what I could say back. Giovanni's logic made sense. My heart wanted him to be right, but my mind ran wild ... wild enough to wonder if saving Armond could be a dreadful thing for the future. Not mine, but the world.

I remembered exactly what *The Gift and the Curse* said about giving life to a time traveler's other half. And Krysta's warning of the consequences of interfering made me think it was possible. I only didn't know how profound a repercussion of messing with life and death might be.

But I held on to the faith that I could figure a way out no matter the difficulties I faced. I was a rare star plucked from the dark universe, unknowingly given a bright light, dimmed and held dormant in the blazing land called Earth. It was time to shine it again to find the end of the unlit tunnel.

I must have fallen back to sleep because I was woken by a feather-light touch to my forehead. I didn't recall something like that waking me up so fast before.

I flinched slightly, but the hazy image of a curly head appeared as I opened my eyes, recognizing who it was earlier than the blur could go into focus.

"How do you feel?" Armond asked in a murmur. "You were beginning to worry me a little, sleeping past twelve like you did."

"Oh …" I tried to sit up, but my head protested with another dizzy spell. "Ah, I didn't realize. I'm fine; I just need rest."

"Yes, you have a concussion. You told me. The nurse explained, but I wanted to hear more from you."

Something kind of clicked for me, a conversation I vaguely remember having about concussions with his ghost.

"Yeah—I …" I laughed. "I do."

"What is amusing about that?"

"Oh, nothing." I brushed him off. "Just a memory."

"Hmm." He raised a questioning brow but ignored me, probably assuming I was still in a confused state. "Here. Have an apple. I found apple trees this morning when I snuck out."

"Armond! You snuck out alone without me?"

"You can't strain yourself; of course I went without you, but no, not alone. Armani came along."

I took the apple with a scowl. "You're lucky I love you," I said quietly enough for no one to hear.

"You wouldn't be so concerned if you didn't."

I rolled my eyes and shook my head gently, biting into the apple and ignoring him.

He began laughing at my reaction. "*Ti amo, cuore,*" he murmured. "Always."

And the melting of my heart had begun again.

Our silence didn't last very long. Armond suddenly grasped my free hand, and I glanced at them intertwined. "Lavinia …"

He was careful to keep his voice down. "I never got the chance to really thank you."

My eyes darted to his wide and earnest ones. "You don't have to thank me, Armond. You'd do the same for me."

"I would, without a doubt ..." He visibly swallowed. "But you are taking the brunt of it now."

"A concussion heals quickly. As long as I am careful, it isn't a big deal. I don't see any reason to worry too much."

"I wasn't just worried," he whispered fervently. "I was scared witless that you were dying instead of me."

"I know. I'm sorry."

I sighed before taking another bite of my apple. I chewed slowly as I thought to myself. I understood that feeling; of course I did. He had died in my arms, after all. I forced those painful memories away, though.

"Well, I should thank you ... for all you have done and the past week. For the record, I was more than afraid, too. This whole time. I was lost when I knew you weren't coming back. Instead, I came back to you, and here you are. But I wouldn't have been able to do it without your help, anyone's help for that matter."

He started to shake his head and speak, but I stopped him.

"No, it's true ..." I whispered, swallowing. I felt around my pocket for the small rock. "I want to give you something." I pulled the red-orange rock and held it between my fingers to show him. "You'll never guess where I found this." I laughed to myself, almost shedding a tear. "It was sitting in our spot by the waterfall when I first visited Italy again, desperate to go back to you. I always kept it in my purse, and I held onto it almost all the way through battle. It's a carnelian ... the bloodstone. Warriors used to wear it in battle for courage. That's what made me keep it on me."

I grabbed Armond's hand and flattened out his palm, placing it there and closing his fist around the amber glow. "I want you to have it."

"Lavinia, this is your rock. Your lucky rock. Don't give it away."

"I'm not giving it away to just anybody. I'm giving it to you, my salvation. I like to think of this rock as our talisman, as our souvenir. I want you to be protected."

I opened his hand and stared at the colors intently. "It's beautiful ... the color is almost like your eyes." Then he looked up at me. "I'll keep it, but it's ours. Not mine."

I nodded and smiled, kissing his knuckles gently.

"La—" Someone's throat cleared. I looked up to see Bartoli standing by the entrance of the tent. He coughed in a very odd and dramatic way. "Excuse me. Sir Luciano? Am I interrupting?"

"Maybe." I deepened my voice with a discreet raised brow. "Yes, Sir Bartoli?"

Bartoli gave us a creepy smile that I imagined was supposed to be pleasant. "How would you like to go home?"

I watched the road outside the tiny window in the carriage, lounging back on the red broad silk and velvet plush as we passed through a village. The area was quaint and upbeat, with small stone houses, stores, and food markets. We had stopped to pick up a few items on the way back, and the warm bread I bit into was one of the things. Delicious.

As I reveled in the taste and perfect crusty crunch on top, my eyes suddenly caught on a familiar figure. A man. A woman was at his side. They walked unhurriedly, hand in hand. He wore a flat cap, and I glimpsed dark curls protruding from his nape.

"Stop ... stop the carriage!" I demanded, all at once breathless, almost too breathless, to pull the whistle out of the pouch and blow it to signal the coachman. Armond's head snapped in my direction, confusion etching his features. "I need to get out, please!"

The coach halted, the two passing figures' legs taking them farther and farther away by the second. I had to move quickly.

"What's wrong, *cuore?*" Armond asked in concern, then added before I could answer, "Wait. This isn't like the last time you ran out of the carriage, is it?"

"No, I ..." I couldn't get into depth with my explanation yet; there was no time for that. "Hold on, I need ... I need to catch him before it's too late."

"Catch? *Whom?*" Armond asked as he raised a brow, more perplexed than a few moments ago.

"I'll explain later!" I assured him hurriedly as my hands moved to work faster than him.

The driver opened the door just in time for me to jump out before he could pull down the retractable steps. I landed on two feet gracefully, then took off in a sprint. I ran so fast my legs couldn't even keep up.

They were about to turn around the corner, and the man must have heard me coming because his hand gripped the woman more tightly, and he tugged her along faster.

"Hey, wait!" I shouted.

The man's head turned slightly, then he protectively brought the woman behind him and faced me. She peeked over his shoulder, dark eyes full of confusion, not an ounce of fear. He lifted his chin, and his face was finally revealed under the front of his hat, confirming my suspicions to be true. He visibly froze in place.

"Lavinia ..." he gasped, his tanned skin looked ashen, eyes frantically taking me in.

I swallowed, my own eyes wide, approaching him slowly and keeping my voice soft when I spoke. "It really is you."

CHAPTER 19

THE SMELL OF HOME

1848

Luca's grip went limp in the pretty young woman's hand, and then, a split second later, his arms embraced me tightly. My arms reciprocated with the same amount of disbelief and joy. I hadn't seen him in what felt like so long.

Unscrewing my eyes shut, I instantly saw the girl's features contorted with incredulity. Her caramel skin glowed in the sun, and her long, wavy dark hair cascaded past her hips.

"Oh ... I—uh ..." I stuttered. I pulled away and shook my head. Luca turned and his face became red as a tomato. "I am sorry. I ...didn't introduce myself; how rude of me. I'm Lavinia." I elbowed Luca's side. "Luca, tell me, who is this beautiful young woman?"

The woman's demeanor changed, like a wall she had put between us suddenly crashed down. She tucked a long strand of hair behind her ear bashfully.

"Err—oh! Heh ... she is ..." He just stared at her as if the world revolved around her, his words caught on his tongue. "She is Evie."

I sighed. I knew the look, and I immediately knew who she was to him.

Evie ...

She giggled at him and offered me a smile. "My name is Ginevra," she specified. "But he always call me that." Her Italian accent was so thick and noticeably different from Armond's and Luca's.

I grinned softly, already fond of her. "That is *bella*."

She thanked me, a pretty rosy flush rushing to her cheeks. Her wide smile showed her imperfect teeth.

I nodded. "My pleasure to meet you. I apologize again, Luca and I are ... old friends. It's been a while."

I wasn't certain how much she knew. I only gathered she knew nothing of me by her reaction.

"Oh, no—no! It is no bother to me. My pleasure as well. How have you met?" she questioned, glancing at either of us.

Luca cleared his throat awkwardly. "Erm—Lavinia ..." He looked at me in an odd way, in such a way I couldn't decipher his thoughts. He changed courses swiftly. "Um, *sì*, so Lavinia is ... *was* my *closest* friend. I mean, uh ... you are much closer to me now! And, Lavinia, that doesn't mean ... Look ... her and I ..."

I pinched him, and he yelped and lowered his brows at me. Ginevra watched the action intently.

The hell is he doing? And he can't just come straight out with it by being vague. Now, I'm questioning whether or not he is courting her.

I looked at her hand. She wasn't wearing a ring yet.

"Yes, we *are* close." I let out a half-hearted laugh. "He means we used to be quite fond of each other, but we grew apart, as you can see. He's a funny one, isn't he?" She raised a brow and puffed a breathy laugh. "We met in a library, actually."

"Oh! How lovely!"

"Evie loves to read," Luca said, gesturing a hand her way. "Maybe more than you, Lavy."

I laughed and watched them together with a smile as they looked at one another.

"So, are you two ..." Her dark eyes fell on me before immediately darting for his own light brown ones as I trailed off, looking for an answer in them.

"We ..." Luca began. "We haven't really decided that."

She looked crestfallen. "You do not think so?"

My lips made an O shape. "Um ... maybe I should ... go." I hitched my thumb back.

"No, no ... Not so soon!" she insisted. "Come! Come with us. Stop by for lunch."

"Erm—I'd love to, but I ..." I looked back, finding the carriage and the man leaning against it patiently. His arms were crossed in an uncomfortable manner, green eyes laser-focused on me ... and Luca.

"That's him, isn't it?" Luca asked me. I whipped my head around at the question, seeing him stare at Armond closely. "Did you do it?"

My mouth opened and closed; I must have looked like a fish. Finally, I nodded.

"Do what?" Evie asked, obvious confusion in her tone. But obviously, that was too complicated of an answer. Her eyes followed Luca's gaze and landed on Armond, the past question forgotten. "Who is that man?"

"My husband," I whispered, my voice cracking for some reason. Maybe because, for a short while, I forgot he could have been dead again had I failed. Seeing him alive brought tears to my eyes.

"Oh ..." Evie only murmured, blinking in Armond's direction. She looked at my hand. "Oh ... I do not realize you are married."

"She is," Luca said. He shook his head. "He seems ... kind of vexed. Might be best if you go talk to him, Vin."

I laughed. "He just doesn't know who you are."

"You never told him?"

I shook my head, not wanting to explain further, especially in front of Ginevra. I swallowed, and he nodded in understanding.

"I will talk to him," I agreed.

He nodded as well.

I turned and walked back to Armond. The closer I reached him, the clearer his frown became. As I was about ten feet away, he spoke before I could.

"You know this man well, do you not?" he asked.

I froze momentarily, speechless. Almost. "Er—yes. I do." For once, I couldn't really read him. He seemed oddly ... calm.

Too calm.

"Do you love him?" he asked.

A huge lump formed in my throat. I struggled to swallow it down and reply. "Yes ..." I admitted.

Armond closed his eyes and let out a slow breath through his nose. His face screwed up in pain, as if I had just smashed his heart into pieces.

"But I ..." I began in a panic, trying to find the right words. "I don't love him more than you," I murmured with the most conviction I could muster.

His mouth parted with a sharp inhale, and then his eyelids raised, eyes instantly meeting mine and piercing my soul. A clear glaze appeared over his green orbs, his lips slightly trembling.

"I'm not in love with him like I am with you," I continued. "Never have been. Not even close. And I do love him so much. But the love I feel for you is unparalleled."

And one tear fell on his cheek, just like on that day that would remain instilled in my mind. Right before he had gone limp in my hold. A new tear from the same man for a whole different reason. A wonderful reason. Not to say goodbye. That tear was for the promise of new beginnings.

He took three long, determined steps toward me, then reached out for my face and brought his lips to mine.

His kiss spoke for everything. Since the first time, his kiss had always told me he loved me. I only felt it once I knew the depth of my feelings for him. After our second kiss, there was no doubt in my mind I was done for. And in every countless kiss we later shared, the more love and passion it held.

"Lavinia … Um. Sorry to interrupt." Luca's voice came from behind me.

I immediately pulled away and turned to him and Evie as they stood there awkwardly. Luca more so, his feet shifting and eyes averted.

Evie spoke up, finally.

"We have to go now. Would you like to have lunch together?" she asked. "Our home is that way." She pointed in the opposite direction we were headed. "Not too far. It's quiet." She smiled, hopeful we would agree.

"Well, my family is expecting us …" Armond began, then cleared his throat. "We are not much further. Would you like to … stay for a few days at the villa … erm. With us?"

My jaw almost dropped to the ground after hearing that. I almost couldn't believe he would even be friendly toward Luca, the man I had just admitted I loved, much less invite him to stay with us for a little while. Then, of course, Bartoli would surely blow a gasket if he knew his son was bringing in strangers. Bartoli may have changed his attitude a smidgen, but he was still Bartoli.

But Armond must not have cared. Or maybe he wanted to prove something … Either way, I wasn't ready for whatever trick he had up his sleeve.

"You both live in a villa?" Evie asked, eyes slightly widening.

Armond and I shared a look, then nodded.

Luca glanced at Evie, silently asking her what she thought. She licked her lips and pulled them between her teeth, regarding Luca contemplatively.

I swallowed. I was afraid this could be awkward if they agreed, but the excitement I felt that I might have the chance to talk to Luca again made my choice easy. Of course, I wanted them to come along.

Evie gave a long and drawn-out sigh. "My family will notice I am gone," she whispered. A smile began to form on her face. "We shouldn't stay long."

I grinned. "Come aboard the carriage, then!"

The smell of fresh flowers pervaded the air and filled my nose, and then, eventually, the sight of familiar conical roofs came into view.

Being home again felt so wonderful; knowing I could go back to the villa made me want to cry. Almost. Only a smile brighter than the sun shined on my face because Armond was alive this time as we rode in from hell, holding me close with one hand over mine. We could actually begin the next chapter of our life.

I hoped.

My fear was we wouldn't do it trouble-free, although having Armond there beside me through it all made everything seem possible.

A shriek came from the entrance and distracted me, yanking me out of my head.

"*Oi! Oh, mio Dio! Sono qui!*" Chiara shouted with pure happiness. "*Fratelli miei!* Lavinia! *E papà! Sei a casa! Iseppa! Sì*, they are home! I see them!"

My grin widened at her excitement and relief. By the time she was running to us at the speed of light we nearly reached the stables.

Armond guided me out of the carriage. As soon as I turned, Chiara was there to crush Armond into a hug.

"Armond!" she exclaimed. "Oh, *caro Dio! Sei al sicuro!* You are all safe!" Tears escaped her eyes in a waterfall, absolute joy seeping from her. Armond returned the embrace, resting his chin atop her head. He closed his eyes tight, and I could clearly recognize the happiness he felt to be home.

Chiara hugged Armani closely when he approached us, then Giovanni, Bartoli, and lastly, me.

"Oh, Lavinia," she cried as she constricted my breathing in a crushing hold. "Oh, you … You did it." I thought I heard a dejected sound come from deep in her throat. "Thank you for taking care of him. He needs you more than all of us."

Of course, I held her tight. "Well, that's just not true, but you're welcome."

She pulled back and smacked my shoulder, causing my eyes to widen. "Believe what I say! I don't know who he'd be without you."

"Probably a very grumpy and miserable man married to Francesca the piranha," I deadpanned, snapping my teeth for extra effect.

A devilish giggle burst forth from Chiara's mouth, and I couldn't help but laugh with her.

"Luckily," Armond said, squeezing past everyone to stand by us, "piranhas won't survive on land for long."

I covered my mouth to stop the evil bark of laughter from escaping. "Well, that very piranha was pretty tenacious when it came to earning your love and ending my life. I'd say she'd find a way to try even as a dead fish."

Armond rolled his eyes as Chiara tittered some more. She stopped abruptly, though, when a set of footsteps approached from behind me. Her eyes blinked slowly.

"Who are they?" she asked loudly with confusion. "What strangers did you bring back this time?"

"They aren't strangers." I turned to Luca and Evie. "This is Luca, my …" I glanced at Armond, who stiffened, jaw ticking. "Old friend. Evie here is his …" I trailed off, waiting for an answer from either of them.

"Lover …" Luca said.

I looked at him again, raising my brows in surprise. Evie's

lips were parted slightly. I cleared my throat. "Yes, that."

"Wonderful." Chiara clapped. "I do love to see love. Are you ... visiting?"

I sighed obnoxiously loud, practically feeling everyone's tension, tauter than a tightrope. Especially Armond's uncomfortableness.

"He said we could stay," Luca admitted, gesturing to Armond, "for a few days."

"Oh ..." Chiara pursed her lips. "*Oì* ... well then."

"What did the boy say?" Bartoli asked.

I cringed, feeling heaviness in the air creeping in. I felt like a tightrope. Tension put a huge weight on my chest, pushing me down.

When my eyes finally searched for Armond, my rigidness fell, seeing the softness there in two deep green seas. "The *boy* is a friend of Lavinia's, Father. I invited them both to stay," Armond answered firmly. "If you have a problem being generous, we'll leave with them."

Bartoli stared at him and finally nodded a few seconds later. "Very well. Carry on."

Armond blinked at him in total shock. I stood there quite speechless as well. "Before we do, Lavinia and I have something." He reached into his pocket, slipping a ring into my hand. He mouthed, "You give it to her."

I shook my head, but he shoved me forward and said, "Chiara! Lavinia has something for you from both of us."

Armond had reminded me how he always brought her something home whenever he was gone for long. So, I thought I'd contribute to making it special. I wanted the family to have something from the battlefield, too. An object for all of us to admire so we can remember our victory.

Chiara stepped closer, intrigued. "What? You do?"

"But of course," Armond told her, urging me to go on. "Lavinia ..."

I sighed and held out the ring. "We had this ring made for

you. The stone in the middle ..." Her eyes went wide. "That is a small part of the rare rock I found in my time, which we had seated there for you."

She blinked and immediately slid it onto her right middle finger, admiring the shine as she held her hand out. "It is *bella*. So thoughtful, Lavinia! Thank you both!" She brought us both into a tight hug. "Now I own a ring made of stone from the future?" she said in a questioning tone.

I chuckled. "Yes, you do."

When she let go of us, I saw a tear on her cheek. She quickly wiped it away. "Oh, I am elated you're back." Her face brightened. "You brought my brother back."

I smiled softly. "Couldn't have done it without all of you."

She shook her head, waving a hand to brush me off as if that was nonsense.

"We do have a small surprise for you, too. A few people are inside awaiting everyone's arrival."

"Really? Who?" I asked

"We cannot tell you if it is a surprise!" Chiara exclaimed in a teasing tone. "We have been planning for a welcome ball to distract ourselves. We hoped everyone would be back ..."

I heard Bartoli's small grumble. When I glanced at him, he had a grudged smile, which soon turned into fondness as he noticed me looking.

"A ball?" I said questioningly.

"Yes, for everyone's return home! A victory ball!"

"Oh ... boy, I feel special."

"Only the best surprises for the best people," Chiara insisted. "And ... you are the reason my brother is still with us, so yes, we celebrate your bravery and his survival." She had such big doe eyes when she said it. "Oh, well, we wouldn't mention that."

I laughed, then shook my head with a smile. "We all had our part."

She grinned faintly and nodded. We walked up to the door

where Iseppa was waiting, who chirped, "Oh, my darlings, so glad you have arrived safe and sound." She looked a little stricken but relieved we made it. "Carmela and others are waiting inside for you."

After giving hugs or kisses, I was welcomed by the grand entrance. Home. There really was no place like home. I was too busy admiring the ceiling, like the many times I had before, to see the person ahead of me.

Armond's light gasp caught my attention. "Lavinia ..."

Startled by the sound, I leveled my neck. But my body completely froze the moment I felt as if I was looking at a ghost.

"Why, who are these two beautiful souls?" Carmela asked, glancing between Luca and Evie.

"Mother, this is Luca and Evie ..." Armond began to introduce, explaining how we ran into them, but I did not hear the rest, too busy locking eyes with ...

Was I ... seeing a ghost?

Although that could have been a possibility, Armond's reaction and Carmela's words made me think I was very wrong.

Carmela gestured to the man. "Lavinia, I don't think you have ever met anyone in Giuseppe's family other than his children before." As she said that, Giuseppe appeared in the room.

I couldn't even find it in me to run to him like I normally would have. I couldn't move a muscle.

The man with dark wavy hair and brown eyes gave me a familiar, lopsided smile. "My pleasure to meet you."

"Lavinia, this is Giuseppe's brother, Lord Antonio Melrossi."

I blinked, and a stone-cold chill went down my spine.

Antonio.

He stepped closer, but I couldn't move. Much too shocked. "Oh, how strange. Lavinia, you say?"

Antonio.

Yes, me.

His daughter.

I couldn't speak. I stumbled backward, unaware if anyone

caught me since I was already unconscious.

Armond's voice roused me awake, but I could not open my eyes. My eyelids would not move, not even my body. I really dreamt about seeing my dad, didn't I?

Except, the several recognizable faded and rushed voices convinced me it had been real, especially the one voice that stood above them all.

"Is she quite all right? Did I scare her?"

My eyes fluttered open when the sound of that voice found my ears, widening instantly at the face that matched it.

"No, she just … does this sometimes," I heard Armond explain from behind me.

He wasn't lying …

I knew by then that Armond had caught me; the warm feeling of his arms around me could alone prove it.

I opened my mouth to speak. "Dad?" I croaked.

My father cocked his head at me. "Erm … who?"

My expression surely dropped. "Oh …" I panicked. "Never mind. I'm sorry." I rubbed my forehead as I sat up. Armond was quiet since he knew everything. He knew who this man was to me.

"Why are you apologizing?" he asked in answer. "You are the one who almost hit your head."

I held in my laugh.

That was so my dad.

"Lavinia, you made me worried. What is wrong? Are you ill?" Chiara asked, bent by my side and completely confused as most of them were. "What just happened?"

"I—no … That's …" I sighed, unable to explain myself.

I couldn't even speak. All I wanted was to run to him, but my instinct was telling me that was not the right thing to do.

"It's nothing … I—nice to meet you too," I said to my father's earlier question.

My father nodded once and held his hand out for me to grab. I didn't hesitate to take it, and then he gently brought me to my feet. Before I knew what I was doing, my arms were wrapped around him.

I've missed you so much, I thought.

He was still for a moment before lightly patting my back. "Giuseppe tells me you are family." He pulled away from me and looked into my eyes with intense scrutiny. "I definitely see it."

"Um … yes." I glanced at Giuseppe who stared at me in an oddly serene way, then looked at him again. "We are family." I smiled.

And I'm your daughter.

I tried to keep away my tears. "So …" I took a step back and unhooked the sheathed knife from my waist. "I have something for all of you."

"A …" Carmela raised a brow. "Knife?"

"This is …" I side-eyed my father, then my eyes darted back to Carmela. "*The* knife."

Carmela was silent for a moment, but then she understood. "Oh—*sì* … that knife. So, this is what …"

"This knife has killed, yes," I said, and Carmela knew from my face the deed was done … and by me.

"Oh, yes, *the* knife," Chiara whispered, discreetly throwing me a wink.

I nodded at her.

My father hadn't stopped studying me. His eyebrows furrowed inward like the way I remembered he always had them when he was thinking. He always thought things through. He was a thinker. I wasn't sure if that was bad or good in this case.

"Here." I held the knife out on my palms for Carmela to take.

"No, dear. I won't touch a knife that has been …" She didn't continue.

"I'll take it!" Chiara exclaimed, jumping forward.

"No, young lady. You will not," Carmela told her sternly.

Chiara dared to speak more, but her mother's stare stopped her.

"Let me. We shall showcase it," Bartoli chimed, walking over to take the knife from my hands. "I'll have it put in a display case somewhere safe." For some reason, I believed he saw my father was onto me. Though he had no idea who Antonio was to me, I knew he sensed how strange I was feeling, and I didn't put it past Bartoli to figure everything out. He was a smart man; I would give him that. A smart man who usually used his intelligence wrongly.

I smiled faintly. "Thank you ... because ..." I bowed my head and whispered, "I'm not sure I want it anymore after everything."

He nodded. "Understood." Then, he walked out of the room with it in his hand.

Not much silence went by before my father spoke up: "You were at war, *cara?*"

I glanced at Armond, then stammered, "Um—well, no, I wasn't in the war. I just—"

"She wants to be a nurse. I suggested she come to learn by watching and helping. Why not?" Armond stepped in for me.

I threw Armond a squinted look, and he shrugged at me.

"Interesting," my father muttered, then smiled. "My wife had always wanted to pursue the medical field. You should tell me about your experience sometime."

"Had?" I immediately asked, ignoring all else after hearing that. My heart suffered a pang. "Wanted?"

He shook his head. "I am certain she still would. She only never had the opportunity here."

I frowned. I couldn't tell what this meant. If she was alive, just in the future, or dead, just here. I didn't know which situation was more disturbing.

"Well ..." Giuseppe began, "dinner will be served in two hours. Let's make ourselves ready."

I still hadn't explained everything to Giuseppe, and I wasn't sure where to even start.

"Armond?" I turned to him and saw his tense features. He was worried. "Could we run a bath?"

Armond nodded and placed a hand on my back as we went upstairs. "Lavinia ..." he whispered the second we entered our room and shut the door.

"Armond ..." I bit my quivering lip, and he saw my upset expression.

"*Cuore* ..." he jumped forward and wrapped his arms around me.

I let out a small sob. "You don't know how hard it was to pretend he isn't my own father."

"Why pretend? And I thought he was dead. How is this possible?"

"Because I'm not sure what he remembers or how much. It does make a bit of sense ... when I went back, time had moved on without me there, and I remained in that time like I never traveled here in the first place."

There was a long pause, long enough for Armond to soak in all that information. "This is his time ... so that means he remained alive here."

"My mom brought him back to her time. I know the curse probably forbade that ... he might not know what happened to us."

"And he might think he never went back at all."

"Or he doesn't remember anything. He definitely won't remember me growing up with him until I was seven."

"Hey, let's not assume anything yet." He grabbed both sides of my face and tilted my head up to look at me. "Maybe you should try talking to him."

I shook my head. "You didn't read that book, Armond. I

don't know if he should know who I am yet. And even Dino said I shouldn't mess with time. I did because why wouldn't I do that for you? But now I'm scared. This fear is worse than taking the risk of losing my life for you. I could have made our lives awful for all I know."

He nodded against my temple, then kissed my forehead. "We'll figure everything out," he assured me quietly, and I savored the moment, not wanting to let him go. His body was tense as I held him.

"What's on your mind, Armond?"

I heard his tired sigh. "I just can't help but wonder ... What happened between you and ... Luca?"

I became tense after hearing the question. "We, um ..." I cleared my throat. "We met at the library and became good friends. He helped me with research. He really liked me, but I was still all about you. We went years without taking things further. When I first tried to come back and failed, he kissed me ..."

His hard swallow was audible. "Did you kiss back?"

"At first ... but I pulled away."

"And then?"

"I rejected him ... but our connection grew. We were engaged to be married for a couple of years until I found out he had fallen through time."

Armond brought my head up to look at him. "You knew?"

"Yes ... that's why I had a feeling it was him walking down the street."

He blinked a few times in shock. "You didn't marry?"

I shrugged. "No, he was very much in love with that girl. She was still alive. I let him go. I told him to go back and spend as much time with her as he could. I never saw him again. Until now."

"I'm sorry."

I shook my head. "It wasn't meant to be."

"No, but this is." His fingers tucked a few stray hairs behind my ear, smiling fondly down at me. "I'll have Iseppa collect the water and take off your dress for your bath."

I pursed my lips. "Or ... could you just do it?" I gave him a timid and flirty smile.

He gave a long hum, then murmured, "Indeed, I could."

There was a knock, then Armond asked through the door, "Are you ready, *cuore*? You've been in there for a while now."

"Yes, just a minute. I'll meet you in the dining hall."

I listened to his footsteps fade completely down the corridor, watching my slow breaths in the mirror. When I was ready, I walked out the door but was startled by a hand on my shoulder. On instinct, I twisted my arm around, then pinned the person to the wall, only to realize it was my father, who couldn't have been three inches taller than me.

He just gave me a wide smile. "You are a tough one, eh?"

"Oh ..." I backed away instantly. "I'm so sorry. I didn't mean ..."

"No, dear. That was impressive. You had me. I almost thought I would be on the floor for a moment."

I laughed. My father liked to joke. Some people were easily offended by his humor, but I grew up with it. I understood him. I was happy to see he was still the same. "I could have if I wanted to."

"I will be more careful from now on around you," he said with a chuckle. He became serious quickly. "I should have said something before I grabbed you. I am the one who should apologize."

"It's fine." I shrugged. "Like I said, if it was a problem, I could have handled it."

"Of course ..." he trailed and tilted his head at me.

I nervously shuffled my feet. "So, did you need me?"

"Not exactly. I only—you are ..."

I blinked, stiffening, and straightened my spine. "I am what?"

He stared at me for a long moment, more scrutinizing, really, then sighed. "You know what? It is nothing. You go ahead to dinner."

I furrowed my brows. "Are you sure?"

He shrugged. "I am full of uncertainty, unfortunately. And curiosity, usually."

It was a strange reply, one that made me overthink what he meant. "I can be curious myself," I admitted, then a corner of his mouth lifted. "Walk me down?" I asked.

He smiled. "I'm not sure I can stay. I was going to tell the family but saw you."

"Oh ..." I couldn't hide my disappointment. "Are you all right?"

"Yes ... Tell Bartoli I am very sorry. I know from experience he takes anyone missing dinner seriously."

"You're not kidding ..." I rolled my eyes.

My father squinted his own eyes at me. They slanted so thin I could barely see the color of them.

"Um—well, I'll be going now," I murmured. I turned to leave.

"Actually ... Lavinia," he began, and I faced him again. "I may make an exception. I want to hear more about my brother's long-lost daughter."

I gave him a pleasant smile that I hoped didn't show my disquiet feelings. "That is lovely of you to do for me but don't feel like you have to do this to be polite."

"It's not out of politeness. Family is most important. You are family."

You have no idea, I thought.

I stared at him for a few short moments before I nodded in agreement and silently held my arm out.

After hooking his arm around mine, we quickly made it to dinner. Everyone was already seated, talking amongst themselves, and ... they all looked so genuinely happy. Exuberance and laughter poured from each of them, and I couldn't have been more content with the sight. I was proud I had done such a thing as keep an important person in their lives from dying and prevent their family from falling apart. Happy I could bring them comfort instead of being the bearer of bad news.

What was worse than being told someone you love was going to die? Possibly finding out they're dead, knowing there is nothing you could have done. Maybe watching them die like I had, wishing you had done something. I wasn't completely sure. I only knew a lot worse than that existed.

I took a moment to appreciate every detail of the enormous and grand dining area. The beautiful stone fireplace that looked to be carved by a deft hand was burning wood with gentle flames. Not too hot and blazing for the fairly cool March day. Gas mantles hung equally spaced on each tan stone wall to give the room a pleasant ambiance of dim lighting. On the ceiling, a sparkling glass chandelier was capped by an intricate circular medallion that always drew eyes upward. Especially the picturesque painted cherubs that flew in the heavenly white-clouded blue sky inside the surrounding elaborate design.

Then there was the long dining table and its detailed light blue silk table runner embellished with golden embroidery. The center of every dinner plate had different hand painted landmarks in Italy, designed in ash blue. Ornate golden utensils were on either side of each one, accompanied by detailed crystal wine glasses.

The footman was already pouring Bartoli more wine as my father pulled out my seat, and I sat down beside Armond. The one and only Antonio Melrossi then took his seat beside his brother, the singular Giuseppe Melrossi. My eyes met Luca's across the table. He was cleaned up in a white waistcoat and black tailcoat, his hair not tousled like it normally was. He seemed stiff and out of place. Unusually quiet.

"Is everything all right?"

I nodded at Armond's question, silently reaching under the table to squeeze his hand. He squeezed back.

"How did you two meet?" I asked Luca and Evie.

Evie glanced at Luca before answering. "My father found him in the middle of town, just lying on the ground. He took him into our home. At first, I think I liked him more than he did me."

Luca blushed bright red. "Not true. You thought I was grouchy."

"You wanted to leave."

"Until I got to know you."

I smiled at them bickering like they were already married and said, "And now you can't imagine being apart, I assume."

"Yes," Evie whispered, looking over at Luca with heart eyes. Luca's lips upturned softly.

Silence ensued before my father picked up the conversation again. "So ... Lavinia, where are you from?" Antonio began his inquisition. "I reckon it's not anywhere on the Italian Peninsula."

Everyone moved their heads and pinned their eyes on me. They all knew the truth about me except him, and I'm sure they were wondering what I'd say. I pressed Armond's hand even more and answered levelly. "No, I lived in Pennsylvania with my family until I took a trip here and ..." I paused to give Armond a smile, remembering our meeting. "Unexpectedly, we fell in love."

My father smiled. "How wonderful. You know, I have just come from Pennsylvania myself."

My eyes darted back to him, widening instantly. "You did?"

"Yes, I settled there in 1829 and haven't looked back until now. It was time."

I blinked. "You came all the way back from the Unit—I mean ... America?"

After giving me a peculiar look, he nodded.

"So did you, if I remember correctly, Lavinia," Bartoli taunted, and I sent him a scathing look.

"How remarkable; I do hear it in your voice. Then, you know how difficult the trip is," my father said.

"Difficult but worth it in the end."

"*Sì*, since eventually, those two love birds met," Bartoli added, waving to us, "coincidentally after she came from America."

I refrained from rolling my eyes. He was enjoying this way too much.

"Oh really? How did you two meet?" my dad quickly asked, seeming happy to divert the subject.

I glanced in Armond's direction again. "Well, Armond found me in the woods while on patrol with Bartoli to spot rebels, and there I was knocked over by the one they were chasing down."

"Oh my, were you injured?"

"I was fine. But I had been wandering around, and he offered to help."

"You were alone? How dreadful. Why leave home at all? Were you running?"

I suddenly felt like this was more than him being curious. Though his questions were definitely harmless, I didn't want to have asked them and chance slipping up.

"Sometimes people need an escape. But I wasn't running away; I was leaving to chase my dreams in the hope of finding adventure. And I found that and much more."

His eyes slanted in the slightest way, assessing me thoroughly. "And what are those dreams of yours?"

I froze completely, and everyone must have noticed because they all seemed to glance at each other awkwardly.

"Lavinia is an excellent artist," Carmela spoke up, throwing me a side-eye. "She painted Armond herself and a lot of our lands. She has many talents. She also often helps the cooks in the kitchen."

Bartoli had a look on his face that said, "Not this again." And my father stared at me in interest, questioning, "A painter, a cook, and a nurse?"

I sighed. "An artist, sure. A nurse, probably not. And I'm no cook. You're the cook," I blurted. I gasped when I said it and tried to talk over myself. "You're the cook's favorite," I attempted to rectify. But I only worsened the situation for myself.

A long pause ensued, with him studying me so carefully that I thought a hole would burn through me. "I do cook well on occasion," he admitted, turning his head toward his brother. "Did you tell her about Mrs. Capri?" Giuseppe gave him a shake, leaving me confused, and then he continued. "I used to sneak into the kitchen with the head chef, Mrs. Capri. I would watch her all day long, even begging her to teach me until she finally gave in. She'd offer me food as she made it and divulge bits and pieces of her secret recipes. Do you remember that, Giuseppe?"

The corners of my mouth lifted at hearing something I never knew about him. I never knew anything about his life here. This was my chance to soak in as much as I could.

Giuseppe's smile was large as he chuckled. "How could I forget? I remember the time you showed up at dinner with flour all over your face and clothes."

My father waved a hand. "I was only proving something to our father."

Giuseppe nodded, seeming to mull over his memories silently. Then, "You were always the rebellious one going behind our father's back, doing things even when he forbade you."

"Well, Father was too serious and protective. All I wanted was to be able to do things my way."

"And only your way," Giuseppe added. "You were more stubborn than a mule. Still are."

My father rolled his eyes dramatically. "Are you at all stubborn, Lavinia? You seem like you are resolute."

I raised a brow, wondering how he could even tell that. "I definitely get it from my father, yes."

"Hm ... Giuseppe *is* stubborn when it comes to his family and ruling his lands, of course."

I didn't meet his eyes as he replied; they immediately went to Giuseppe, who looked beside himself. "What was I supposed to tell him?" His face read. I only nodded and welcomed our first serving. Giuseppe helped himself before everyone dug in. For a while, we ate in silence, other than the awkward sounds of utensils and dishes clanging and us eating before my father broke the quiet.

"So," he began, "tell me about nursing. What gave you such an interest?"

I gulped down a bite of food. "Uh ... my mother, actually. She's very educated in that."

"She must have been an extraordinary woman."

I nodded. "She is. I bet you'd like her."

He chuckled. "If she's anything like you, I'm sure I would." I tried not to show my agitation but was almost certain it was obvious. "Anyway," he continued, "you must cook with me while I am here. I've learned quite a lot from Mrs. Capri."

I raised my eyes up to him. "You're staying?" My face must have lit up because he did, too.

"Well, I certainly can't miss this very important ball, now, can I?" He winked, then I smiled. "So, *sì*. For a few days at most before I have to return home."

"Why go back?" I asked, regretting if that sounded disrespectful in any way.

He chuckled. "I do have a life back home. A farm and a son to take care of."

I blinked. "A—a son?" I echoed, almost crushing Armond's hand at that point. "You have a son?"

He smiled faintly. "Yes, his name is Marcello. He must be

around your age."

Oh.

Armond's hand pressed on mine, and I felt his heavy eyes on me as my heart leaped. Mark. Mark existed in the nineteenth century? In America? What did that mean for me, then?

"Do ... Do you have a daughter, um, by any chance?" I stammered again.

My father's eyebrows went inward and something dark came over him, a stormy look I had never seen in his eyes. "The only daughter I ever had died many years ago," he muttered in an abrupt tone. "She passed away from the measles, I'm afraid."

Dead silence fell. It was so awful that I had half a mind to leave the table. My father thinks I died as a child with the measles. My mom had mentioned how they traveled to her time so I could be hospitalized and given proper care. But the part of me that remained here ... did not make it.

How was that possible?

I wondered, though, if there was a reason for this.

Maybe Guinevere Powers didn't know everything.

I gave a sincere smile, contemplating my next question only for a few seconds before deciding I didn't care if it was a bad idea to ask. "What happened to their mother?"

I saw Armond's eyes visibly widen in my peripheral vision and my dad's face fell, the color it held draining fast. He made sure to look away from me as he muttered. "Their mother is gone and won't be coming back."

"What happened to her?" I pressed, and Armond put his other hand on my thigh, bringing my attention to him. He shot me a look that made me question what I was doing. But I had to know.

"She disappeared," he rasped shortly, almost seeming to lose his breath as he said it aloud.

"I'm sorry," I murmured, glancing down at my lap with our clasped hands. "Well," I began again, "I hope I can be like a daughter to you in the future." The sentence had a hidden double meaning.

"You already are," he whispered with a smile, and I faintly offered a grin in return, giving a firm nod.

At least I hadn't angered him.

"Well, that was depressing," Bartoli grumbled, then clapped his hands. "Where goes the next course?"

Dinner went smoothly from there; laughter filled the room and brought me joy. But my father's mood had changed, a despondency remained there with a dark shadow behind his grin. I wasn't ready for anything to ruin it. I hoped life wouldn't find a way to stop it. But life seldom does offer breaks.

CHAPTER 20

DANCING INTO A CORNER

1848

The morning light shone through the kitchen window as my father worked on chopping herbs. My eyes followed the familiar movement with a smile.

"Good morning, Lavinia. I'm making spaghetti today. I thank you for joining me."

"It's my pleasure." I came to stand next to him. "What can I do for you?"

"Are you fine with chopping?" he asked. I nodded, and he handed me the knife. "Please, be careful. Make sure your fingers are completely out of the way of the knife."

I bit my lip to hide my giddiness. "Yes, so I've been told."

When his head turned to me, his eyebrows drooped in an unsettling way. I quickly switched my focus on chopping, afraid to look any longer. He watched me intently for a moment before starting to mix ingredients for homemade pasta, naming the four of them off to me as I listened to him. The only difference was that the dough would be made from wheat.

"You know, the secret to the sauce is including the right

herbs. If you forget one, forget the sauce."

I chuckled. "It really does make a difference."

"So, you know the taste of good sauce?"

"I know the taste of the best sauce, yes."

"Good," he said thoughtfully. "Then, you'll know this is even better."

I didn't mention how I was referring to his sauce as *the* best sauce.

"Indeed, you'll have to prove that to me."

He gave me a smug grin. "That will be the easiest thing I do all day."

I laughed. It was nice to spend time with him and laugh with him again. How did I get so lucky to see the two people I thought I lost forever?

"So, you mentioned you have a farm back home? Is farming what you do for a living?" I wanted to ask him as much as I could and learn about his life. Once he was gone, all I remembered were the things I never knew or couldn't ask.

"Not always. I used to be a professional rider. A jockey."

I tried not to show my surprise. I had not known that he was a professional and did races. But that explained why he worked with Calabrese. "What changed?"

His eyes darkened. "A friend betrayed me. Many things happened that led to the reasons we left. I didn't continue riding. I focused on what was important. My wife and children."

I frowned. He had given up his passion for us. "Betrayed you how?" This could be my chance to find out.

He looked at me squarely, tone cold. "He threatened to tell a secret of mine."

I swallowed thickly. Must have been about time travel. "I'm sorry."

"You should not be sorry. He should be. I'd just rather not talk about it."

I nodded and changed the subject, his mood instantly brightening. I never liked to see my dad angry. He rarely ever was. If he felt angry, the situation was very unpleasant.

Once we finished and he made a plate for me, I twisted my fork in my pasta. He watched me with his head tilted and hands on the counter, awaiting my reaction.

If it was at all possible, that sauce tasted better than I remembered him making when I was a child. My guess was that because of all the fresh and traditional ingredients. "This is absolutely the best sauce and best spaghetti I've ever had. You win."

"*Sì!*" He clapped. "I knew you'd agree."

I smiled. "Hmm, yes. Well, a recipe has no soul without the heart of a cook. And you definitely put all your heart into what you cook."

For a brief moment, pain erupted on his face, and then it flattened, frighteningly earnest. "My wife has said something like that to me before."

I swallowed my tongue and instantly felt a twinge and gnawing in my belly. That was my tongue burning in the acid in my stomach, not the fact I had probably given him reason to suspect something of me!

I tried to smile fondly. "Your wife sounds so wonderful."

"And that's even an understatement. She was extraordinary. But as I can clearly see, you are too."

My breathing wavered as I discreetly hid my wince with a smile. I glanced over at the clock, seeing it was almost noon. I turned away before I could show too many of my emotions and reached behind me to untie my apron. "I'm going to get cleaned up for the luncheon."

He nodded. I stepped away, about to leave the room, when he spoke.

"Do I know you from somewhere?"

The question stopped me in my tracks. I faced him again. "What?"

"I think perhaps I know you from somewhere. You are ... too familiar."

I blinked. The huge lump of lies in my throat gave my tongue some company, but one stayed and was forced to burst out. "Maybe we passed on the streets of Pennsylvania one day. But other than that, I can't think why that is. You must be mistaking me for someone else."

He seemed completely muddled as I said it, furrowing his eyebrows and shaking his head.

"I'll see you in a bit." I began to walk away before he could say another word, but his hand grabbed mine to stop me, and a tingling jolt went up my arm. A visual of our memories together played like a movie before my eyes. I saw him laughing and joking. I saw him cooking meals for us. I saw him dancing around the room with me. I saw his dead body at the morgue.

My father let go of me, and suddenly, his widened eyes came into focus. His jaw unhinged, and his body trembled as he backed away from me. "I—what did I just see?"

Oh ... no ...

It had happened. I was the kind of Seer who saw visions and could transfer them into other minds. I had a feeling I might have even seen one in a dream already.

I swallowed thickly and ran, quickening my pace in a hurry to reach Armond. "Armond," I spoke his name loudly. He turned as he was fixing the collar on his shirt. Seeing the worry on my face, he walked closer and asked me to tell him what was wrong. "My father knows who I am. I'm not sure I'll be able to hide the truth from him much longer. I think—I think I'm having visions."

He stepped toward me. "What happened?"

"He—he just touched me, and memories of our life together flashed before our eyes. He looked at me like ... I betrayed him."

"Oh, cuore." Armond wrapped me in his arms and kissed my head. "He'll understand once you explain."

A knock sounded on our door. "Lavinia, you can't hide from me. I know everything."

I shook nervously, but before I could reply, my father burst into the room uncaringly. I watched him cautiously, waiting for his next move, but all he did was rush toward me and gather me in his embrace. I cried. And he did, too. I didn't have to explain. We already understood each other.

The ball came quickly. As soon as the music hit my ears, a familiarity I hadn't felt in a while filled my heart with warmth. The cheery atmosphere the people brought to the ballroom through their dancing gave me a happiness I couldn't put into words. There was something thrilling about being swept away by the music as one song poured onto the next. I knew somehow that I was born for this, dressing in a fancy ball gown and dancing till my feet hurt. I felt it down to my bones. This was my time. I was meant to be here.

"Can I cut in for a minute?" Luca asked in the middle of a dance. Armond reluctantly stopped us. His eyes seared hot with intensity as he fixed his gaze onto Luca, contemplating the idea for a moment. Finally, he leaned forward and kissed my cheek. "I'll be waiting, *cuore*."

His hand slipped out of mine, then he walked off. Luca, clueless as to what to do, had to let me lead him.

"You'll learn eventually," I encouraged him. "It's not as difficult as it seems."

"To you," he mumbled. "Everything comes easy to you."

"That's not true."

Luca's sigh was agitated. "Did you tell your husband about us?"

"I did, yes. Did you talk to Evie?"

"Not yet. I haven't had the chance," he said. "How did he take it?"

"Well. He was dead when I met you. There was nothing wrong with what we did, and he knows that. He's just as grateful as I am you were there for me."

"He's a good man. Good for you."

I looked downward as I exhaled gently. "And Evie is better for you than I could have ever been. I was still in love with a ghost."

"Who is alive, apparently." He chuckled. "Only you would succeed at that." I laughed with him until he became serious. "I did love you, you know. But I understand now. My love for her is unshakable."

"It's the soulmate bond."

"Right."

"I loved you too. Still do. Just not like I love him." I met Armond's eyes as we turned, and his eyes darkened even in the bright lighting.

"I know exactly what you mean." I knew he was looking at Evie as he told me that.

"You should tell her how you feel, Luca," I whispered. "Don't wait."

He pulled away from me slightly and frowned, disappointed in himself. "I will."

I gave him a soft smile and hugged him close, realizing at that moment how much I had missed him. I only wondered why I never saw him again once I told him to go back to Evie. I thought it wouldn't matter since the future was his time, but he never showed. I hoped he would save Evie from her doom.

"Lavinia!" Giuseppe called. "Come this way!"

I whirled around with a sigh. "Sorry, Luca."

He shook his head. "Go ahead."

I thanked him and began to walk in Giuseppe's direction, noticing another man by his side.

"I'd like to introduce you to someone," he said with a proud smile. "Count of Umbria, Lord Arturo Carmine Mattio Bazolini, may I present to you Lavinia? My dear, the count was in the war and survived two life-threatening injuries." My eyes fell to the leg splint, and nobody could miss the crutches. "He has traveled all the way from Umbria just to be here this evening despite how much pain he endures."

My eyes set on a pair of dark ones, dark as onyx, his skin a deep maple and black hair down to his shoulders. Chills swept down my back. His overpowering presence instantly put me off, but I ignored it and gave him a polite simper with a curtsy.

"Lovely to meet you," I said impassively.

"Pleasure is all mine, *signora*," he murmured, grasping my hand and kissing it gently. That awful chill crept back up my spine, and the hairs on my neck stood on end as he did it. I quickly retracted and discreetly wiped my hand on my dress.

"What is an important man like you doing at a celebratory ball?" I asked, speaking in a hurry, trying not to sound curt.

"I'm a good friend to the family."

That was hard for me to believe, but Giuseppe had introduced me to him.

"How come I haven't met him sooner?" I pointedly asked Giuseppe.

"I've been occupied," Arturo answered instead. "My son was in training for the war and still hasn't returned."

"Hopefully, he is all right."

"My son, I would think so. As for my dear friend, I cannot say the same."

"You think he is going to die?"

"He is dead," he muttered. "He was killed in battle a few days ago."

"I'm sorry to hear that."

Although if he was anything like him, I was glad he was gone.

He shook his head, brushing it off. Suddenly, the music changed and picked up. "Hm, would you have a dance with me?"

"I regret that my dance card is full for tonight," I said too quickly. "Besides, aren't you a little too impaired for a dance?"

"I may be a little wobbly. But I think I can manage. I *insist*."

I swallowed but nodded, and he took my hand, dragging me to the middle of the floor. I felt Armond's eyes on me, watching closely.

"You know, I hear you are quite astonishing. Helping in the kitchen, saving Mrs. Alessandro and your husband, riding horses ..." he paused. "Fiddling with knives and pistols ..."

I tensed immediately as his mouth formed a slightly devilish smirk. "I don't *fiddle* with them, my lord. If you don't mind me correcting you on that. It is simply to defend myself in times of need."

"And when would that be? Women are hardly in the setting of danger."

I gave a contemptuous smile. "They are in plenty of danger, my lord. Especially when on the streets alone."

"Well, no good gentleman would let a lady out on the road alone." He chortled.

I sighed, biting back my less polite words. "Not all men are gentlemen, my lord. Women want the comfort of feeling safe on their own."

"Surely that is true. But women are incompetent, which is why men are their protectors."

I narrowed my eyes, tightening my grip on his hand. "I could very well prove you wrong."

His gaze went to our tightly joined hands. "Hmm," he hummed shortly, not seeming the least bit phased by my tone.

"I'd like to go now," I murmured tersely.

Letting go of his hand and stepping away, I tried to leave, but his hand stopped me when it wrapped around my forearm firmly enough to pinch my skin. His hot breath as he spat his words made the hairs bristle on my neck. "I will decide when we are done speaking and dismiss you as I see fit."

My breath quivered. "Remove your hand, or I will," I snarled. "We can calmly finish this conversation, or I can publicly embarrass you. Your choice."

I felt his brutal stare on the side of my face, and he still hadn't let go before a voice startled me.

"Is there a problem, Lord Bazolini?"

Bazolini's eyes shifted to Armond, and he gained composure in an instant. He shook his head, the pressure of his fingers lifting from my skin.

"Is there a reason you had a hand on my wife?" Armond asked, chillingly calm. His eyes darkened, and not in a good way.

"I want to finish our dance. We were having the most stimulating conversation. She is a lovely girl as you would know. You're a lucky man."

Yeah, stimulating. More like suffocating.

"I am," Armond admitted steadily. "Although, it doesn't really look like she wants to dance with you, does it?"

"Very well." Arturo bowed his head and retreated, narrowing his eyes in my direction, then soon enough I felt his gaze turn away.

"What did he want?" Armond asked in a rush to say the words.

"I think he knows something. He said I *fiddle* with knives and pistols."

"If so, what could he actually do about it? He has no proof anyway."

"I wouldn't put it past that man," I muttered, scanning the crowd until I found him laughing boisterously. I quickly looked back at Armond. "I need fresh air. I will be back."

He nodded, grasping my hand to kiss it. "Don't be long. I heard they are playing our favorite dance soon."

"I won't be," I assured, and our fingers slowly lost grip before I went to exit the ballroom.

I maneuvered my way through the hundreds of men and women, receiving several grunts of irritation. Then, peeking past the crowd of people to look for the doors, I stopped when a man in a butler suit I'd never seen before slipped into the door leading back to the kitchen. The door I used to sneak in for the ball that had me thrown in a dungeon. He seemed suspicious, and that worried me. I furrowed my brows and decided to follow him.

Once I reached the kitchen, something fell with a resounding thud and it seemed to have come from the drawing room.

"Hello?"

I entered the room and looked around, but saw nothing. The eerie silence was deafening. As my eyes traveled along the walls, they stopped on a book. I hesitantly walked toward it, inching closer and closer …

My heart clenched at what I saw.

But the next thing I knew, a hand wrapped in cloth clamped over my mouth from behind. I tried to scream, tried to take action, but a sweet smell filled my nostrils. I was out like a light.

CHAPTER 21

ASCEND THROUGH DARKNESS

1848

My eyes flickered open, and the residue of sweetness remained in my mouth. I knew what it was that had knocked me out. Mr. Maki had gotten me familiar with the smell. And taste.

Chloroform.

"Ugh ..." I groaned, smacking my chapped lips.

I tried to move, but my wrists strained against a rope-like texture while tied behind the chair I was sitting on. And my ankles and midsection were bonded to it well.

I struggled to blow away the hair that was fanned over my face so I could see my surroundings. And I wish I hadn't. My eyes locked onto the walls of a dark, abandoned shack. Skeletons and bones were scattered around the room, and huge cobwebs were up the walls and in high corners. Gruesome. I wouldn't be surprised if animals lived in the place.

Completely skeeved out, I began trying to loosen the bonds by wiggling around. "Is anyone there?" I screamed, with a loud echo following. Silence followed, except for the wind whistling through the unstable wooden door and birds flapping their wings as they flew away from atop the holey roof, scared by the sudden noise of my voice.

I hadn't been awake when whoever had tied me up, so I couldn't have made sure the rope wasn't tied too tight. I focused on twisting my hands to first wiggle one hand out and then release the other.

A bang on the door startled me, and a rugged man wearing animal fur walked inside, pointing a gun my way. "Don't move, little girlie; I will use this."

I raised a brow, unimpressed. "It's not as if I can move, now, can I?" I squinted at him, and he shifted his feet in return, seeming more afraid than I was. "Who the hell are you?" I still worked on freeing my hands as he spoke.

"I'm the one who makes sure you don't escape."

"Oh, hmm. I gathered that." The rope was definitely loosening. I kept him talking. "You don't really look much like the guarding type to me, though," I lied.

He glanced down at himself for a moment, then snarled and marched closer, pressing the muzzle to my forehead to crane my neck back. "I am one of the count's finest guards, thank you very much!"

"Is that right? Then why aren't you in uniform?"

He glared with a grunt. "I'm not supposed to give myself away."

"So, you are decrepit and dead from the neck up. How are you a guard then?"

"I am not old nor dead!"

I grimaced; he clearly had no idea what I meant. "Oh ... Have I insulted your poor impenetrable heart?"

He cocked the pistol. "Don't, girl, My temper is short. And I have more interesting ways to kill you."

I didn't feel like I had the first time I was held at gunpoint. I didn't feel much of anything in the face of danger anymore other than thrill. "You can't kill me. Whoever is in charge of you will have your head if I'm killed."

His lip curled. "Although you are right, I still have ways to hurt you."

"I hardly care if you hurt me, but someone else does," I told him with a snarky smile. My wrists were burning at this point, but almost free.

"Well, I *don't* care," he deadpanned, putting more pressure on my head with the gun. "You are only a stupid fairy girl. You mean nothing to me."

"Fairy?" I asked, furrowing my brows. "You think I'm a fairy?"

He was angry when I asked about that, moving to knock me out. But my hand slipped free, and I quickly grabbed his wrist, wrapped my other hand around the barrel of the gun in case of a discharge, and disarmed him. I redirected the pistol at him, cocking it straight away. "Untie me, or I will kill you because, unlike you, there's nothing stopping me." I gestured my head behind me.

I was sort of afraid of the person I was becoming, but another part of me felt powerful. I reminded myself I don't think of killing as a sport. In fact, I really didn't enjoy it, but in these times, it was necessary to stay alive.

The man put his hands up, eyes wide, and sidestepped around me to undo the knot at my back. I kept the weapon on him. "You said you are one of the count's guards, correct?"

"Y-yes, ma'am," he stuttered.

"That's milady to you, fool." I narrowed my eyes, and he withered. "Which count?"

"The Count of U-Umbria, milady."

I swallowed. Arturo. The man I met hours ago. I knew he was up to no good. "Hurry up," I muttered, becoming impatient.

"Please, milady. I will let you go; don't do me any harm."

Of course, I didn't believe him. I kept the gun at his head

as he undid the ankle bonds, then knocked him out with my elbow the second he finished. He fell to the hard floor with a resounding thud. I sighed, not really enjoying that part.

I couldn't get past him calling me a fairy as I tucked away the pistol in the top of my dress and then slipped out the wonky door. The only conclusion I could think of was that someone else knew who I was and where I was from. Again.

I was in danger. Again.

More importantly at the moment, I had no clue where I was. I checked to make sure it was clear, then began walking through the trees. But before I could go too far, the sound of commotion and hooves stopped me. I sprinted and ducked behind a bush as a group of uniformed men on horses rushed by further up the hill near me. Dozens of them.

The hair on my neck stood on end. Like a sixth sense, I felt something creep up on me from behind. Or someone.

Definitely someone.

Pistol in hand, I whipped around, put them in a neck hold by the arm, and pressed the muzzle to their head. "Not very wise of you to sneak up on a woman like me." I froze at the man in my hold.

"Not wise, indeed, especially my woman," a deep, velvety voice purred.

I gasped. "Armond Alessand—" Before I could get out his full name, he flipped me around deftly and pocketed the pistol I had been holding. His hand clamped my mouth shut.

"Shh, *cuore*," he whispered. "We don't want them to hear you."

"But, Armond!"

"Hush!" He ushered me to the ground, his body hovering over mine. The heat of him close to me, the fact I'd been away from him for a while, just made me want him. He watched the men pass us until they were gone, hand still keeping me quiet. I blinked up at him lazily as he brought those stunning green eyes to me. They filled with fervor, and then he finally uncovered my lips, diving for them.

I gasped into the kiss, embracing his frame, and pulled him against me. He devoured me, putting all of his emotion into it as I did the same.

"How did you find me?" I breathed.

"When I hadn't seen you in an hour, I began to worry and went around the villa looking for you. I sent search parties when I realized you were gone ... and so was ..."

I cut him off with another passionate kiss, hands roaming everywhere. The rest of the story could wait. He broke away to connect his mouth to my neck, and I sighed, but a quick noise startled me. The moment that I tensed at what I saw, he felt it and stopped. "Armond," I muttered in a tremble.

A few men dressed in uniform were standing over us, rifles pointed directly at our heads.

My heart was beating fast for a completely different reason than seconds ago. One man stepped forward, mustache moving as he gave us orders. "Move away from the lady," he barked, knocking the barrel of the gun against Armond's head for emphasis. "Slowly. I don't want to have to use any more bullets today."

I stared at Armond as he nodded at me and gradually rose to his feet, backing away. Two men grabbed him and held him still.

"Please, let him go. He wasn't doing any harm. Whatever it is you want from me—"

"Whether he was doing harm or he wasn't, we care not. We have strict orders to escort you to the train station."

"You mean bring me there against my will?" I countered, beginning to glare. "And if I refuse?"

"We have something of yours that holds much value."

Armond was visibly nervous, staring at me intensely.

"And if I don't care?" I asked.

"We have no choice but to persuade you accordingly."

At those words, a man pulled out a knife and pointed it at Armond's throat.

"All right! I'll do whatever you ask; just please let him go home."

"I'm not leaving without you, Lavinia!" Armond gritted between his teeth.

The man inched the knife closer.

"Shut up!" I shouted at him, turning to the other man. "I'll go. Just free him, or I will have no choice but to take that knife and use it on you."

Armond scowled at the man as he returned the knife to its sheath, and as soon as the men released him, he ran to me. "Lavinia, you can't do this alone."

"Armond, they just threatened to torture you. I'm not letting that happen."

"Not only that." He swallowed.

My heart sank at his whitened face. "Armond ... What?"

He grasped my hand and looked me in the eye. "I know what they have. Your painting was stolen. That's what I tried to tell you ... When I looked in our room, it was missing. They have it. I know they do. They're going to blackmail you for something."

I searched his eyes for any reason he could be wrong, but there was only certainty. "No ..."

He nodded, eyes searching my features for my emotions. "Whatever you choose to do, I'm right behind you."

My blood ran cold, and I stood to my feet, glowering ahead at the men. I took three long, angry strides until I was planted in front of them. "Take me straight to the man in charge of you. I need to have a talk with him."

"That is our direct order, yes," the man said, stepping closer to me. "Although, there are a couple things you're missing ..." he trailed. My narrowed eyes turned to sharp daggers as I imagined them going into him. "He told us you have a sharp tongue and are good with weapons, so we should be certain you weren't awake." I tried to take action, but a few men grabbed me. Then, he focused on Armond. "And that no one follows our trail."

A thud against the ground started me from behind, and I jerked in their hold. "Armond!" It was too late; he lay on the ground, knocked unconscious. "You bastards!"

The man smiled at me evilly. "Sleep well, *Lavinia*."

Soon, a black veil welcomed my senses.

"I want you to lay down, close your eyes, and hold on to my voice, Lavinia. There something we not go over," Mr. Maki commands in an unusually serious tone.

I did as I was told, then popped a question. "What is that?"

"Hardest lesson of all," he said. "You can't control universe. Universe has own plans. You can only control how you react to what happen. And you might take hit hard."

"I won't let that happen."

"You need to be ready if it does," he whispered firmly, "because you never be too sure."

I swallowed.

"So, when you are down. If you are down. As you there, seemingly defeated. As he stand over you, ready to kill you. Smile inside because you have upper hand. He unaware of your strength. And you can end him."

My eyes shot open, and then pain flooded in my head. My limbs were trapped once again, tied to a more comfortable chair this time, at least. The tremble of moving fast and riding over tracks pulled me further out of the dark. I was already on a train.

And then …

There was the Count of Umbria across from me, sipping a teacup on a luxurious bench, one bushy eyebrow arched. "Ah, you're awake. Finally. How was your peaceful slumber, hm?" He gestured to the teapot. "Coffee?"

I cracked my neck to the side, scowling fiercely at him. "The chloroform from before was a nice touch," I muttered, voice heavy with sarcasm.

He hardly seemed surprised. "You liked it, then? I knew you'd be a hard one to kidnap. And poison is an art, you know." He glanced downward at the table in front of us. "Say, is that a no to coffee?"

"No ... to all of it. I'm hardly impressed or comfortable while trussed to a chair. And chloroform isn't a poison; it's a toxic drug. When it reacts with air, it produces a poisonous gas—"

He snorted, cutting me off. "All right, encyclopedia. I've heard enough of the lesson. Poison or not. It still takes a proper dosage. Too much or too little causes very different results." He rolled his eyes. "Who knows what you'd do if you weren't 'trussed to a chair' at the moment? I should gag you."

I chuckled humorlessly. "I'm surprised you have faith in my fight."

"I don't." He threw me a wicked grin. "That is not why you are bound. I simply take pleasure in it."

I grimaced. "Get to the point. Why am I here, *Arturo*?"

He leaned back in his seat and tapped his fingers on his legs menacingly. "I'll let you in on a little secret." He grinned wickedly before whispering dramatically. "I'm not really the Conte of Umbria. My real name is Ferox. Ferox knows you have something he wants."

"I'm not even surprised." I wanted to roll my eyes. "So why would someone like you want anything from a weak woman who is difficult to kidnap, has a sharp tongue, and is yet harmless?"

He gritted his teeth, then rose to a grand height and began walking back and forth in front of me. "I'm going to tell you a story, *Lavinia*." I didn't know why, but the sound of his expensive shoes dragging on the floor infuriated me. "Years ago, I was imprisoned for arson. I was content to be left alone and not bothered. But not too long ago, a prisoner was put into the cell beside mine and spoke of things I found ridiculous. He said a woman could help me bring back my son. He told me everything about you. Your name. Where you lived. I escaped last week, not expecting a strange woman to appear out of nowhere not too far away from the villa." My breathing quickened, and so did the pace of his words. "I began to believe the man."

"Was this man Eduardo Calabrese?"

His smile widened frighteningly, confirming the answer to my question. "I followed you and watched you for days. Fascinated. And then ..." he paused. "I went to war and was saved by a small gentleman." His look turned dark. "I was grateful, especially when I went to thank him and realized he was she. You were the one who helped me. You had been successful. I needed you."

"That was you who tried to kidnap me."

"I had you. I let you go easy." He stopped pacing abruptly and slammed his hands on either arm of the chair. "You have the future. The past," he rasped, lifting my chin with a single dirty finger. "You have the ability to change it. You could even save your own husband's life."

I gulped down the lump in my throat. "I enjoyed every second it took to end the man who was responsible. I don't regret it one bit. Matvei was a horrible person, just like you. You're not getting anything from me."

His hand struck my cheek hard, enhancing the ache in my head and creating a lingering sting. He began to leave when I spoke:

"I know you have the painting," I told him, and he instantly halted in his tracks. "You want to bring him back. You want to go back and ensure your son stays alive, don't you?"

"Yes," he hissed.

"Well, you can't."

He faced me faster than the crack of a whip. "And why

not? You did it!" he barked.

"Because you can't time travel. Only I can."

"And how do you know that?"

"The painting is a linked talisman. It's connected to me and therefore doesn't work on others."

"Then, you will take me with you."

I shook my head. "I doubt it is possible."

"You will find a way to make it possible. Because I will stop at nothing to have what I want. We'll go together." Ferox stomped over to me in a fury, hands working fast to untangle the bonds on my chair, which was a mistake on his part.

I had him on the floor so fast he didn't have a chance to think twice. "If I go with you, will you leave us alone?"

"Yes," he groaned under the pressure of my armlock.

The door several feet away from us suffered a loud bang, followed by more before it flew open and the one and only Armond Alessandro appeared. "You're not going anywhere with her without me," he growled.

I was so distracted by his entrance my grip on Ferox loosened and he escaped. "We do not need you tagging along, Alessandro. We'll do this alone."

"Then find another time traveler!" Armond stalked close to Ferox and grabbed him by his neck, pinning him against the train wall. His back slammed so hard the breath was knocked from his lungs. He gasped for air and struggled to sputter out his reply. Armond whispered to him, threateningly enough for Ferox to visibly quake in his boots. "Before I have to end your miserable life in front of her eyes."

"Fine," Ferox seethed in an air-constrained wheeze until Armond pulled back marginally for him to continue speaking. "Take your hands off me, Alessandro. You can come."

Armond let him go reluctantly and Ferox uncovered the painting in the corner, standing it up. "You're right. When I touched it, nothing happened." He stared at the painting, cackling evilly. "But now I have you."

I turned Armond around to face me. "This will get rid of him," I assured Armond. "Wherever we end up, we can always come back."

He smirked. "You have a plan, don't you?"

I nodded with a smug smile, kissing him gently.

"I'm waiting," Ferox said, his tone impatient.

I stepped forward with Armond's hand in mine, and Ferox roughly grabbed my free one, yanking me closer to the painting. I stared ahead at Armond's painted eyes, anticipating its allure to surge through me. Luckily, it did, and the pull brought me a step closer. I reached forward with Armond's hand that slid down to grasp my wrist so my fingertips could brush the painting. A strong jerk dragged us through the void, and we were falling. Falling down, down, down deeper into the darkness, through the veil between life and death.

Quickly putting my plan into action, I sneakily slipped my hand out of Ferox's grasp so he could be swept away in another direction, lost in the void. He screamed in anger until he disappeared. I didn't dare let go of Armond before our landing knocked us unconscious.

Something strange had occurred between us. I recalled recollecting all of our memories together the first time I went back after he had died. The same thing happened again, only I had flashes of Leo being born and ones of him growing up. And I somehow knew Armond saw them, too.

The air fed my heaving lungs as I roused with a groan, comforted by the feeling of Armond's tight embrace. He was still with me. As I peered down at the man that I sacrificed everything for, his eyes shot open and met mine, the black night of his pupils consuming a sea of green.

Rain pelted against our faces, the vague memory of Leo lingering in our thoughts. Suddenly, I knew where and when we had ended up and that all I had done was worth it. He *would* visit his family whenever he wanted by traveling together back and forth through the painting, our masterpiece. He *would* see

Leo and hug him closely for the rest of our days. We *would* grow old together. We *would* die gazing at the sunset if fate let us.

Acknowledgments

To my loving family, who always support me in climbing the large mountain of success. To my editor, thank you for all you do for me, but especially for making me laugh and putting up with my awkward sentences. A big thanks to the Atmosphere Press team since my book would not be as amazing without everyone involved. And thank you, readers, for reading my books and any others in the future.

About Atmosphere Press

Founded in 2015, Atmosphere Press was built on the principles of Honesty, Transparency, Professionalism, Kindness, and Making Your Book Awesome. As an ethical and author-friendly hybrid press, we stay true to that founding mission today.

If you're a reader, enter our giveaway for a free book here:

SCAN TO ENTER
BOOK GIVEAWAY

If you're a writer, submit your manuscript for consideration here:

SCAN TO SUBMIT
MANUSCRIPT

And always feel free to visit Atmosphere Press and our authors online at atmospherepress.com. See you there soon!

ABOUT THE AUTHOR

Quinn Jamison's first novel, *The Art of Time*, was written in three months when she was sixteen during the Covid-19 pandemic. Quinn has been dancing from the time she could walk and discovered her love for writing along her journey of being a dancer. She enjoys writing historical romance the most but sometimes explores other genres. Born and raised in Pennsylvania, her family is the most important thing in her life, and she is very close with her sisters and parents.